Even in the
Breaks

HEND HEGAZI

First Edition, 2020

Copyright 2020 by Hend Hegazi
www.hendhegazi.com

Design by Reyhana Ismail
www.reyoflightdesign.com

ISBN: 978-1-7340921-2-7

Chapter One
AYDA AND DIDI

Inside her private office, Ayda sat staring at the computer screen, her stockinged legs crossed at the knee, her high-heeled foot bouncing up and down. Cigarette smoke filled the room and crept out the bottom of her closed office door. She often imagined the smoke forming phantom hands, slowly curling around the necks of certain employees. How many times had they complained about her smoking? How many references to the danger of second-hand smoke had she heard? *Bunch of wusses.*

She spoke into the phone as she clicked away at the keyboard. "I know it's been a long time, Auntie, but I'm swamped with work. Soon *In sha' Allah*. The important thing is that you see your cardiologist to regulate your blood pressure. Yes, and send him my salaam. *In sha' Allah*. Will do. *As salaamu alaikum*."

She hung up with one hand as she continued typing with the other.

The knock at her door didn't divert her attention, only caused her to call out, "Yes?"

A woman in her late twenties entered and stood directly in front of Ayda's desk. Her hair was pulled back in an untidy ponytail, her rumpled blouse, sporting a wet blotch just by the shoulder, was sloppily untucked. The woman panted as she spoke, unable to catch her breath. But Ayda noticed none of that.

"Why were you late today?" she snapped, still staring at the computer and typing away.

"My son wasn't feeling well this morning. It took me a while to find a sitter."

"Next time, you should plan these things in advance. I'll let it go this time, but next time your pay will be docked. I want to see the final proofs on the cereal account by the end of the day."

"I sent you those last week, Ms. Faisal."

"What you sent was crap. I cannot use those images in a professional ad. Maybe for a middle school project they'd be good enough, but here... they're crap. Redo them."

Cynthia stood silent. A moment later she asked, "What should I change about them?"

Ayda stopped typing, pulled a cigarette from the pack which lay on her desk, lit it, and took a deep drag. She puffed the smoke directly at Cynthia and stared at her as she spoke.

"If I wanted to do them myself, I would. But this is your job. Go figure it out."

Ayda refocused on the computer, oblivious to the look of hatred that came over her employee, as Cynthia walked out and closed the door behind her.

Making eye contact with one of her co-workers, Cynthia shook her head and mouthed, "Bitch!" Her friend rolled her eyes and shook her head, agreeing with Cynthia's sentiment.

In fact, everyone in the office agreed with Cynthia's sentiment. And they had some interesting nicknames for Ayda to prove it: A-Hole, Bitch Boss, AF.

"We could probably get a good one using where she's from," one guy suggested as a group of them huddled around the coffee machine later that afternoon. "Where's that again?"

"Hell," Cynthia said.

Through the laughter, a few more nicknames were created.

"Hell Boss."

"I like Ayds of Hell."

As the laughter subsided, someone said, "She's from Maryland."

The guy rolled his eyes. "You know that's not what I mean."

"But she *is* from Maryland."

"Oh, God! Where are her parents from?"

"Her parents are dead."

"What is wrong with you people?! Where were her parents from *before* they died?"

No one answered. As the fridge closed behind them, they all turned to see who had joined the party.

"My parents were from Egypt," Ayda said casually as she popped open her can of soda and took a sip. "And I'm sure you can come up with something more imaginative than Ayds of Hell. Your jobs are based on your ability to be creative, for God's sake."

Paying no attention to their open jaws or their red faces, Ayda walked nonchalantly back to her office and kicked the door closed behind her.

"What in the world does she have on the CEO that makes him keep her?"

"She doesn't have to have anything on him," Cynthia said. "We all know that without her talent and hard work, this place wouldn't even exist."

"Still. I'll bet she's blackmailing him."

◆ ◆ ◆

"Good morning, *habibi*. Come on... You have to get up, or you'll be late for work."

Didi stroked her husband's head and kissed his cheek as Saef only moaned to show he'd heard her.

"I've already got breakfast on the table. *Yalla*...come on."

He wrapped his arm around her and pulled her under the covers.

"Isn't this so much better," he whispered.

She giggled. "Yes, of course. But we have to go to work."

"Ok then... I'll go to work." He nudged his face against the nape of her neck.

With a giggle she said, "Come have breakfast first."

He started placing soft kisses all over her neck. "But Didi, I want dessert first."

She let out a loud chuckle. "You know I love when you call me Didi. But we have to save dessert for later. You're already late." She got up and pulled the covers off the bed.

Didi and Saef's days were pretty routine. Every morning they ate breakfast then drove to work together. Didi would enter the building from the front while Saef circled around to the side entrance. Sometimes they'd meet for lunch in the company's courtyard. On their ride home, Saef loved listening to Didi chatter about her day. He listened attentively when she told him which accounts were a waste of their time and which were great but challenging.

"If I ever decide to open an ad agency instead of an art gallery, I've decided to steal my team from the company," she said.

"You totally would steal your team."

"Too bad I wouldn't have any money to pay them."

"So you don't steal them right away," Saef suggested. "You wait a year for your company to stand on its feet, then you steal them, but only one-by-one. A good kidnapper has to make sure she can feed her hostages before nabbing more."

"This is awesome," Didi giggled.

"What is?"

"You encouraging me to kidnap the people I work with. Not every husband would do that, you know?"

"I totally know. You are one lucky lady."

His laughter made her whole world brighter.

When they had first gotten married, it was Didi who encouraged Saef to improve his relationship with God, to be vigilant with his prayers. Saef had accepted her gentle pushes as signs of love and acted upon her suggestions. After their third year of marriage, Didi no longer had to remind him; prayer and other forms of worship had become second nature for him. Once they arrived home from work, Saef would tell Didi to wash up so they could pray together. He did the same thing for each one of the five daily prayers. And after each one, he would kiss her hand and say, "May God accept this prayer from us and grant us eternal togetherness in Paradise."

They always prepared dinner together, often continuing the conversation they had started on their ride home.

"I thought for sure she hated my idea, the way she just sat there staring at me with those squinty eyes. But when I had finished, she said, 'Good job, Didi. Get your team together and put it into motion.'"

"That's wonderful, *habibti*," Saef said, "I'm so proud of you."

"Yeah, it would have been an awesome day, if Derek would just stop with all his inappropriateness. Today he had his disgusting eyes all over me as he hissed, 'Nice skirt.' Ugh... I hate it."

"We need to report this, Didi. That man has gone far enough."

"What are we gonna say, 'He said he liked my skirt'?"

"It's not about *what* he said. It's about *how* he said it and how it made you feel. Everyone knows he's a creep."

"But he *is* the CEO. No one will listen to me."

"You still have to speak. Now he's just making remarks, but next he might try to touch you or one of the other women. Who knows what he's capable of."

They placed the food on the table and sat down to eat.

"I'm gonna hire someone to beat him up," Saef said.

"No you won't."

"No, I won't. But I want to."

"Let's just find another job first, then we can beat him up. Deal?"

"Deal."

Saef watched Didi eat for a few minutes with a smile on his face. Her soft brown hair was clipped at the top of her head so that its length fell away from her face to her shoulders. Her lips, now moving with the rhythm of her chewing, were naturally bright red, and her eyelids were a shade darker than the rest of her caramel skin.

When she finally felt Saef's eyes on her, she stopped chewing and looked up. "What?"

Saef kept smiling, but said nothing.

"What? Why are you staring at me?"

"You're so beautiful. I just like taking it all in."

"Oh," she chuckled. "You're just making sure I haven't forgotten about 'dessert,'" Didi said.

He let out a laugh. "I'd forgotten about that." He walked over to her and started kissing her neck, pulling her up from the chair.

"We're in the middle of dinner!"

"The food isn't going anywhere."

She giggled as he continued to kiss her neck and led her to the bedroom.

Chapter Two
AYDA

At the office, the backbiting about Ayda didn't stop even after she confronted the offenders. Most of them thought that if she didn't want people to talk about her, she shouldn't be such a bitch.

"Wonder what she was like as a child?"

"Bully. Definitely a bully."

"You think so? I think she was probably too aloof to be a bully. Bullies are all in your face; she's weird and rude, but she's a loner."

"How old do you think she is?"

"Somewhere between 37 and 42."

"No way, man. She's not a day older than 35."

"I've seen her driver's license. She was born in 1971. That makes her 47."

"Forty-seven! You've got to be shitting me!"

"I am not. She's 47."

"Wow. She looks great for that age."

"She looks great for any age."

"Does she have a boyfriend?"

"I think I heard she used to be married."

"Can't blame him for leaving. If I were a goldfish in her place I'd find a way to get out."

"Too bad she's the devil. Otherwise, I'd get me a piece of that."

The group chuckled, then one of them said, "Women like that don't look at men like you, Ed."

"What? What you talkin' about?"

"Yeah, man. Bitch or not, she's totally out of your league."

"You guys are all trippin' on me. I'll show you."

He walked up to her office and knocked on the door. They watched as he went in. Less than thirty seconds later, he was back.

"What happened, man?"

"She asked me what I wanted, so I said I'd like to take her out to dinner sometime."

"Yeah, then what happened?"

"She blew smoke in my face and told me to fuck off."

They all erupted with laughter.

The jeering didn't bother Ayda even when she heard them; as far as she was concerned, it was all air, light and invisible. What surprised her was that they couldn't find anything better to gossip about. What about the woman in HR who was caught—by her husband!—in bed with another man? Was this not more worthy of their idle jabber? Or the man from IT who received court order after court order to pay his outstanding child support? Was none of that more deserving?

But circumstances change and events get forgotten. Ayda's personality, on the other hand, was a staple of the office, making it a staple of their daily babble.

As she did every evening, Ayda walked into her home at about eight. She locked the door behind her and reached for the TV remote on the table beside the door. As the hushed sound of a newscaster reporting all the tragedies of the day broke the silence in the house, Ayda sat down on the couch and began to sort through the mail she'd brought in. But it was only a solitary square envelope which grabbed her attention. She could tell immediately that it was a wedding invitation.

One of her distant relative's kids was getting married. Ayda never attended weddings, but even so, a hundred thoughts now raced through her mind. Should she send a gift? If so, money or something from the registry? Should she call? Better yet, should she call and tell them her true thoughts on marriage? Should she tell the young bride not to love too intensely, not to let herself get too attached? *That never does anyone any good.*

With a heavy sigh, she placed the invitation back in the envelope and threw it, along with the rest of the mail, onto the coffee table, making a mental note to send a gift, knowing full-well she would probably let it slip her mind.

She climbed the stairs to her bedroom. Kicking off her heels, she instantly shrunk by nearly four inches. She shed her clothes and walked to the bathroom, not bothering to close the door. The water coming down from the shower was so hot it could have scalded her skin, but she liked it that way.

When she finished, Ayda toweled off and stepped into a silky nightgown. She loved the feel of it against her skin; the way the sleek fabric clung to her breasts and bottom made her feel sexy. She never went to bed in pajamas or even a cotton nightgown. Even when the weather outside was freezing, she slept in satin or silk.

Ayda's house had two bedrooms, three baths, a large living room, dining room, and kitchen. It was always spotless—the maid who came twice a week saw to that—and far too big for just one person. But the hassle of finding another place and sorting through her things to decide what should be kept and what should be thrown out made her dismiss the idea of moving. Her aunt and uncle had invited her to live with them, but she couldn't do it. She'd gotten used to being on her own. And she had no reason to feel guilty about not being there for her relatives since their daughter stayed close to them.

♦♦♦

Derek called her into his office and told her to close the door behind her

Now hidden from view of the employees, he stood opposite her.

"Ayda, I want you to know that I see you. I see the long hours you put in. I know that you were the brains behind the sneaker account, and you were the reason we stayed out of court. I know how hard you work, and I appreciate it."

"Thank you," she said with a straight face.

"And I'd like to reward you. What would you say to a nice bonus?"

"I'd say I deserve a bonus, a raise, and a promotion."

He laughed, but when he looked at her face and saw that she still maintained the same stern expression, he stopped and took a step closer to her. Putting his hand on the small of her back, he leaned in and whispered, "I think we can arrange something." Then he kissed her neck.

She kept still as his hands pulled her hips toward him and his kisses continued.

"Aren't you married?" she asked.

"Shh. Don't ruin our first kiss."

He kissed her on the lips, forcing his tongue against her own. A moment later, she put her hands on his chest and pulled away slowly.

"Not like this," she said. "I'm worth more than that." She left his office quietly and didn't close the door behind her.

Back at her own desk, at that time still just a cubicle among all the others, she sat and stared at the computer screen. Anger welled up inside of her as she pretended to focus on the work on her desk. After all her hard work, after she'd proven herself time and again, it was still not enough. She'd get nothing for her effort, but would be rewarded with wealth and success for remaining silent to his harassment. Her CEO had made advances at her before, but this was the first time he'd laid a hand on her. She was disgusted by his lack of professionalism, lack of morals, lack of loyalty. It reminded her, albeit distantly, of a time she'd worked hard to forget.

Were all men cheats? Was it in their genes? They saw a beautiful woman, they immediately needed to fuck her?

But unlike the last time she was cheated, this time she could do something about it. It would take a bit of planning, but she was going to make sure Derek would think a thousand times before letting his dick lead the way and harassing another woman ever again. And like it or not, he would give her that promotion.

The following day, Ayda arrived at the office before anyone else and snuck into Derek's office. Moments later, she was back at her desk, looking over slides for the new project. She had a regular workday, content in the fact that her plan was self-actualizing, requiring little to no effort on her part. Ayda knew she wasn't the only one Derek was hitting on. Now, he would be the cause of his own destruction.

A week went by. Each day he'd called Ayda into his office. Each day he'd drawn the blinds and rubbed up against her. Each day she pushed him away and walked out of the office quietly, without anyone noticing. Then one day she decided it was time.

"I won't come in here again. I've already told you, I'm worth more than this."

"You're absolutely right; a woman like you deserves to be wined and dined. So, I've made reservations for us at the Four Seasons for tonight at eight. But," he continued, narrowing the space between them, "can't I get a down payment until then?"

Ayda pulled away when he moved to put his hands on her hips. "Good things come to those who wait, Derek. And trust me," she said, patting his groin, "I'm worth the wait."

As the door closed behind her she heard him say, "I'm sure you are."

That evening, Ayda ordered the most expensive steak on the menu and the oldest champagne. Derek didn't even notice that she didn't take so much as a sip of it.

"Our first date," he said, raising his wine flute. "It's bound to be memorable."

"You have no idea," she replied.

Throughout dinner Ayda smiled and laughed, making small talk. Then after they had finished dessert, she looked Derek straight in the eyes and said, "You're not serious about me, Derek. If you were, you wouldn't be having an affair with that girl from accounting."

"You mean Kim? Kim is just..."

"Don't lie. I can't stand men who lie."

He held her gaze for a moment, seeming to gauge her degree of seriousness. Her flat expression and half-raised eyebrow told him Ayda was not to be messed with.

"Ok, I won't lie. But Kim is for fun."

Ayda laughed out loud. "Oh, and you were planning on marrying *me*?"

"I think we can be a great team. At work and... personally. There's chemistry between us. I think if we experience it, it could be electrifying."

"I don't want to be electrified."

"I'll give you that promotion. Head of the department."

"And?"

"And a raise."

"The raise goes with the promotion, Derek. Don't be an idiot."

"Sorry. Ok...and...and a bonus."

"And a company car."

"What? I don't have that kind of leverage, Ayda."

"Derek, don't fuck with me. You and I both know that you do."

"I can't."

"Then," she said, starting to stand up, "I think dinner is over."

"Wait, wait," he said, grabbing her hand. "I'll see what I can do."

She rested back into the chair as she stared into his eyes. Taking a final sip of water, she said, "Let's get started then." And she got up and walked out.

He stared after her in disbelief for a moment then dropped some cash on the table. In his haste, he forgot to grab his keys and had to go back for them.

In the lobby, Ayda licked his ear and whispered, "Did you book us a room or a suite?"

He tripped over himself to get to the reception desk to book a suite.

With the key in his hand, he led her into the bellhop-operated elevator. As soon as the doors closed behind them, she grabbed him by the crotch and whispered, "You've never been fucked the way I'm going to fuck you tonight."

The bellhop pretended not to notice, but Derek's eyes grew wide and the tension she felt in her palm indicated she was close to getting what she wanted.

She let him open the door then grazed her body against his, kissing him forcefully as his back was against the wall. Grinding her hips against his, she didn't back away until he was fully aroused.

"Come into the bedroom," she commanded, throwing off her blouse and pulling out some rope from her purse.

"What's that for?"

"I told you—you've never been fucked like this before. Take off your clothes and get on the bed."

She kicked off her shoes, but when she noticed he wasn't doing as she demanded, she kissed him again and asked, "Don't you want me?"

"Oh God, I'm about to explode I want you so badly. But... I've never done... this." He pointed to the rope.

"It'll be memorable. Trust me." She forced her tongue against his and undid his zipper. When she stepped back again, he pulled down his pants, underwear attached, threw off his shirt and jumped on the bed. She got on top of him with the rope in her hands.

"Aren't you going to undress?"

"Be patient," she said, kissing him and tying his hands to the bedposts. When she was sure the rope was secure, she got off the bed and put her shoes back on.

"What're you doing?"

She pulled her phone from the inside of her skirt, pressed a few buttons and waited.

"What's going on?" he said, his eyebrows beginning to furrow.

"Don't get yourself worked up. What I really wanted to do was to cut off your dick. I think you'll prefer this option. Ah...here it is."

She turned the phone toward him. He watched himself on the screen standing in his office. A moment later, the girl from accounting appeared on the screen, and soon, they were undressed and on top of each other on his desk. The phone was playing back the audio as well.

"I've recorded every minute you've been in the office for the past week. Every time you had sex with her, every time you came on to me or anyone else.

"So what's going to happen now is up to you. You can either keep your word—give me the promotion, bonus, and car—and no one will ever see any of this footage. Or you can resist. Fire me, tell me to get lost. And in that case, not only will your wife get copies of these videos, but so will the board of the company. And I'll manage to convince...what did you say her name is? Kim? Yes. I'll manage to convince Kim to be a plaintiff in the sexual harassment suit I'll file against you."

As Derek stared in shock, Ayda took a deep breath and began to put her blouse back on. "What's it going to be?"

"You are such a bitch!"

"Yes, so I've been told. What've you decided?"

"I'll give you that promotion, you dumb bitch, but if you don't honor your word..."

"I'm a woman, Derek. Only men go back on their word; otherwise, I wouldn't have had to go to all this trouble. You have nothing to worry about. And let me congratulate you on your decision; the other option would've been too messy. I'll see you at work on Monday."

"Wait!" he screamed as she made her way to the door. "You can't leave me like this!"

"You know," she said, backpedaling into the room, "I know I shouldn't. I should untie you. For the sake of the cleaning lady—I really do feel bad that she's going to walk into this. But at least she'll get a kick out of it; she'll be privileged to have seen the world's smallest dick."

Ayda paid no attention to Derek's rantings as she left the room.

Chapter Three

DIDI

Didi and Saef had met at work, and quite by accident. There had been a glitch in one of her paychecks, so when she went to sort it out, she eventually made it to Saef's office.

"There's a mistake in my paycheck and they sent me to see you," she'd said as she walked into his office.

"Sure. Let me take a look."

When she handed him the check, she explained that the company had paid her twice for the same project. "It's sort of a bonus we get, but they gave it to me twice."

Still holding the check, he dropped his hands against the desk. "You're here because... they overpaid you?"

"Exactly. I guess you need to cancel this check, fix the mix-up, and get me another one."

"Cancel it?" he said.

"Yes. Well, it's not accurate."

"Are you serious?"

The woman looked around, confused by his question. "Why... wouldn't I be serious?"

"Because no one gives back money."

"They do if it's not rightfully theirs. They do if they're honest."

He was quiet for a minute. "I guess you're right. Ok, I'll fix this and have the new one printed out for you by the end of tomorrow."

"Thank you." She pulled the door to leave, but he called out to her.

"Would you... like to have dinner with me sometime?"

She felt her cheeks warming up and her palms begin to sweat. "That's very flattering, Saef, but... I don't date."

"It won't be a date then. We'll meet to discuss your paycheck issue."

"Look, I appreciate the invitation. But I just can't."

"Give me a good reason why and I'll drop it."

"Because I'm a practicing Muslim. So I don't meet strange men on my own."

Saef's eyes grew wide. Then he began to giggle. Within seconds his giggle turned to an all-out guffaw. She felt humiliated and stormed out of his office before he could say another word. Her face grew red with embarrassment and anger. When she sat back down at her desk, she thought of what she would say to him if their paths ever crossed again. It took her a minute to formulate it all into words, but she got it eventually. "You racist pig. What gives you the right to laugh at my religion or mock me? People like you make this world the horrible place that it has become—your supremacist complex is disgusting. The world would be a better place without you in it. And no, that's not a threat—just a fact." *Perfect.*

The following day, she sat deliberating which image to use for the upcoming project. She was immersed in thought, her face inches from the storyboard on her desk, when a soft tap on her shoulder broke her concentration.

"I wanted to apologize for yesterday," Saef said, holding out her updated paycheck. "You left before I could explain."

Snatching the envelope from him she snapped, "Oh is there an explanation now for xenophobic behavior other than being a prick?"

He blushed and nodded, looking down. "I totally get why you'd say that. But I'm not racist; I'm Muslim."

She crossed her eyebrows and looked up at him. "You're serious?"

"Yes," he replied. "But clearly not as dedicated as you are."

She took a deep breath and shook her head. "Well, I did not expect that." She remained quiet for a moment then said, "Sorry for calling you a prick."

"I deserved it." They nodded a truce to each other then Saef left, going back to his office.

The next morning, as she was working at her desk, an email notification popped up.

From: Saef Tawwab

Subject: Not a prick

It was just one line.

"I'd still like to take you to dinner."

She replied immediately. **"Thanks, but no. I told you, I don't date. You should understand that. And please don't use my company email for personal communications."**

She hoped that would be the end of it, but later that day, as she strained her eyes against some proofs, she heard a voice behind her say, "So bring your mom. Or sister. Or brother. Bring the whole family if you want." When she turned around, he was standing with his hands in his pockets and a grin on his face.

"Why won't you let this go? Maybe I just don't want to have dinner with you," she said.

"No, you do. And I want to get to know you better."

"Why on earth do you want to get to know me better, Saef? You are clearly not marriage material, and *I* do not waste my time."

"I am serious. I would like to see if... maybe I am marriage material after all."

She huffed loudly and said, "You aren't going to leave me alone until I agree, are you?"

He shook his head, the grin on his face getting even broader.

"Fine, but I'm bringing the whole family. You better be on your game or you may end up in all sorts of pain."

"I'm looking forward to it," he said.

That Friday evening, she met him at the local Italian restaurant. He was already seated when she arrived. They chit chatted for a few minutes, then she suggested they order. "My parents won't mind if we start without them."

The two ordered and began their meal. Saef laughed at her jokes, they talked about their family life and career ambitions. Saef learned that she dreamed of opening an art agency. "I don't know what shape it'll take yet. Like, will it be a graphic design ad agency? Or an art gallery? Or something else? I don't know yet. I just know that I want to be on the creative side, and also the one calling the shots. The company refused a project last month that could have been great. And some members of the team get paid a fraction of the others. There's so much politics involved. I would love to end all that—have it all be about the client and nothing more."

Saef learned that Didi's parents owned a bakery in town, and they did well for themselves. They had always encouraged her artistic side despite so many "religious" people telling her it was against Islam.

"They always stood up for me," she said. "They'd say, 'she's not hurting you nor is she depicting illicit things as permissible. Advertisements are part of the world today; it's how word gets out about new merchandise or services.'

"They always encouraged my drawing, but they would try to guide me," she continued. "They registered me for a calligraphy class so I could learn Islamic art. And then they enrolled me in a digital art program; that's what has helped me the most."

Saef enjoyed listening to her, but Didi didn't dominate the conversation. He told her about his family as well. He said his parents always wanted him to be an architect, and they were disappointed that he had gone into accounting. "I think they still have hope that I'll go back and get another degree. My sister tells them point blank that it won't happen, and they respond with, 'Be quiet! What do you know anyway!'"

"Were they as adamant that your sister get a particular degree?"

"No." He laughed. "They didn't have too much hope with her. She was a straight C student all through high school. She blew us all away in college when she graduated Summa Cum Laude in business. She and I are pretty close; we have to fend off my parents." Saef's face brightened as he listened to her loud chuckle.

At the end of dinner, Saef insisted on paying.

"I had a nice time. Thank you," she said.

"Thank you for agreeing to come. I had a great time. I'm just sorry your folks couldn't make it."

"Yeah, well... my parents died a few years ago. Everything I told you about them was true, they just aren't alive. I'm all the family I have, but I couldn't very well let you think I was okay with meeting you alone. It was the only 'protection' I had."

Saef stared at her, unable to formulate any suitable words.

She got up and said, "But now that you know the truth, I won't be able to meet with you anymore. I'll see you around the office."

He continued to stare in her direction even after she was completely out of sight.

◆ ◆ ◆

The week went by, and as she had expected, she neither bumped into Saef in the office nor got any emails from him. *I knew he wasn't marriage material*, she thought.

But on Thursday morning when she got to her desk, she was surprised to find Saef sitting, twirling around in her chair. He didn't even bother to get up when she arrived.

"I wasn't avoiding you. I know that's what you think, but you're wrong. My mom wasn't well all week. My sister and I each took a few days off to look after her. You can ask anyone in my department."

"I believe you," she said, not quite sure that she did. "Hope she's better now?"

"Yeah, she's better. *Alhamdulillah*. But the reason I'm here is she wants to meet you."

She was silent for a moment, absorbing what Saef had said. But the words seemed indigestible.

"My parents want to meet you," he repeated.

"I... I...." She still couldn't find the words. Then suddenly, they came to her. "Why?"

"What do you mean 'why?' I told them I met a nice woman..."

"Did you really use the word 'nice'?" she interrupted.

"Actually, no. I said, 'I met this strong, independent, funny, Muslim woman, and I want you to meet her.'"

She raised her eyebrows and crossed her arms, but she couldn't help the half-grin that wriggled its way to her lips. "Did you really say all that?"

"Yes, Didi," Saef said. "I really said all that. And now they want to meet you."

"Didi?" she repeated, her eyebrows knitted.

"You're totally a Didi."

She shrugged, nodded slowly, and shooed him out of her chair. He stood beside her, his hands in his pockets, his forehead raised in anticipation of her answer.

She swayed back and forth in the chair; her eyes focused on his shoes. A few moments later, when she still hadn't said anything, he spoke up. "Well? What do you say?"

She stopped swaying and looked up at him. "What do you want from me? I mean, really. What do you hope to get?"

He shrugged. "I see something here. I don't know exactly what it is or exactly where it will lead, but I'd like to explore it. With the hope that it might be something real. Something... special."

Her eyebrows went up in surprise and she stared out in front of her. A moment later, her shoulders rose just the slightest bit, and she nodded gently.

That weekend Didi met Saef and his parents out for breakfast. His parents smiled and his mother hugged her when she arrived. "*As salaamu alaikum.* Hello, Didi. It's nice to meet you," his father said.

"*Wa alaikum as salaam.* Nice to meet you, too, Uncle."

"So, Saef tells us you're a graphic designer," his mother said.

"Yes. I work on the creative side of the agency."

"Humph. Doesn't seem like something like that would require any special degree. You know Saef was going to be an architect?"

Didi nodded and said, "Yes, he told me."

"He's very smart," Saef's mother continued, sitting straight up with her hands folded in her lap and her face blank as stone. "We think he should continue with his education and go after that architect's degree. Then, he can marry a nice engineer like himself. Or a doctor. Someone worthy of being with him."

"Ha ha," Saef's father forced a laugh, trying to lighten the mood. "We did want Saef to be an architect. And he would have made a great one too. But he enjoys numbers and money and accounting. Good for him that he enjoys his job. You too, Didi? Do you enjoy being a graphic designer?"

"Yes. I'm a very creative person. I just wish I could do it on my own, outside of the framework of this company. There's too much politics involved; it gets in the way of the work."

Saef and his father both nodded.

"So you're thinking of quitting? You want to just have no job? How will you live? You think you'll marry a nice man like my Saef and he'll have to support you? These days both the husband and wife have to work. Saef, you shouldn't be thinking of anyone who doesn't want to work."

"She didn't say she was thinking of quitting or that she doesn't want to work, Mama."

Didi remained quiet, shocked into silence by his mother's audacity.

"You know our daughter, Saef's sister, Siham, she's a business major and has been thinking of starting a graphic design company. Maybe, Saef, you can ask her. Maybe once she starts it, she can hire Didi in the mailroom or something, to help get her foot in the door."

The morning continued in much the same way: Saef's mother degrading Didi at every opportunity, and Saef and his father trying to cover it up. Didi thought for sure, after his mother's atrocious behavior, she would never see him again. The thought relieved her.

But when she got to work on Monday, there he was, sitting in her chair again.

"Why won't you leave me alone? What, your mom didn't humiliate me enough? She wants to plan another day to take it further? Maybe you're here to tell me I should come by and clean your parents' house for them sometime this week? I'm sure your mom's already prepared my maid's apron."

"What? My mom loved you!"

"Get out of my chair, Saef." She continued talking as they switched places. "And don't lie; I hate men who lie. Your mom hates me. And to be honest, I didn't like her. You were probably right to check the chemistry between me and her before thinking about beginning a relationship. And now that you have, I'm certain you have no reason to keep coming by my desk. Next time, don't bring someone home unless she's an engineer or a doctor, to save the poor girl her sanity... and your mom the aggravation. Now leave me alone."

"I don't want to leave you alone."

Didi huffed loudly and shook her head, staring at him with wide eyes.

"I did want my folks to meet you. I wanted them to like you. But you're right; my mom probably won't like anyone. But I've come to terms with that. It's fine with me if she doesn't like you. I know she'll learn to."

"I don't want her to learn to, Saef. I am not a dramatic person and I do not enjoy that kind of nonsense in my life. You have absolutely no reason to pursue me. I barely know your name. Find someone they'll approve of. It'll make your life easier.

"Now, please leave me alone. I have a ton of work to do if I don't want to find myself *demoted to mailroom clerk*."

He nodded. And left without saying another word.

Two weeks went by, and she never thought of Saef once during that time. She did, however, think of his mother and all the ways she would like to return her proverbial slaps, but somehow, Saef was never in the picture. Until one day, she arrived at work in the morning to find a dozen red roses in a vase on her desk. The card attached said, "Please let me try again. Saef"

"Oh, come on!" she said, throwing herself down on her chair. A moment later, her nose began to tickle and her eyes began to water. The allergy hit her rather suddenly. She held out for all of one minute. Having had enough, she picked up the flowers, sneezed her way to the farthest end of the office, and threw them in the trash. When she got back to her desk, Saef was standing there.

"Sorry. I didn't know you were allergic."

"You don't know anything about me."

"I want that to change."

"I have no idea why."

"Honestly, I don't either. But something about you keeps calling me back."

"Nope. Nothing about me calls you."

"Something about me keeps being pulled back to you."

She sighed heavily. "Saef…"

"Just let us try again, ok?" he said, cutting her off. "Just give me a second shot."

His tenacity impressed her. Ignoring the fact that she might eventually encounter his insufferable mother again, she reluctantly agreed.

"Why were you so persistent in courting me?" Didi asked him a few years later.

Saef had replied, "I can't really put it into words. I just knew, somehow, that we fit together, that I would be happy with you. And I wanted to make you happy. I thought of your smile all the time. I imagined making a joke and hearing your laughter. I wanted to be there for you to make sure you were always happy and that no one ever said or did anything to bother you."

"But your mom. What did you say to her to make her stop being so... so... unpleasant?"

"She wasn't unpleasant."

Didi had looked up at him with one eyebrow cocked.

"I told her if she wanted to stay in my life, she'd have to respect my choices and be kind to my friends, all of them." He paused for a minute. "And anyone I wanted to be more than a friend. She told me to take a hike. So I did. I turned off my phone and stayed with a friend for a week without them knowing where I was. When I finally showed up at their house, she was so glad to see me that she agreed. And, if you remember, that lunch she invited you to, the first time you came to my parents' place, that was her idea, so she could apologize."

"I don't remember her apologizing."

"Her being nice to you and not making you clean the house, that was her apology."

"Makes sense. But I think she likes me now. Or is that just part of the agreement?"

"No, they both love you now. They see that you make me happy, and that makes them love you."

Although Saef's parents had always wanted someone better for their son, his sister loved Didi. Siham was a few years older than Didi and often discussed the idea of the two of them opening a graphic design company together.

"You can handle the art and I'll handle the business. And you *know* there's a strong market for graphic designers right now. There's really no downside."

"Of course there's a down side: how do we attract clients? And if we do manage to attract them, where do we get the artists to do the jobs? And how do you pay them? A percentage? What about taxes and all that messy stuff..."

"I'll take care of that!" Siham had said. "And at first, *you* can be the only artist, then once we start to make a profit and roll in the high clients, we can hire more."

"But high clients tend to go with full ad agencies, not startup graphic design teams."

"I still think it's a good idea. Think about it."

But what Didi hadn't said to Siham was that her real concern—her only concern actually—was that she had learned never to mix business with friendship. Years ago, when her parents had the bakery, their most trusted friend, Ghazi Dabbour, invited them to partner in an import/export company. He had stayed with them for over a year when he'd first moved to the US. The still-young Didi had called him Uncle, and her father treated him like his brother.

"We'll be 50:50 partners, and all you have to do is front the money. I'll take care of the business and run it. We'll have a contract to insure you get your profit. And," Ghazi had added, "you'll even get access to flour and sugar and all sorts of ingredients for your shop for a fraction of what you're paying now."

The deal had seemed perfect. The Faisals' had wanted to expand their business, and here the perfect opportunity—partnering with their most trusted friend—had been laid at their feet. Didi's father gave Ghazi the thirty thousand without hesitation, and they signed the contract.

"But you know what business is like," Ghazi had said. "We can't expect a profit the first year."

During that first year, Ghazi paid them their monthly share of the sales even though no profit was being made. At the end of that time, they had made back only half of their investment. They remained patient, knowing it could take time to make a profit.

Then Didi's mother had a stroke and needed medical care and physical therapy to recover. But they didn't have the money. And Ghazi had stopped delivering his monthly checks. And then he disappeared altogether. When they went to the location of the business, the guards told Didi's father that Mr. Dabbour had liquidized the remaining assets because the business had gone broke. They called him over and over, but he never answered. When they called his family, they learned he had moved out and wasn't providing them with any details about his whereabouts. It was the biggest stab in the back, and it hit them right when her parents were desperate for that money. Didi's mother's health deteriorated, and she passed away shortly after. Her father couldn't take the passing of his soulmate of over twenty years. He died of a broken heart just a few weeks later. Didi was left to deal with the bakery, and with life, all alone. The betrayal turned her sour. And she vowed that once she had the means, she would find that Ghazi Dabbour and take back what was rightfully hers. And ever since then, she'd avoided entering any kind of business arrangements with friends or family. It's one thing to be cheated by a stranger; it's another thing altogether to be cheated by someone you thought would always have your back.

Respecting Didi's reservation, Siham found another partner and opened a graphic design company. "But I still want you on board," she'd said to Didi. "Once we start making a profit, I'm going to make you an employee—not in the mailroom, by the way. And then you're going to want to buy in."

Siham was Didi's only friend. But she was all the friend Didi needed. She was the first one Didi called when she needed to vent, even if it was about Saef. She was always fair, so Didi valued her input. Siham was the first one—directly after Saef—that Didi shared her good news with. She knew that her friend would be as happy for her as if the good fortune had been her own. That kind of love wasn't common to find, and Didi knew how precious it was.

When Didi had received the results from her doctor all those years ago, she showed up on Siham's doorstep with tears in her eyes. Siham embraced her before she even knew what was wrong. The best part of crying in Siham's arms was that she never told her to stop; she always let Didi cry as much as she needed. Once she was all cried out, Didi would explain her situation, and Siham always listened intently.

Siham had married when she was very young, but her marriage had lasted only one year. Although she'd always wanted to be a mother, she was thankful that her failed marriage hadn't produced any children.

"So, here we are, two hopeless women who won't ever bear children."

"But you *can* bear children," Didi had objected. "If you overcome your aversion to men, you could have children. I can't, whether I want to or not."

"You might not be able to bear a child, but you can still be a mom, Didi. There are millions of children already born who need parents to love and raise them. Biology is not the only way to have a child."

"But it's the only way I would want to have a child. I get adoption—and I try to give to orphans and help out. But if God made me unable to bear children, that may mean he doesn't want me to raise them."

"Or it could mean He wants to see how you'll deal with this situation, how you'll redirect your maternal instincts. Maybe He wants you to be someone else's mom."

Didi just shook her head. "I'm not going to tell Saef."

Siham didn't react. When a few more moments passed in silence, Didi repeated herself, "I'm not going to tell Saef."

"I don't agree with your decision, Didi. He has a right to know."

"I have my reasons for keeping it to myself."

"I think you're wrong, but I won't overstep my bounds. It's not my news to tell."

And Siham kept her word; she never told anyone about Didi's infertility. And she was never able to convince Didi to tell Saef herself. Being the keeper of Didi's secrets was just another way that Siham proved she was an awesome friend.

Often if Didi needed to get away, she would call Siham to hang out with her. And Siham never let her down; she was a true friend who always made herself available. Often the two women just sat and had coffee at the local coffee shop or perused through the local bookstore.

"I want to own a bookstore one day," Didi said as they moved through the aisles.

"I thought you wanted an art agency?"

"Not an art agency, an art gallery—in a bookstore, with a coffee shop. Where you can view works by local talent on the walls and painters can even hold workshops. We could have art classes right there in the shop."

"Okay," Siham said.

Didi laughed. "What do you mean 'okay'?"

"I mean, okay; if that's something you want, then we've got to start working toward that goal."

"Yes, I guess you're right."

"I'll do the research and let you know the budget and merchandise suppliers. Once we do that, we'll search for an appropriate venue and research its market to see that it'll be profitable in that location."

"You're serious?"

"Only if you are," Siham said. She waited a few moments then asked, "So... are you?"

Didi fingered the books on the bookshelves as she walked by and thought about it.

"I am."

"Alright then."

"Alright," Didi said with a determined nod and a wide smile. She would start moving forward to achieve one of her dreams.

As promised, Siham did the research and wrote up a budget. Once they had the plan, they spent months searching for the perfect location. After about nine months of active searching, Didi decided they should take a break. "Some things come when you stop looking for them."

"Okay," Siham said, joining Didi in her feeling of disappointment. "But this is not over."

"Definitely not."

"We're going to do this. Maybe not now, but we are, *In sha' Allah*."

"Definitely, *In sha' Allah*."

But the right location never appeared. As the years passed, the project kept getting pushed back into Didi's land of unfulfilled dreams. Along with motherhood. The only dream she had actually managed to achieve was marrying a loyal, compassionate, kind man. And working in her field; she did love her job. She knew lots of people never achieved as much as she had already, and she was grateful. But, true to human condition, she wanted more.

Her in-laws asked her and Saef when they were planning on having kids every time they saw them. Every. Single. Time.

"You've been married for three years now. Don't you think it's time you started a family?" Sumayya would say.

"We are a family, Mama," Saef would reply.

"You know what I mean."

"Nothing happens without God's will. We're leaving it in His hands."

"You aren't using birth control then?"

Didi was too astonished to answer, and Saef acted like he hadn't heard.

"But if you try for six months or so with no result, you should see a doctor."

The invasion of privacy was so overwhelming that Didi had to leave the room. If Siham happened to be present during those interactions, she would usually speak up. "Mama, that's none of your business!"

"The hell it isn't! I have a right to see my grandkids before I die. You've basically turned into a lesbian, so my only hope is these two."

"You have no such right, Mama. Only they can decide when—or if—they'd like to have kids. But on a related note, I'm bringing my girlfriend to dinner next week." Siham winked at Didi as the in-laws began another tirade altogether.

"Your what?! Girlfriend?!"

"Chill out, Baba. I was only joking."

"We don't joke about that!" Saleh screamed.

Although she'd almost given her parents heart attacks, Siham had gotten them off of Didi's back.

"If your parents ever found out," Didi had once said to Siham, "they'd make Saef take a second wife."

Siham thought for a moment. "Yes, they probably would."

Chapter Four
A SURPRISE

After threatening to blackmail Derek, Ayda had gotten that promotion. She knew she deserved it, so bending the rules a bit to get it didn't bother her. If she'd been a man, she thought, she would have gotten it long ago. Her position was now secure, and Derek never bothered her. He let her have full creative control, and whenever anyone complained about Ayda or her work, he explained that she had a vision which he respected. Everyone in the office knew he'd never side with anyone against her. For Ayda, that meant he remained aware that she could bury him at any moment. She was glad he knew who was in power.

When she had first moved into her office, all those years ago, she stood in the middle of the room with the door closed and the blinds down. She held her hands up before her and made a prayer that God would grant great blessings in her work.

"Forgive me my shortcomings, Lord. And help me to improve. And make my job a source of blessed income for me."

Ayda was not necessarily a religious person, but she believed in God and she believed that she could not lose hope of His mercy. Losing hope, she knew, was a sign of a disbeliever, a sign that the devil was closer to her soul, and she wouldn't let that son-of-a-bitch win. She held onto her faith, despite the thin thread that connected her. She breathed in the new smell of *her* office and sat on *her* chair behind *her* desk. She called her new assistant, Colette, into her office. "Where are we with that information technology account? Has everything been signed off?"

"The group was waiting for your approval on this last board," Colette said, handing her the images. "They think it adds some humor to the ad and will grab the attention of some of the younger viewers."

Ayda took her time reviewing the board while Colette sat quietly. "Yes, that's good. Tell them to move forward with that and set up the final meeting with the client for early next week.

"The other thing I want from you is to get me that jewelry company on the line."

Colette shook her head slightly, a confused look on her face. "What jewelry company? Oh, you mean from last week?"

"Yes."

"But we dismissed that client already."

"I know we dismissed them. Just get them on the line."

This is what she had been waiting for—the power to make the calls, to decide which clients to work with and which to decline.

Ayda remained patient on the phone with the representative from the jewelry company for a full hour. Colette watched her through the glass partition as she nodded, sometimes laughed, sometimes spoke with authority. After she hung up, she took a deep breath and informed Colette that they had taken on the jewelry client and that the team should get started on the account right away. Despite thinking that she was too tough and often bitchy, Ayda's team admired her hard work. She recognized their talent and never denied them appropriate credit. Because she dealt with them honestly, they felt a loyalty towards her even though they didn't particularly like her.

The team cheered at their desks for the acquisition of an account they had all hated to lose. That had been the first time they'd seen her acquire an account undeterred by the CEO's disapproval. Her actions gave her team the sense that she would use her position to do good by the company, and they respected her for her gall. They all watched with open mouths as Colette informed Derek that they had acquired the account.

"Didn't I decline that client?"

"Ayda made a new deal with them." She handed him the contract and waited for his response.

"I'll look this over and get it to her by the end of the day. Thank you."

Colette left Derek's office and everyone in the department watched him disappear as he drew the blinds. They had bets going about how long it would take for him to fire her after pulling this stunt. In whispered voices, they discussed who might take her place.

Suddenly cutting into their conversations were muffled yet discernible screams of "That bitch! Bitch!" coming from Derek's office. They heard him go crazy making unintelligible noises, apparently fighting himself in the office. Then they all watched his secretary go in and reappear with the contracts.

"Flip to the last page," they urged her. "Did he sign?"

"Of course he didn't," someone said. "There's no way he did."

In the few seconds it took for the secretary to flip through the pages, it seemed like everyone in the office was holding their breath. When her eyes found the last page, the secretary's face lit up; she held the page up for them to see. "He did."

They cheered quietly, not quite believing it. "What would make him change his mind?" someone said. "Wonder what she has over him," someone else commented. In their excitement, none of them noticed Ayda standing in her open doorway until the secretary handed her the contract.

"This is my show now, ladies and germs. Congratulations on the new account. Let's not fuck it up."

Ten years had passed since that day, and the politics of the company remained very much the same. Ayda's team, including Colette, was more or less stable. They all agreed it was better to work beneath an unfriendly boss who recognized your work than to work with a smiling hypocrite who'd take credit for it. Ayda always made sure that any bonuses paid by clients—for finishing projects early or for extra splendid execution—got distributed to those who truly deserved them. Her team recognized that other bosses might hoard all that praise and money, and they appreciated her integrity. It didn't stop them from gossiping about her, of course, but it did strengthen their loyalty—that same type of loyalty seen in families where members mock each other one minute, then if an outsider makes the same derogatory comments, stand up for each other. In this same way, if the team caught members of other departments talking about Ayda, they would stick up for her. "She's not that bad," they might say. Or, "Say what you will about her—she doesn't really care anyway—she works her ass off."

Those same team members would ask Colette, "Does she ever get any personal phone calls?"

"Just from her aunt and uncle and every once in a while from a woman named...Sam? Simone? I can't remember the name exactly, but something like that. But that's all. No one else."

"It must have been devastating," someone remarked.

"What was?"

"Whatever happened to make her like this. You don't actually think she was born a bitch, do you?"

But except for a remark here or there, no one cared enough to give it any real thought. And of course getting close to Ayda, to find out why she had such a rough exterior, was completely out of the question.

One day an unfamiliar man showed up at the office and asked to see Ayda. Her secretary informed her that he was a lawyer.

"What does he want?" she asked.

"When I asked him what this was in reference to, he said it was personal."

Ayda fiddled with his card for a moment then told her secretary to show him in.

"Good afternoon, Ms. Faisal. Thank you for agreeing to see me. I apologize for coming without an appointment."

"Have a seat, Mr. Williams. But do get to the point because I'm busy."

"Of course," he said, setting his briefcase down on the floor and settling into the chair. "I'm here to inform you that you have been named guardian of a twelve-year-old girl after her mother passed away last week."

The man handed Ayda a notarized will clearly stating that Ayda was the mother's choice to raise her daughter should anything happen to her.

"Look Mr. Williams, there must be some mistake. By some freak accident there must be another Ayda Faisal out there somewhere. I have no family, so I certainly can't have inherited a child to raise."

"There is no mistake, Ms. Faisal. The girl's mother provided your full name, home address and place of work. You are the Ayda Faisal intended."

Ayda stared blankly at the will before her, trying to understand what was happening.

"Who in their right mind would appoint me the guardian of a child?! I have no children of my own. I'd have no idea what I was doing. Who was this woman?"

Then Ayda flipped the papers back to the front page, and there, staring back at her and slicing her heart open again, was the one name she hated even more than the devil: Leah Robinson.

"Get out," Ayda said a bit too softly.

"Excuse me?" Mr. Williams said, leaning forward to hear her better.

"Get out. Get out!"

He stood but did not leave. "Ms. Faisal, I must know where you stand with regard to this matter. I cannot simply..."

"I said get out! I have your card. I'll call you. Now leave!"

The man grabbed his briefcase and dashed out of the office as though he were escaping a fire.

Ayda pulled the blinds down, still holding the will in her hand. That name—Leah Robinson—had haunted her every day since her husband's death. Every day, for the past ten years.

The audacity of that woman to think that even in her death she can poison me! During her life she destroyed mine, and now she wants to continue with this destruction even in her death?! What kind of a woman appoints the widow of her dead lover as her daughter's guardian? Who does that?

Ayda was on her fourth cigarette, and still pacing around her office with the will dangling from her hand when her assistant knocked and entered. "The sports apparel team is ready to present to you now."

"Not today. Reschedule it for tomorrow. Or... on second thought, reschedule for next week."

"But you wanted it finished before the weekend," Colette reminded her.

"And now I'm changing my mind! Next week!"

Ayda grabbed her purse and the pack of cigarettes from her desk and ran out of the office. She got in her car and sped off. In her haste, she nearly hit a young woman riding a bike, but Ayda didn't slow down to apologize. She needed to get away. Away from what exactly, she didn't know. Away from that villainous will that now sat in the passenger's seat? Or away from the life she had failed so miserably to forget? Or away from herself, the idiot who was always the last one to find out about anything? Because as much as she hated her husband for his betrayal, she hated herself more for only discovering it after his death. She hated that she'd given him the benefit of the doubt, that she'd trusted him enough to believe he would remain faithful.

She drove madly through town, her rage fueling the car. After about ten minutes of aimless driving, she realized she had no real destination. Where could she go to escape herself? There was no place. And then it came to her.

She slowed down as the turn approached, and as she turned into the cemetery, she brought the car to a crawl. As she made her way to the section for Muslims, she rolled down her window and said the prayer she'd memorized all those years ago when her parents had been brought to their final resting place, leaving her an orphan at the age of twenty-two. *"As salaamu alaikum ya ahl el diyar, antum el sabiqun wa nahnu el lahikun. Nes'al Allahu lena w lekum al 'afia.* Peace to you, dwellers of this home, you have gone before, and we will follow. We ask Allah for well-being for us and you."

Her first instinct in going to the cemetery wasn't to visit her folks; her first instinct had actually been to remember that eventually the pain would be gone. Once her body was laid to rest here, in that plot she'd already purchased beside her parents, the worldly pain would disappear. Only that didn't really appease her worry; she did believe in an afterlife. She did believe in heaven and hell. And she knew that her temper alone was an indication of which direction she'd be going. But as she stood there, staring at her plot, she prayed that the day her body would be placed there would be the last day of her suffering. She prayed that God would have mercy on her, in this world and the next. Then she sat down at the bench beside her parents' plots, and as sacrilegious as she knew it was, she lit another cigarette while praying for them. She prayed for them every night, but when she came to the cemetery—once or twice a month—she extended her prayers and afterwards she talked to them, never really sure whether her words had been heard or not.

"He did it again, Baba. That bas...he did it again. Even in death he's found a new way to break my heart. He had a child with that who... with his mistress. A child that he never told me about. A child that, now that both of her parents are dead, is apparently going to be my problem."

She put out the cigarette and lit another one.

"Am I supposed to take on that responsibility? I have no idea how to raise a kid. Do I want to make that leap now that I'm 47? Or can I just say, 'This isn't my responsibility. Find someone else to take care of her'? Or would that be like throwing away a gift? It could be a gift, right? Shit. I don't know what to do."

She smoked a third cigarette, hoping some kind of clarity would come to her. It didn't. When she left a few minutes later, she headed home, feeling the weight of the decision she had to make and at a complete loss as to how she should come to that decision.

After her shower that evening, she didn't feel like eating a full meal. She pulled out the left-over salad and when she'd finished it off, grabbed some grapes and sat on the couch, nibbling them. Even though the TV was off, she still stared at it. The will sat beside her on the couch; she stared straight ahead of her to avoid it.

When she went up to bed, she left the will in the living room. It had made her entire day unrestful; she didn't want that negative energy near her when she slept. But the truth was, she couldn't escape it. She tossed and turned for hours before falling asleep.

What seemed like only minutes later, she woke from a nightmare with a lurch. Breathing heavily, she looked around the room, as though searching for something. When she found nothing, she held her hand to her chest and repeated a short prayer she'd learned as a child whenever she felt scared. She didn't really understand what she was scared of, but her fear was undeniable. When her breathing had slowed to normal, she reached for the clock. It read 5:16. The sun would be up soon. She replaced the clock and took a cigarette from the pack on her nightstand. When the lighter didn't work on the second click, she sat frozen in place, deciding if perhaps there was a better escape than the cigarette.

◆◆◆

Since Saef refused to help Didi with the housework, she refused doing the jobs that weren't technically considered "housework." She was fully capable, for example, of getting on a ladder and changing a light bulb. But she insisted that he do it. And he always did it right away, fluffing out his chest. She asked him to take out the trash every evening, and eventually he began doing it without her needing to ask. When she wanted to hang some pictures on the wall of the staircase, she handed him the hammer and, again, he accepted the task like a hero saving the day.

"Should I add this one at the top, above the one of us at 'Eid, or at the bottom, below the one with us and my parents?"

She came over and looked for a moment at the wall of pictures. Their wedding picture, with both of them clearly laughing, stood tall in the center. Above it was a photo of Didi staring out at a purple sunset. Above that was the 'Eid picture of them both. Below the wedding photo was a profile of Saef in a suit, looking down at something on the ground that had caught his eye. At the bottom of the staircase was a picture of both of them with Saef's parents and sister. They were all smiling; it was one of Didi's favorites.

"Should we start a second row, above them all?"

"But with just one photo, won't that look strange?" he asked, holding it up.

They examined it for a minute then Didi said, "Oh, wait! I have another one I wanted to hang. You can put them both up, towards the middle, starting a second row. That should even it out."

She got the other photo and handed it to him, and Saef did as he was instructed.

As he hammered the nail into the wall, he asked her, "Do you remember what we were laughing about in our wedding picture?"

She laughed, "Are you kidding? I'm never going to forget it. The photographer said on the count of three we should say who we love the most in the world. 'One, two, three.' I say, 'Saef' and I hear you say, 'My mom.' The guys snapped a couple of pictures of me beating you up first, then you said, 'I mean Didi, Didi.' He kept snapping away as I beat you up, then finally your laughter became contagious. I still have a few of those shots of me beating you up."

"You know that was planned, right?"

"What do you mean planned?" she asked.

"I never told you? The guy told me beforehand. He said, 'When I ask who you love most in the world, say your mom.'"

"You're lying."

Saef burst out laughing. "I swear I'm not. I can't believe I never told you!"

He didn't surprise her often, but when he did, it was always big. Like never telling her about the staged wedding photo fiasco. Or never pulling out the gift from his pocket...

Early on in their marriage, several loads of laundry had been ruined by the tissues Saef invariably forgot to take out of his pants. She quickly got into the habit of searching her husband's pockets before sticking any item of clothing into the machine. Once she'd found a hundred dollar bill, and thanked God she'd caught it before it went into the wash. One day, she found a medium sized box. When she opened it, a shiny silver charm bracelet glowed back at her. The only charm attached was a tiny cherub with the engraving "True Love." She couldn't contain her elatedness at the wonderful surprise. She ran down the stairs and threw her arms around Saef.

"*Habibi*, this was so thoughtful of you. Thank you, I love it!"

He hugged her back and chuckled at the good mood, but she didn't notice his crossed eyebrows. "You're welcome, *habibti*. What is it you love?"

"The bracelet you got for me." She held it out for him to see. "It's perfect. Such a beautiful way to surprise me." She kissed him again.

And again she missed the expression on his face.

Chapter Five

A CHILD JOINS THE FAMILY

Just as Didi's in-laws pressured them about having a baby, they tried incessantly to find Siham an appropriate husband. They asked all their friends and relatives, even members of the mosque who they knew nothing about except that they were Muslim, to introduce them to any available men. Siham sometimes met with the potential suitors just to appease her parents.

It was Siham's nature to do shocking things. Only, she never did them to be shocking, no matter what her parents thought. She simply preferred to keep her private life private. On occasion Didi sensed that Siham was seeing someone, but she never mentioned it. Then one day at their weekly family dinners, the reason for her recent secrecy and odd behavior became clear.

Siham said, "I need you all to appear in court next week to speak on my behalf."

Sumayya, Saleh and Didi all froze and stared at her.

"What did you do now, Seema? Pour burning coffee on one of your employees?" Saef joked, still focused on his food.

"No," she replied, continuing with her meal as well. "I'm in the process of adopting a child. He's just a few months old. His entire family was killed in Syria; a neighbor found him under the rubble and rescued him. The man had planned on raising the child as his own, but he died shortly after arriving in this country. I know I can raise this baby; I feel it is my calling. The next step is the court needs to meet my family. Make sure we're not a bunch of wackos."

Saef dropped his fork. "You're serious?"

"Of course I'm serious." She took a sip of water gingerly and resumed eating.

"You want to adopt a child? On your own?" her father asked.

"Yes. I figured if I had a biological child, I'd end up doing everything for him anyway. I mean, how much did you really contribute to our upbringing, Baba? Basically bringing in the paychecks...and that's about it. Well, *Alhamdulillah*, I don't need financial help. I do well on my own."

"But raising a child without a father?"

"Come on, Mama. You know better than anyone here that fathers' roles are overrated, at least the way they've been fulfilling them. Where was dad when I got appendicitis? Where was he when Saef broke his arm playing basketball? Or when you caught him skipping school that day he hid in the shower?"

"He was at work, but when he came home, he supported my decisions. He helped instill my rules and punishments. He shared the responsibility of raising you."

"I don't mean to sound mean or ungrateful, Mama and Baba. But the truth is Mama shouldered the task of raising us almost by herself. Most mothers do—that's just the way it is..."

"As boys get older they need a father, Siham. They need a man to be a role model, to guide them," her mother protested.

"And that's what Saef and Baba are for. There are plenty of uncles and grandfathers who step up when their single-mother relatives need it. I expect you'll both do that."

"But this child...this baby...you have no way of knowing what family he comes from, what kind of people they are, what diseases they had."

"I'm pretty sure a baby won't get up in the middle of the night and try to murder me, Mama."

"I'm being serious!" Sumayya snapped, slamming her palm against the table.

"So am I," Siham said calmly. "May God be merciful on them and reward them for the pain they suffered, but the type of people they were means nothing. I will be raising him. If he does wrong, it'll be because I didn't guide him, not because it's in his genes to be a criminal."

The family sat in silence for a few moments exchanging glances while Siham continued with her meal.

"Didi, maybe you can knock some sense into your sister," Saleh said.

Didi looked down at her plate. "I don't think I'm the person you want, Uncle. I think what Siham is doing is not only admirable, I think God will reward her many times over for being generous with her love and not hoarding it solely for her biological kids."

"What biological kids?! She'll have no biological kids! No man will want to marry a woman who's adopted a child and raising him on her own!" Sumayya replied.

"Perfect. You just gave me another incentive to push forward with this, Mama." Siham winked at Didi while her mother left the table in a huff.

"This isn't going to be easy," Saef said. "Not on you, and not on this family. You need to think about that."

"I know it isn't going to be easy, Saef. But I also know that no one ever received any honor for not doing the right thing simply for the comfort of their family. God told us to care for orphans. I can't care for them all, but I can care for one. You standing in my way is like you telling me not to follow God's word."

It took them all a few days to calm down. But when the time came, they all showed up at the adoption hearing to support her. It was a long process, but at the end of it, Siham returned to her home with her new son in her arms. As she and her family walked in the house that first day, Siham told them, "I know that according to Islamic law, he doesn't inherit the same way he would have if he were my biological son. So if I kick it, he gets a third of everything, as is permissible. But if he needs a place to live, then let him live in my home for as long as he needs. After that time, you can sell it and disperse it as appropriate."

"What kind of talk is this on such a celebratory day?" her father said.

"I just want everyone to know that I understand and respect and will always follow my religion. I know he doesn't take my name and doesn't inherit the same as a biological child. I know, and I don't want to do anything against God's law. I'm going to tell him all about how he came to live here... he will know I didn't give birth to him. I just want him to be loved. And he will be, even if I'm gone."

Her mother, who had been her strongest opponent, became her biggest ally. She showed her how to bathe him, how to swaddle him, how to burp him without his spit-up making too much of a mess. She spent the first few days and nights with her.

"Thank you, Mama. I know you didn't want this baby. Thank you for helping me anyway."

Her mother grabbed her forcefully in a hug. "I didn't *not* want this baby. I wanted your baby. And now we have him. And we all love him very much. I think it's honorable and brave what you're doing. But I know the difficult days you're yet to face, and I just didn't want you to face them alone."

"God keep you safe and here for me always, Mama."

Siham proved to be a wonderful mother, one of those super-moms who did it all and succeeded at it. She took Rizq with her to the office, never missed a meeting, feeding time, opportunity to make a new client, or to kiss her son. He became the reason she invested in a childcare room at the office and made sure any parents in the office took advantage of it. Rizq's first few years were spent in the office, by his mother's side. On the weekends his grandparents spent hours playing with him and spoiling him.

"He doesn't need all those toys, Mama."

"No, he probably doesn't. But he loves them so they're staying!" Sumayya would say. She had fallen well into the role of grandma despite her earlier reservations. She bought him clothes and toys, told Siham she was dressing him too light or not feeding him enough. She spent hours with him on the weekends even when Siham had no errands to run or plans to go out. And when he spiked a fever—as children tend to do—she sat with Siham and calmed her fears, telling her she was doing a great job and whatever virus had had the audacity to attack him would be gone soon. And it always was.

"Thank you for your support, Mama."

"It's nothing. You just make sure to take care of yourself, too. You look too pale. Are you eating enough meat?"

Siham hugged her mother. "I love you, Mama."

When Didi first found out about Siham's plan to adopt, she was hurt that Siham hadn't confided in her.

"I get why you didn't tell your folks. But why didn't you tell me? I'd support you. You know that."

Siham hugged her. "I know. I just...I didn't want to get your hopes up. Or maybe I didn't want to get my own hopes up. I think that might be more honest. Telling you meant I was really in this, really fighting this battle. I guess...I'd feel like I let you down if I didn't succeed, and I couldn't handle that."

Although she was still hurt that Siham seemed to have prerequisites before sharing her news with her, Didi fell easily into her role as aunt. And Saef was a great uncle. He bought Rizq a nerf baseball set when he was only two years old.

"You know he's just going to whack you in the crotch with that, don't you?" Didi had said.

"What? What are you talking about? This is going to teach him how to play the American game!"

"If you say so."

When Saef gave the toy to Rizq and took him outside to show him how to use it, Didi grabbed her phone and switched on the camera.

"What's going on?" Siham asked, coming up behind Didi.

"We're about to win the next America's Funniest Home videos. Just watch."

The women sat outside watching Saef teach Rizq how to play. Once he thought the little boy had it down, Saef stood a few steps back and lolled the nerf ball. Rizq swung and missed.

"That's okay," Saef said. "It takes some practice. Let's try it again."

Saef bent to grab the ball, and as he stood back up, Rizq swung the bat to position, only it connected with Saef's groin first, sending him to the ground in pain.

Didi turned off the camera, and she and Siham, both laughing out loud, went over to the victim.

"I'm pretty sure it is all-American to get whacked in the balls with a nerf baseball bat. You did a great job here today, Saef. Keep it up. Actually, you probably won't be able to *get it up* for a few days, but you did it for a good cause, so Didi, don't hold it against him."

Saef rolled around in pain for a few more moments as Siham picked up Rizq and took him in for lunch.

"Do you need some ice?" Didi asked him.

"No," he groaned. "I'm fine."

"Yeah, you look totally fine."

Rizq's presence had made her in-laws stop asking about kids. Or maybe they assumed something was up; Didi wasn't really sure. In any case, she enjoyed not having to deal with their questions and comments. And Rizq himself made Didi feel like God had blessed them with children even though she couldn't have any. She helped her sister-in-law as much as possible and followed every one of Rizq's milestones, every new tooth, every step. She didn't have to deal with the night wakings that drove Siham up the wall the first few months, nor the immunization shots that somehow always sent the new mother into a crying fit, but Didi figured she wasn't really missing much. She considered Rizq a blessing for all of them, and she thanked God for him every day.

She didn't know that soon after Rizq's second birthday, Didi's biggest blessing would be taken away from her.

Chapter Six

AYDA MAKES A DECISION

The coolness of the floor shocked Ayda's feet for a moment, but when she stood and pulled her robe on, she could no longer feel the chill. In the bathroom, she waited a few seconds for the water to warm up, then she performed ablution. When she finished, she dried off and made her way back to her bedroom. She pulled on the prayer gown that covered her from head to toe, aligned herself to face Mecca, and prayed the pre-dawn prayer. It had been years since she'd prayed, but even as she stood there, she recalled her parents telling her that prayer was more beneficial than sleep. She hoped it was true.

Once she'd finished praying, she remained seated on the prayer mat for several minutes, contemplating the events of the day before. She'd been named guardian of a girl whose existence she had purposely ignored. She'd been forced to face the fact that her husband's indiscretion had produced this innocent child. And now, this child's mother—her deceased husband's mistress—had trusted her enough to raise the child.

And suddenly, she knew that she had no choice. She hadn't seen a vision or heard voices, but something told her—something screamed out from her soul—that she had to accept her husband's little girl into her life. If the young girl was alone and Ayda had the opportunity to help her, then it was her duty.

Without standing up, she reached for her purse which rested on the nightstand beside her. Fishing out her phone and the lawyer's card, she dialed his number. A groggy, gruff voice answered.

"Yes, Mr. Williams, this is Ayda Faisal. I'm calling to inform you that I will honor Leah Robinson's will; I will accept responsibility for the young girl."

"Do you know what time it is?"

"I'll wait for you later today so we can finalize everything." Ayda hung up without thanking him or saying good-bye.

As she replaced her phone in her purse and folded up the prayer mat, her breathing became lighter. She still hadn't a clue what to do with a child, but at least now that the decision had been made, she felt like the most difficult part was over.

When Mr. Williams arrived at her office several hours later, the secretary showed him in immediately.

"Good morning, Ms. Faisal. Although it would have been a much better morning if a phone call hadn't awoken me before six."

"Don't cry over spilled milk, Mr. Williams; you're far too old for that. Have a seat and tell me how we move forward from here."

"There is not much more you need to deal with. I'll take care of the legalities, and Shams should be with you in a day or two. But first, Leah had advised that you be given this letter. I meant to give it to you yesterday, but you kicked me out before I could."

Ayda took the envelope with both hands and stared at it.

"I don't need anything else from you, so I'll leave before you kick me out again. You'll be hearing from me in a day or two. In the meantime, you should make sure you've prepared your home to welcome Shams."

The words snapped Ayda from her trance. "What do you mean 'prepare my home'?"

"I mean make arrangements to have her there with you. Where she'll sleep, where she'll hang her clothes. That sort of thing. Good day, Ms. Faisal."

Ayda stared at the door long after he had left, the mysterious envelope still in her tight grip. It was plain white all around, and Ayda thought it was strange that it hadn't even been addressed. She wondered if it were possible that frazzled lawyer had given her the wrong envelope, an envelope for another case altogether. She knew the only way to find out was to open it, and read the enclosed letter, but she feared what she may find. Already her husband had made a fool of her: once in his life when he'd had an affair, and now in his death, when his child—a child he'd fathered with another woman—would be brought out of secrecy and into the light. He'd already humiliated her enough, she wasn't eager to learn how he could do it again. She shoved the envelope in her purse and lit a cigarette.

"Colette," she said into the receiver, "have the sports apparel team come in and make their presentation."

"But you said next week?"

"They were ready with it yesterday, Colette, surely they'll be able to do it today. Let them know I expect them in fifteen minutes."

"Your office or the meeting room?" Colette asked innocently.

"My office!" Ayda screamed and slammed down the receiver.

The team members flew into a panic as soon as Colette told them Ayda was waiting for them.

"I knew she was going to do this to us! When she postponed yesterday, I knew she was gonna call us in unprepared," one of them said.

"Well hurry up and get your shit together. We can't screw up the presentation for the biggest client we have."

The five of them hastily reviewed the storyboard and their presentation before walking into Ayda's office accompanied by Colette.

The errors they made during the presentation were minimal. Once they finished, the team stood before Ayda, holding their breath.

"The colors aren't quite right," Ayda noted. "Try a shade of green instead of the blue. Show it to me by the end of the day. Besides that, good job everybody. Practice it a few times before we present to the client next week. Colette, set that up for Monday or Tuesday. Now everybody get out."

The members began gathering their materials and shuffling out of her office.

"Cynthia," Ayda called out. The same woman who had accused Ayda months before of being from hell turned around. "You did a great job on this project. If you keep it up, you'll be going places."

Cynthia stood there, her mouth ajar, staring in disbelief at the woman from hell who had just complimented her work. When a moment had passed, Ayda said, "Now get out." In her haste, Cynthia didn't even thank her for the compliment. Walking out of Ayda's office in the same zombie-like trance, she stood with her back against the closed door.

"Did she chew you out?" one of the team members who had left before her asked.

Cynthia shook her head, still in a daze.

"Well, what did she want then?"

Cynthia looked at her colleague, knitted her eyebrows, and asked, "She complimented me? She complimented my work? Were you there? Did that really happen?"

"Cyn, man, are you losing it? I don't know what she wanted; that's why I asked you."

"But could it have possibly happened the way...the way my brain processed it?"

The two women stood there staring at each other for a moment, then the other patted her on the shoulder, shook her head, and headed back to her desk.

"Maybe she's not from hell after all," Cynthia said aloud. Just then the office door swung open and Ayda collided into Cynthia with an aggravated huff as she barreled her way out of the office.

"Or maybe someone spiked my coffee."

◆◆◆

Ayda stood in the middle of her living room. "Is this place fit for a child?"

She walked to the guest bedroom and looked around. The bed was comfortable enough, and the closet was spacious and clean. Still, the room gave off a cold, hotel-like vibe.

"Marge!" she called out.

"Yes, Ms. Faisal?" the maid replied, appearing beside Ayda.

"What do I need to make this room fit for a child?"

"For a baby?" the woman asked.

"No, she's about twelve or so."

"Well, my daughter has lots of dolls and teddy bears and throw pillows decorating her bed. Last time we repainted she asked for a lilac color in her room. She has a few posters hanging up and a drawing that she drew."

"So I need teddy bears and dolls?"

"Perhaps your visitor will come with her own things?" Marge asked.

"I don't know." Ayda was quiet for a moment. "Make sure you clean this room exceptionally well. Dust even the drawers and the closet. Don't forget the windows. Then change the sheets; use those lavender ones I keep for my bed—you'll find them in the linen closet. I'm going to buy some teddy bears."

"Yes, Ms. Faisal."

As she walked the aisles of the toy store, Ayda realized a child would need to be fed properly. She'd need three meals a day and healthy snacks. Back at the house, stacking her new purchases on the guest bed, Ayda asked Marge if she could come the following day.

"No problem, Ms. Faisal."

"Do you cook, Marge?"

"Yes, I do."

"Good. Then I'd like you to spend tomorrow cooking. Make as many meals as will fit in the freezer. Go through the pantry tonight before you leave so you can bring with you any necessary ingredients. Here's some cash for that."

Marge took the money and they both stood admiring the bed.

"You think it's okay?"

"I think you did well, Ms. Faisal. Excuse me so I can go make that grocery list."

Ayda stood there staring at the bed. She hadn't felt so anxious and excited and completely scared in quite a while. Since her husband's death, her life had been her work. She met with her relatives rarely. She wondered what it would be like to have someone else living with her, what it would be like to be responsible for the well-being of another human being.

The following day at work, the lawyer informed her that Shams would be brought to her residence that evening. "It's recommended that you take a few days off from work, to have time to spend with her, to get to know her," he said over the phone.

Ayda remained quiet.

"Ms. Faisal, are you still there?"

"Time off from work? I *never* take time off. I don't even take holidays off."

"Well, that's about to change. She'll be at your place at about five, so make sure you're there to welcome her. Good luck, Ms. Faisal."

Ayda kept the phone to her ear even after he'd hung up. Time off from work? Seriously? Obviously this arrangement was going to require some sacrifice, but right off the bat like that? It seemed a bit too cruel.

She sat in her office for a while outlining the things that needed to be done in the next few days. Once she was confident she'd gotten down every account and all that would be needed to have everything run smoothly in her absence, she called Colette into her office and told her to gather all the teams in the meeting room with their materials.

Ayda waited until the last stragglers entered the room, then she followed. "I have some great news for you, ladies and germs. For the next few days, you'll be getting a break from the Ayds of Hell. I need to take some personal days. Before I do, does any team need me to sign off on anything? Anyone have any questions regarding their account?"

She paused and a few people asked some questions. Once she'd addressed their concerns, she continued, "I've printed up the timetable for each account here. Make sure you stick to it. While I'm gone, Colette will be taking my place."

"What?!" Colette screamed in shock, crossing her eyebrows at her boss who stood directly beside her.

"Exactly," Ayda continued. "If any of you have any issues or questions, direct them to her. She knows me enough to know how I would respond."

"But, Ms. Faisal... what if they need your feedback on something?"

"Come on, Colette. I'll prove to you that you know my taste. Vic, hold up your storyboard. Colette, would I pick the blue background or the orange?"

Colette stared at them from across the table. "Blue."

Ayda smacked the back of her head.

"I mean orange."

"See," Ayda said, "exactly as I'd like it. Did you already set up the meeting with the sports apparel client for next week?"

"Yes," Colette said. "We're scheduled to meet with them on Monday."

"Well call them back and reschedule for Thursday or Friday. Don't call them today so we don't look like a bunch of fucking morons, but *don't* forget to call them. And that covers everything."

She grabbed her phone from the table and left. The rest of the office stood frozen, not believing she'd truly be gone for a few days. But when they saw her through the glass walls walking out of the office with her purse, briefcase and several files in hand—which she'd never done before—they all cheered.

Marge was still in the kitchen fixing supper when Ayda arrived. "Did you get everything you needed?"

"Yes, Ms. Faisal. And I've already placed a few dishes in the freezer, labeled with reheating instructions. This is the last one. Shall I put this away too?"

"No. Once you've finished you can leave it on the stove."

"Very well."

"The house is clean, right?"

"Yes, Ms. Faisal. If there's anything you'd like me to go over again, let me know now because I'm about done here."

Ayda walked around the house, inspecting it for dust or disorganization or anything out of place, but as usual, she found it in perfect order. The guest room was also well prepared; Marge had even hung a few scenic pictures and framed loving sentiments on the wall.

"Everything looks fine, Marge. And thank you for getting those pictures."

"I hope your guest likes them."

Ayda didn't reply. She went to her room and washed up. When she came back down, Marge was packing up her things. "Will you need me again this week, Ms. Faisal?"

"No, Marge. Next week at our usual time."

"Very well," Marge said as she left.

With Marge gone, Ayda had a couple of hours before her guest was expected to arrive. She walked through the house again, inspecting it for any faults. When she found none, she went to her own bedroom to put away her clothes and fold the laundry. When she picked up her purse to place it on the nightstand, she noticed the unopened white envelope inside. It remained the thing she least wanted to do, but she knew she should read the letter before Shams arrived. She tidied up her room, then pulled the envelope out and sat on her bed. With a deep breath, she began to read.

Dear Ayda,

I know that you must be finding this hard to digest now. And unfortunately, I cannot promise that this letter will clarify everything, but I hope it will at least shed some light on why I have chosen you to be Shams's guardian.

Shams was born into a loving family. Her father and I loved her very much...and we loved each other. Tawwab was such a wonderful father.

Why the hell did she call him by his college nickname?!

He never made me worry about finances, and, as often as he could, he spent time with Shams. He'd even volunteer to change her diaper. Of course, we only had him for a few hours each week, but somehow, we made it work. Shams was too young to understand then, but he used to tell us about you often. He would say he wished he could introduce us, wished we could be a complete family. He talked about your sense of humor and your love. We experienced your generosity firsthand when you gave us the money we needed for Shams's operation when she was just a few months old. Do you remember that? He was very distraught when he came to you that evening and explained that a friend's daughter needed an operation, but they didn't have the money. That was us. He told me you didn't even hesitate; you told him to write a check right away.

"If we give them that money, it will make a huge dent in our savings. We'll barely be able to get by," he'd objected.

"If you don't write the check, then I will," you'd said.

When he still hesitated, you got up, and wrote the check yourself.

"There must be another way for us to help," he'd said.

And you'd said, "This is how we can help. Give it to your friend. God sends us these opportunities as tests; do you really want us to fail God's test?"

"But maybe we don't have to carry the full load," he said.

To which you replied, "But if we can—and Alhamdulillah we can—. Then we should. Take it. Go. Give it to them."

Do you remember now?

Ayda lowered the papers, recalling the incident. Through a haze, it all started to come back to her.

But if I had known the money was for you, you bi...

"No. No cussing the dead. *AstaghfarAllah*."

It was your generosity that saved my little girl. And I can't tell you how thankful I am. I've prayed for you every day since then. Every day.

I know you're thinking my prayers mean nothing when I messed up your life so badly. But I truly did not intend to mess up your life; that's why Tawwab and I decided to keep our marriage a secret. He sought me neither to spite you nor harm you in any way—he truly loved you, more than anything. He sought me simply to be the bearer of his child. He wanted someone to carry his name—dying without a son was something that even Prophet Zachariah feared. And a daughter is not a son. But Tawwab felt satisfied nonetheless.

Without knowing it, you were an integral part of our lives. He was always happy leaving me and returning to you. And in the rare occasions that you two were in an argument, he would stay with us even less than usual. "I need to get back and make things right with her," he'd say. Your love was his fuel. And that's what kept our family strong.

And that's why I have chosen you to take care of our daughter. I know that you are loving and generous. I know that despite the hurt you felt when you found out about my relationship with Tawwab, you still love him. I'll bet you still pray for him. Is there any higher proof of love? He always prayed for you.

Please take care of Shams. Motherhood is by no means an easy feat, but you are certainly qualified. You are, after all, one of the strongest, most successful women in your field. Yes, I do keep up with your professional achievements. Seeing you rise and succeed makes me happy.

I know you will treat Shams with love. I pray God guides you through this new stage of your life, and makes it easy for you.

Sincerely,

Leah

A whirlwind of emotions washed over Ayda as she read. Part of her felt violated, that a woman she'd never met knew so much about her. Part of her felt vindicated—that in the end, her husband did love her more after all. Then her inner voice reminded her that love can never harbor betrayal.

But the letter left so many things unsaid, resurrected so many questions that she'd managed to bury for years. How had the two of them even met? Was the story as she'd claimed in the letter? Or was that just the story they appeased their consciences with? Conflicting words and emotions shot around her head until she felt like it might explode.

"Stop!" she shouted, hoping the noise would block the silence that was opening the gates to chaos.

Just then, the doorbell rang. The only one who might be able to answer any of her questions stood on the other side of her front door, waiting to be let in.

Chapter Seven
GOING FOR A RUN

Didi was Saef's best friend. Yes, he enjoyed being with his guy friends and was diligent about meeting them every weekend. But when he had a problem at work, whether technical or interpersonal, Didi was the first to know.

"What do you think?" he'd ask her. And she would think aloud with him until they came to some sort of solution. He valued her opinion over anyone else's. When his supervisors preferred one of his colleagues for a promotion, his friends and his parents told him to just be patient, his time would come.

"This is bullshit," Didi had said. "You line up another job, and you go in there and quit! You deserved that promotion and everyone in your department knew it."

"He'd even hinted that it would be mine. Last time we spoke he said, 'You're next in line for the big break.'"

"Then you go in there and ask him what happened. Why'd he overlook you?"

"You don't think the guy who got it will be pissed I do that?"

"I think that if he's pissed, then he's not a friend. A friend would want you to at least get answers. It's not like they're going to fire the new guy and hire you in his place. But they have to know that you expected something from them that they had hinted at, and they didn't deliver. There is nothing keeping you in this company, and if you find something better, you'll take it."

Saef had taken her advice. The next day he went into his supervisor's office and told his superiors that he had passed on a better position in another company because they had promised him a promotion. He had been loyal to them, and they hadn't kept their word.

"And so now I want to know why. Before I decide this team no longer deserves my hard work and loyalty, I want to know why I was overlooked for the position that you had promised me."

"We knew you'd feel this way, Saef. But this isn't the promotion we had in mind for you. By next month, you'll be happy you stuck around. And if you're not, I'll accept your resignation without any notice, *and* I'll write you a glowing recommendation letter. Just be patient."

Two weeks later, his immediate supervisor was promoted, and Saef took his position.

"See," his parents had said, "you just had to be patient. There was no reason to cause tension."

"He didn't cause any tension. He simply asked why they'd overlooked him for a position they had promised him. This shows he's not a sucker and isn't going to put up with less than he deserves. Yes, he got a better position, *Alhamdulillah*, but they needed to know that he wasn't just going to sit back and let others advance while he remained stagnant. It showed ambition," Didi had said.

His parents simply shook their heads, but Saef leaned down and gave her a kiss.

Loving to spend time with his wife and wanting them to try something new, one Saturday morning after they had prayed the pre-dawn prayer, Saef suggested they go for a run.

"A run?!"

"Yeah. Come on, it'll be fun. Running together through the neighborhood. We'll get to see the sun rise."

"We are not runners, Saef."

"Who says we can't start?"

"My jiggly butt, that's who."

"Come on. We'll jog. I'll keep pace with you."

She buried her face in her hands and said, "Why do you do this to me? Why do you like to torture me?"

"You're going to enjoy it. We'll connect with nature and get our hearts pumping."

They got dressed in their sweat suits and were out the door with their house key and a cell phone within ten minutes. They jogged for a few minutes, then the rhythm of their feet against the asphalt began to cheer her on.

"Let's speed it up."

"Isn't it good," Saef asked her through panting breath.

They ran past houses and through the hilly neighborhood. Up the road beyond which was the wood with the blackberry bushes, down the one that led to the open four-way intersection. The birds flew above, spurring them on with their songs.

Breathing in the crisp, early morning air, Didi thought, *Saef knew what he was talking about when he suggested this.* Just as she was about to speak the words, she heard a loud thud and turned to find Saef lying motionless on the ground.

"Saef! Saef, answer me!" she screamed, rolling him over. "Saef!"

She tried slapping his face, but there was no reply. Her shaky hands pulled the phone from her pocket and dialed 911.

Through her fear and nervousness, Didi continued administering CPR for what felt like hours until the ambulance finally arrived. Her breathing was heavy, and her heartbeat was the loudest sound she could hear. She kept her arms wrapped around herself as she watched the emergency medical technicians attempt to revive her husband.

A few minutes later the EMT turned to her and said, "I'm sorry."

She stood frozen, unable to speak, unable to breathe, trying to understand what the EMT had said.

"Sorry? Sorry for what? No! No, we just went for a run. We were home just a few minutes ago and he was totally fine. He's going to be fine! He's fine! Saef! Saef, wake up! Saef!" Tears streamed down her face as she continued to scream his name.

At the hospital, the doctors told Didi that Saef had probably suffered a stroke. She had left the house that morning with her partner, her life, and now she had nothing. She was exhausted, and cold, unable to control the shaking of her body, or the wails which erupted from inside of her. Her chest heaved, and tears burned her eyes.

She didn't feel the nurse's gentle touch on her back. She didn't hear her when she asked if there was someone they should call. The nurse sat in the chair beside her and kept rubbing her back. Sometime later, when her wailing had calmed to sobs, the nurse tried again. "Sweetheart, is there someone you'd like to call?"

Didi looked at her blankly with her red swollen eyes, tear streaks shimmering on her cheeks. "Did you say something?" she managed to ask through her sniffles.

"Do you want us to call someone?" the nurse repeated.

Didi pulled out her phone and stared at it for a moment. "Who do I call? Who do I call?"

Eventually her unsteady fingers pulled up Siham's number.

"Call the sheikh," Didi said into the receiver without returning the greeting. "And come to the hospital with your parents."

She couldn't bring herself to say it. They'd find out when they arrived.

◆ ◆ ◆

Her in-laws remained inconsolable all day. The funeral, as common in the Islamic faith, was performed later that day. Didi remained in her sweat suit, but an older woman had pulled a black *abaya* over Didi's clothes. After the prayer at the mosque, the funeral reception drove to the nearby cemetery. Didi kept her arms wrapped around herself as the casket was lowered, still unable to believe the nightmare she'd stepped into, still hopeful that her beloved husband would push open the casket and give her his bright smile.

Siham's tears did not cease, but she held up her mother. Her father stood apart, his eyes wide with disbelief. After Saef's body had been lowered and the dirt placed on top, his father fell to his knees and cried. Both Siham and her mother fell beside him, and they held each other tightly. Didi remained frozen where she stood, listening to the sheikh's supplication, still trying to wake up.

The next couple of days, people swarmed in and out of Didi's home. Siham had insisted on staying with her for a few days. Rizq was the only light she saw during that time. He came into her bedroom several times a day just to pat her head and give her hugs.

"Wuv you, Didi. Wuv you."

She was too dazed to answer him, but his words did make it to her. She lay in bed still hoping that somehow she would wake up. "Any minute now, I'll wake up and thank God that it was just a nightmare."

"You need to eat something," Siham said, coming in with a tray filled with food.

"I don't want to eat."

"Yeah, I know. But you have to."

"If you come near me with that tray, Siham, I will flip it over your head. Leave me alone."

Siham sighed heavily and left with the untouched tray in her hand. She tried again the following morning. "Come on, Didi. You've got to get out of bed and wash up. People came yesterday and we told them you weren't well, so they're coming back today to pay their respects. You need to receive them."

"I don't want to see anyone."

"Yeah, well, you have to. Come on."

She pulled the covers off her and threw them to the floor.

Didi tsked. "Come on, Siham. I'm cold. Give those back."

"If you want them, you'll have to get out of bed and get them."

Before Siham left the room Didi murmured, "Pain in the ass."

"I heard that!" she said from the hallway.

But Siham's plan worked. Once she was out of bed, Didi figured she might as well wash up. As she stared at her reflection in the bathroom mirror, she decided to jump in the shower. Although she felt refreshed afterwards—the smell she'd been smelling had been her all along—she still felt weak, her chest still tight, and each breath she took infused her body with more pain.

When she finally stepped out of her room, Siham embraced her and led her to the living room where condolers were already waiting to pay their respects. The group of Saef's friends stood when she walked in. It looked as though they, too, had been crying.

"We're very sorry for your loss, Didi. He will be missed."

"Yes," she said. "Who's going to kick your asses at FIFA now?" She wasn't smiling, but she was trying to.

But the men looked at her with furrowed eyebrows. "What do you mean?" one said.

"I mean your weekend guys-nights. When you usually play PlayStation and he beats you all at it."

They exchanged glances then looked back at her. "Didi, yeah, we do get together on the weekends, but Saef almost never joined us. We always invited him, but he always said he couldn't."

She looked at each one of them, a blank stare in her eyes, the hollow in her chest widening, the pain increasing.

"Well, we should go." They all lined up and said their goodbyes, leaving Didi with her head spinning.

How could what they said be true? He'd spent hours away from home every weekend for as long as she could remember, saying he was hanging out with his friends. If he hadn't been with them, where had he been going regularly all those years?

Chapter Eight
SHAMS ARRIVES

Ayda wiped her palms on her skirt, took a deep breath, and opened the door. The girl who stood before her was skinny with curly brown hair falling down her shoulders. She didn't make eye contact. The woman beside her looked even more nervous.

"Hello, Ms. Faisal. I'm Shams's aunt, Ann. Here are her things." The woman handed Ayda a bag. "Take care, Shams." She kissed the girl brusquely on the top of her head, got in her car, and drove away as both Ayda and Shams stared after her.

"Come in, Shams."

The young girl wore a mismatched outfit: a bright yellow top and striped red and purple pants. She wore long earrings which hung to just above her shoulders, and more than a few rings adorned her fingers. Her bag was equally colorful, covered in "Girl Power," "Flower Power," and "Harry Potter" pins.

They sat down on the couch, and Ayda, wishing for nothing more than to grab a cigarette, rubbed her cold, sweaty hands together, mentally ordering them to stop shaking.

"Did you guys find my place okay?" she asked.

Shams shrugged. She kept her eyes glued to some spot on the ground.

A moment later, Ayda couldn't take the silence. "Come on," she said. "Let me show you your room."

She climbed the stairs with Shams just behind her. Walking into the room, Shams placed the bag she'd been carrying on the bed.

"Can I help you put your stuff away?"

"No, I got it. Thank you."

"If you think of anything you need, just let me know."

The girl nodded.

"I'm going to heat dinner while you unpack. Just come down when you're finished. And feel free to explore the house. I want you to feel at home, so go into each of the rooms and check them out. I'll see you downstairs in a bit."

Ayda ran down the steps, grabbed her cigarettes and lighter from the drawer, and stepped out onto the back porch. Smoke filled her lungs, shooting new life into her body. She pictured the nicotine seeping into her veins and traveling to that spot in her brain that helped her relax. The harder she pulled in and held that smoke, the quicker relief came. Her mind had begun to buzz with insecurities and worries, but the smoke drowned out their screams. *If I were a drinker, I'd be drunk by now. Alhamdulillah.* She'd always avoided alcohol. But she understood it. She understood the need to escape, to forget, to become numb. It scared her that she understood it; she feared where that empathy might lead.

She finished off the cigarette and went inside. In the kitchen, she started the oven and placed Marge's dishes inside. She then took out the silverware and a couple of plates and began to set the table.

"You have a beautiful home."

Ayda jumped. She noticed Shams's face fall when she saw her reaction, and Ayda immediately felt guilty. "Sorry. I'm just used to being alone. Thank you. But it's *our* home."

Ayda tried to smile at the girl, but her face would not cooperate.

"How come you don't have any pictures up anywhere?"

Ayda continued placing the silverware as she said, "Nothing is important enough for me to look at all day."

Shams nodded. She stood awkwardly in place, unsure of what to do with herself, crossing then uncrossing her arms. Leaning from one foot to the other, she finally said, "Can I help?"

"Please do. You finish setting the table, and I'll make us a salad."

A few minutes later, Shams was back in the kitchen. "Where do you keep the glasses?"

"Explore. Find them." Ayda waved around the knife she was using to chop up the vegetables.

Shams opened one cupboard before finding the one she was looking for. She took two glasses, placed them on the dining room table, and popped back in the kitchen. "Can I do anything else?"

"I think the rest is all set. Have a seat. Keep me company while I finish up."

They sat in silence for a few moments.

"Did you unpack everything?"

"Yes."

"And is there anything you need? There are fresh towels in the bathroom. And it's got all the toiletries as well, even a new toothbrush for you."

"Thank you. I don't think there's anything I need."

Ayda continued to chop the salad, feeling like she needed another cigarette, feeling overwhelmed by the silence.

"I guess on Monday we'll need to get you enrolled in school."

"I guess so. I hate school," the girl said almost under her breath.

"Why's that?"

Shams just shrugged.

"There's no such thing as," then she imitated Sham's shrug. "You have to know why you don't like it."

Shams sat quietly.

"Is it the teachers? Do you not like being told you have to do this or study that?"

The girl shook her head.

"You don't like studying? You find it too hard?"

Again, she shook her head.

"The kids? You don't like other kids your age?"

Shams sat quietly.

"Yeah, you've definitely got a point. Kids your age tend to be real pains in the ass...or so I've heard."

Shams nodded.

"Are they mean? Do they say mean things to you?"

"They make fun of how I dress, and how I don't talk very much."

"Em hmm." Ayda threw the chopping board into the sink and drizzled some dressing on the salad.

"Come, let's go eat."

As they ate, Ayda told Shams about herself. She told her that she was the manager at an advertising agency.

"Among other things, I oversee accounts. My teams do the actual work, the actual art."

"Could I come to work with you one day?"

"Only if you pretend to be that long-haired ghost girl that shows up in horror films. We need to wake up those clowns who work at the company."

Shams giggled.

Ayda continued to tell her about work and that she knew no one on her team liked her. "I don't go out of my way to be nice to people. But when they do good work, I let them know. I also let them know when they do shit work. And, apparently, those talks are the ones that stand out more to everyone. Whatever. Doesn't bother me because I'm just being honest. But I do like my job."

Shams asked her a few questions about the nature of her work, and Ayda answered frankly.

When they had finished eating, Shams volunteered to do the dishes.

"Let's do them together," Ayda replied. "I'll wash, you rinse."

For the next ten minutes, they stood beside each other over the sink, Ayda washing and passing an item to Shams, who rinsed it and placed it in the dishrack.

"You have good organizational skills. You stacked them just like I would have."

"I have a lot of practice. Mom made me do the dishes every night. 'I cook, you clean,' she would say." Then she became quiet, the smile which had been on her face just a moment before disappeared, and a shadow came over her.

"I'm sorry for your loss."

Shams just nodded.

"Do you want to talk about it?"

The girl shook her head.

"Good, neither do I. I mean, I'd talk about it if you wanted, and I'm always here to listen if you need. I never say things I don't mean so...just remember that."

Shams remained silent.

Ayda spent the next hour asking Shams about herself, trying to get to know her. She learned that Shams liked romantic comedies and reading anything and everything. She liked to draw and hoped to take an art course at the local high school to improve her talent.

"Maybe we could turn the basement into a studio," Ayda said. "It would help me go back to drawing for myself, for fun. The only art I do now is for work. I enjoy it, but I'd enjoy it more if I could do it for myself."

Ayda was surprised that she didn't feel at all awkward around Shams. Was it because she was still only a child? She didn't know, but it helped her relax about the situation.

The weekend went by, and on Monday morning, before Ayda and Shams left to enroll her in school, Marge showed up.

"Good morning, Ms. Faisal," she yelled as she entered the house. She stopped with a start when she saw the girl in the kitchen.

"Good morning, Marge," Ayda said. "This is Shams. I've kidnapped her so she'll be staying with us from now on."

Shams giggled and held out her hand to Marge. "She's kidding," she said with a shy smile.

But Marge was slow in reaching out her hand. "Ms. Faisal never jokes," she whispered.

"Are you kidding?" Shams said. "She jokes all the time. I promise you, she hasn't kidnapped me. But I am moving in here."

"Nice to meet you, Shams."

"She liked that pasta you made with the white sauce Marge, but not that mushroom dish."

"Very well, Ms. Faisal."

"Is there anything you need before I leave?" Ayda asked her.

"Shall I clean the guest room?"

"Not the guest room, Marge. Shams's room. Shams, does your room need cleaning?"

"I think it's fine, thank you."

"Next time then, Marge."

"Very well."

"Okay, we're off to enroll Shams in school so that this kidnapping looks legit. Let's go, Shams."

As they walked out, Shams heard Marge mumble something under her breath.

In the car, Shams said to Ayda, "I think you're freaking Marge out with this kidnapping thing. I hope she doesn't call the cops."

"She loves me. She never would."

"Does she have kids?"

"Yes, she's got a daughter about your age."

"Then she totally would."

"You're right. Let's see what kind of adventure she'll get us into."

Shams shook her head. "You're horrible."

"Thank you. I do my best." Then she took out a cigarette and lit it.

After they had finished at the school, Ayda took Shams to the outlets.

"What are we doing here?"

"Walking around. You might find something you like."

"But I don't need anything."

"Yeah, you keep saying that. But, maybe if you see it, you'll think of something you need. Or just want."

They walked around for a while and visited a few shops.

"Do you have a backpack for school?"

"I use the bag I brought my stuff in."

"No. You need a school bag. Come in here, let's see what they have."

Ayda eyed the bags and pointed out a few she liked. But she followed Shams's eyes and noticed one in particular that seemed to appeal to the girl. "You like that one?" Ayda asked.

"Anyone of these is fine."

"Shams, I'm asking you which one you like the most. Is it that bright yellow and orange one?"

Shams shrugged.

"I think it's beautiful. Just like you. Shall we get it then? Final answer?"

Shams smiled and nodded.

When they walked out, she thanked Ayda.

"Oh, don't mention it. We're putting it on Marge's credit card. Can't leave any kind of trail for when they come looking for me."

She always said her jokes without laughing, and for some reason, that made them even funnier to Shams.

"But I don't want you to do that again," Ayda said, lighting a cigarette.

Shams face went red with embarrassment. "I told you I didn't need a bag."

"I don't want you to hesitate to tell me what you really want. When you see something you like, something you want, tell me. I'm not saying I'm going to buy you every little thing your heart desires. But you needed a bag. And you saw one you liked, but you hesitated to tell me. I don't want you to do that again. I'm open with you, and I hope you'll be open with me. Deal?"

Shams nodded.

"What did you say? I didn't hear you."

Shams looked up and said, "I think Marge should buy me a pair of shoes."

"Good answer."

When they finished shopping, Shams with her new bag and shoes and Ayda with a new lighter, they sat in an almost empty restaurant for lunch. As they waited for their food, Ayda asked Shams if she still felt worried about starting her new school the following day.

"Change can be good. Mom always used to say that. But I'm a little nervous."

"Do you want me to take you tomorrow? So you don't have to deal with the bus on the first day?"

"I think I just need to begin...begin everything all at once."

Ayda nodded. "Good girl. You're going to do just fine."

About half-way through their meal, as they had been quiet for more than a few moments, Ayda asked Shams, "Do you know who I am, Shams?" She had stopped eating, put her fork down, and stared down at her plate, avoiding eye contact with the young girl.

"Yes. You were my dad's other wife."

Chapter Nine
NO MORE DIDI

The hustle of condolers swarming through her house made it hard for Didi to focus on anything. She sat in the living room, greeting her visitors with a blank face and a handshake. Days passed, and as the number of visitors dwindled down, Siham made sure Didi was well enough to keep functioning. She had more than a few casseroles lining the fridge, but they did have to take care of laundry and the general tidiness of her home. When Siham saw that Didi was beginning to recover, she asked her when she was thinking of going back to work.

"I'm not sure," Didi had answered. "I hadn't thought about it."

"Well, you should think about it. They all know your situation, so no one's expecting you back tomorrow. But it's already been a week. Give yourself one more week, then try."

Didi nodded. Throwing herself into her work would probably be the best medicine. And that's what she decided to do. Two weeks after Saef's death, Didi drove herself to work, crying the entire time as she remembered her daily commutes with her husband. He'd known how much she hated driving, so he always did it happily. When she pulled into the parking lot at work, she sat there for a few moments wiping her eyes and trying to compose herself. "God, please help me through this," she said aloud. "I am in so much pain. Please grant me ease."

With that, she pushed the car door open and got out. Her first few weeks back would remain hazy in her mind because she worked with an inhuman intensity, focusing all her energy, all her thoughts, into the projects. Lunches brought more tears, but her co-workers simply sat with her in silence or offered her a gentle touch. She appreciated that no one told her to stop crying or to buckle up or any of the other completely insensitive things people say when someone is mourning. She needed to shed those tears and gradually, as the days turned to weeks, the tears decreased, but the pain in her chest remained. The awful feeling that her biggest blessing had been taken from her was a weight she carried everywhere. Her loneliness grew. Eventually she stopped crying at work completely.

One weekend shortly after, Didi decided she needed to go through Saef's closet. Someone else could benefit from his things. She knew he would have hated that she'd waited so long already. So with a deep breath, she opened his closet and began folding his belongings. She filled several large bags and called the local charity to pick them up the following day. She'd kept a couple of his sweaters and one pair of pajamas for herself. A few of his things had never been worn and still had the tickets attached. Those she put aside to give to her father-in-law.

The experience brought with it a whirlwind of emotions. She remembered certain occasions where Saef had worn an outfit, and that memory would bring a smile to her face. But the present truth was that he would never again wear it. And then she wondered who would go through her things once she passed. Would the house simply gather dust until it was reclaimed by the city? The thought made her draw up a will and name Siham proprietor of the estate and all she owned. A third of her assets would be donated to the Islamic Relief Fund and the rest would be divided according to Islamic law. If, she stated, in the case no heirs were present, then Siham was free to take it all and keep or disperse as she saw fit.

A couple of weeks later, her in-laws brought dinner over and sat to eat with her. "Didi, why don't you sell this house? It's so big, you can get a smaller place. Or if you'd like, you can come live with us."

"I can't leave the house. This is our home. My home. I don't want to leave it." She couldn't imagine selling the home they had worked so hard to buy. And fix. It had been a mess when they had purchased it. Not only had the plumbing needed to be completely redone, but the floors had needed to be replaced and the water damage in the ceiling fixed, and lastly, all the walls had had to be repainted. Didi and Saef had spent months making all the repairs themselves. But when they had finished, it was a home. "Good enough to raise some kids in," Saef had said. And although the kids never came, the two of them enjoyed it just the same.

"I could never sell this place. This was our masterpiece, the work of art we built together."

Her in-laws never suggested it again.

Although she'd cleaned out all of Saef's clothes, she hadn't gone near his papers. It seemed too daunting a task for her. But one evening she decided she couldn't put it off any longer; she opened the drawer to his nightstand. Resting on top of a large stack of papers and files and books, was his cell phone. She plugged it in and turned it on. She looked through his videos—things he'd downloaded from social media. A few were funny, and others he had already shown her. There was a picture of a baby. For a second she thought she recognized the child. But no, she'd never seen her before. She wondered why Saef would have the picture on his phone. It had been taken with his camera, not downloaded. Didi didn't understand, but she moved on.

She scrolled through the names, not looking for anything in particular nor noticing any unusual contacts. Then she clicked to see his messages. The last one had been sent the night before he died. It was to someone named Leah, and it said: "I'm spending all day tomorrow with Didi. I'll see you on Sunday."

The woman replied: "Enjoy yourself. I miss you."

The message before was dated one week prior and read: "I'll be there soon."

Didi scrolled back through all the messages Saef had exchanged with this Leah. And as she did, she couldn't believe the nightmare she was uncovering. Message after message indicated not only that he'd had a relationship with this woman, but he saw her regularly. He ate with her. Brought her the groceries she needed. He even went with her to the doctor. The messages on his phone only went back two years, but it was clear their relationship had begun before then.

Didi couldn't wrap her head around it. Was this really happening? Did she really just discover that her dead husband had been having an affair? Could Saef really have cheated on her?

It all seemed too cruel. It was bad enough that he was gone, but realizing he hadn't even been who she thought he'd been was a stab in the back that pierced her heart until it felt like all her blood had been drained. "No," she said. "He'd been a loyal husband. He was good to me. We never fought, we always made up after any argument. He called to check up on me. He loved me. He wouldn't do this."

And yet the evidence he left behind was stronger than all those truths combined. He'd betrayed her. He'd had an affair with a woman named Leah. And, what's worse, the messages about visits to the obstetrician and meeting her for lunch afterwards could only mean one thing. She flipped back to the picture of the baby. Examining it closely, she understood why the child looked familiar: she had Saef's eyes.

Leaning back against the headboard, her breathing became rapid, the world began to spin. She had to be wrong. She had to be. She wanted to show the messages to someone so they could prove her wrong. They would give her a different explanation. There had to be a different explanation. But who could she tell? She had no one to tell. If it turned out to be true, she couldn't tell her in-laws—they wouldn't believe his betrayal and would hold it against her for even coming to that conclusion. And more than that, much more, she simply didn't want them to know that Saef had been capable of being so deceitful. She didn't want to ruin their image of him. Or anyone's image of him. There was no one she could discuss this with. No one to show the messages to. And as she scrolled through them again for the hundredth time, she remembered the words of his friends at the funeral: "Saef almost never joined us for guys' night."

All those times he'd told her he was going to hang out with the boys, he'd been going to his mistress. He'd taken advantage of her trust and in her not wanting to smother him, giving him ample space to spend time with his friends. She'd trusted him, and he'd deceived her. He'd cheated on her. How could she now believe anything between them? How could she believe anything he'd ever said to her? He hadn't loved her. He couldn't: you don't cheat on someone you love. You simply can't. Everything between them, all those beautiful moments, were all lies! Every advice he'd given her, every word he'd ever spoken...all lies! And why? Why had he preferred another woman to her? Why had he given this woman importance and precedence over her? How had she fallen short with him? She had supported him. She had been there for him every day they had been together. She had valued his opinions and his suggestions. She had provided him with her best ideas, her best advice. Where had she fallen short?!

Was it the child? Did he have an affair because she couldn't have children? Was that really it? Would he really betray her, go behind her and break her heart, all so he could call himself a father?

The thoughts drove her crazy. She paced the room and threw his mug against the wall. She pulled out his pajamas that she had kept and tortured them with a pair of scissors. She picked up the framed photo of him that sat beside her bed and smashed it to the ground. Unsatisfied that only a few cracks had formed, she stomped on the picture until the glass had turned to dust, and she could no longer make out his face. She then raced through the entire house, smashing all the pictures, the ones on the mantle and on the wall. No photo of him, whether he was alone or with her, escaped her wrath.

She made a conscious decision to block everything about him out of her life. Anything he'd liked, anything he'd been fond of or advised her to do was now banished. His deceit nullified any possible good intentions he may have had. She rejected everything that originated with him, including her nickname. He had, after all, been the first to call her Didi. She stopped praying because, even though she had encouraged him at first, it was something they did together. And she wanted no reminder of such moments. She began to smoke, even though she'd always hated the habit. But he'd also hated it. Her first couple of cigarettes resulted in coughing fits and shortness of breath. "Stop being a wuss!" she said to herself. Quickly, she learned to hold her smoke like a pro.

She exchanged her long skirts and conservative outfits for miniskirts and form fitting dresses. Her favorite was a tube dress that exposed her shoulders and a bit of cleavage.

Some thought her change was brought on by heartbreak, from losing her husband. Others thought this was her true self, one Saef had stifled, and was only now free to emerge. True to her new persona, she didn't bother to discuss her personal matters—simply waved questioners away with her hand and a puff of accurately aimed smoke.

A small voice inside asked her who she was spiting, who would gain by her transformation. But she was already too far gone to hear that voice. The flames of her anger blinded her, but she feared without it, she would have no bearings. Everything she had known had turned out to be a lie. Her rage was the only truth.

"Are you okay?" Siham had asked her.

"Fine."

"Really? Because you don't seem fine. You seem...different."

"Nothing stays the same, Seema. Everything changes. Everything transforms."

"True. But usually things transform for the better."

"Yeah, well, I've stopped giving a fuck about usually."

"Didi..."

But she cut her off. "Ayda. My name is not Didi. It was never Didi. Call me Ayda."

Chapter Ten
FAMILY REUNION

When Ayda heard Shams refer to her as her father's "other" wife, she wanted to scream. She wanted to protest, "No! I was his *first* wife! Your mother was the *other* wife!" But she didn't. She kept quiet as the girl continued.

"I was too young when Dad died to know or understand anything, but since I was about seven, Mom started talking about you. Maybe it was even before then; I can't remember. But I know that when I turned seven, she gave me a necklace and told me it was from you. 'She's your second mom,' she used to say. 'Your dad loved her very much.'"

Ayda looked up, her eyes were cloudy and her eyebrows furrowed. "Did that make sense to you?"

Shams shrugged. "I asked her why we never saw you. She just said you loved us but you had your own life. She said people only need one mom. But God had given me two to keep me safe, so I'd always have someone to take care of me if anything happened to her."

Ayda had never been one to suppress her feelings. People around her were always quite sure what kind of mood she was in, whether the topic at hand was agreeable or not. She often told people their opinions were "shit" and never cared about hurting anyone's feelings. At that moment she wanted to scream, "Your mother was a whore who took my husband! We didn't need you people in our lives!" She wanted to scream it. But she held back the words, swallowed them and pulled back her tears, lighting up a cigarette.

"I don't think you can smoke in here," Shams told her.

Ayda lit the cigarette anyway, took a couple of quick drags, and put it out before the waitress had a chance to reprimand her.

Just then, Ayda felt a tap on her shoulder. She looked up to find Siham and Rizq standing beside her.

"As salaamu alaikum," Siham greeted. Both Ayda and Shams returned the greeting. Hearing Shams's salaam surprised Ayda, and she turned in the girl's direction as she stood to give Siham and Rizq hugs and kisses.

"Funny running into you here at lunch time," Siham said.

"I've taken a couple of days off of work...to help Shams settle in. Shams, this is Siham and Rizq. Rizq, Siham, this is Shams. You guys can consider her another member of the family. She's moved in with me. Rizq, you finally have a cousin."

"Awesome," the boy said, and sat down to chat with Shams as Siham pulled Ayda aside.

"I'll explain to you later. For now, sit. Let's have lunch together," Ayda said.

"Ayda, where did this girl come from?"

"I told you, I'll tell you later.

"You better not have done anything stupid."

"I never do anything stupid. Sometimes stupid things just happen to me. Anyway, this isn't one of them. Come on, sit."

"No. Rizq, come on. It looks like they're finishing up; we don't want to keep them. Let's grab a table over there. We'll see you guys later. Nice to meet you, Shams."

"Nice to meet you too," the girl said.

"See you later, cuz."

Shams smiled and waved at her new cousin.

"Come on, Shams," Ayda said. "We should get moving."

Ayda was quiet most of the drive home. When they pulled into the driveway, Shams asked, "Are you embarrassed by me?"

"What?! No, of course not. Why would you say that?"

"Because I'm dressed in a fluorescent pink dress with bright yellow earrings dangling to my shoulders and rings that cover my fingers. And you're... in a gray suit. With only that emerald ring on your finger."

"I love that your clothes are colorful and expressive! I do."

"Then why were you all flustered when you were introducing me to Siham and Rizq?"

Ayda sighed heavily then reached for a cigarette. Before she lit it she said, "I was flustered. But not because I'm embarrassed by you." She lit the cigarette and took a drag. "I didn't know...I don't know how I'm supposed to introduce you to them. Siham is your dad's sister. As far as I know, neither she nor your grandparents know about you. I don't..." She paused, taking another drag and thinking. "I don't know how they'll react. I don't want to shock them. Or upset you. I just.... I need to tell them about you first, before introductions."

Ayda finished her cigarette as Shams sat quietly.

"Does that make sense to you?"

Shams shrugged.

"Yeah, I don't know either. But I'm trying to do what's best for you, Shams. I don't want them to react in a way that might upset you. Or them."

"Rizq seems cool."

"Oh, you're going to love him. He's a good kid. His mom did well with him.

He used to have a great time with your dad. Rizq was only two when that happened."

"So he's basically my age?"

"Yeah."

A moment later, Shams was still sitting quietly.

"Come on," Ayda said. "Let's go see how we can further scare the piss out of Marge."

That evening as they sat watching TV, Shams asked, "Do you think you'll tell them about me soon? I think I'd like to meet my grandparents."

"Yes, I'll tell them about you soon. And we'll have them all over here for dinner Saturday night so you can meet them. Is that good?"

"Yes. Thank you. But what about...what about your side of the family? Your parents and siblings? I'd like to meet them, too."

"My parents died a long time ago. And I'm an only child. Siham and your grandparents are my family."

Shams nodded. "And now me."

Ayda looked up at her with a smile on her face. "And now you."

Shams got up and said good night.

"I'll get you up in the morning so you're not late for your first day of school."

"I probably won't sleep very well. That always happens when I'm nervous. See you in the morning. G' night."

The following morning Ayda watched from the window as Shams boarded the school bus. She then made her way to work and called Colette into her office as soon as she arrived. "Fill me in."

Colette recounted what had happened over the past couple of days. She said the team working on the electric fan account had given her their presentations the day before, and she'd made some suggestions. "Their changes should be ready for you by tomorrow. As for the fleece jacket team, they seem to have hit a wall. I've made some suggestions, but I'm sure your input will be appreciated. And that's all."

"What about the sports apparel meeting that you rescheduled? When's that?"

Colette's face went white, but Ayda was fidgeting with some papers on her desk and didn't notice. "Colette," she said again, "when are we meeting the sports apparel people?"

Colette's voice shook when she spoke. "I forgot to reschedule."

"What do you mean you forgot to reschedule? The meeting was originally set for Thursday of last week. But I told you to mark your calendar to remind you to call them and reschedule. When's the new meeting set for?"

Ayda was starting to comprehend what had happened. She stood up. "Did you *seriously* not call to reschedule?"

Colette stood frozen, her eyes glued to the floor. She nodded.

"That was our biggest account! We blew it because you didn't reschedule?! We are so fucked! This is going to kill us in so many ways! It's not just one account that we lose, it's our reputation as being a high quality, reliable firm! Get out so I can fix this!"

Ayda smoked a couple of cigarettes in a row as she paced her office. When she had calmed down, she picked up the phone and called the sports apparel company.

"Hello Frank, this is Ayda. Yes, I know. That's why I'm calling you. I had a family emergency to deal with over the last few days so I didn't have a chance to call to reschedule. I know how unprofessional this looks, but you've known me for years, Frank; nothing comes before my work, so you know how serious this emergency must have been. Yes, it's better, thank you. I apologize for not showing up last week, but I'd like to reschedule for Thursday. Friday then? Tomorrow works fine. We'll be there at eleven. Thank you for understanding, Frank."

The team scrambled to make sure their final presentation was ready for the next day. "If I'd been in a bad mood this morning, Colette, you would be fired. If it happens again, you will be."

"Yes, Ms. Faisal. Thank you. I appreciate your..."

"Get out," Ayda exclaimed.

She signed off on a few more boards and images that morning before telling her secretary she didn't want to be disturbed. She picked up the phone and called Siham. After Ayda had invited them over for dinner on Saturday, Siham asked, "Who's the girl that was with you at the restaurant the other day?"

"She's... I found out that she..." Ayda sighed deeply and then decided to just spit it out. "She's Saef's daughter. He had a second wife I found out about just after he died. Shams is their daughter. Her mother died recently and wrote in her will that she wanted me to take care of her."

Ayda lit a cigarette, waiting for the information to register in Siham's brain.

"You're shitting me?" Siham finally said.

"Nope."

They were quiet for a while.

"How do I explain this to Mom and Dad? To Rizq?"

"Explain it to Rizq just like I explained it to you. Shams's happy to have a cousin. I think he will be too. But I'm going over to your parents' now to invite them for dinner on Saturday and tell them about her. I think...they're going to be real happy about it actually."

Siham was quiet.

"Ok, I should go if I want to get to your parents before I head home. See you on Saturday."

When she got to her in-laws' house, they were both surprised and excited to see her.

"Ayda! So good of you to come by. We miss you, you know. You're always busy with work. We'd like to see you more often."

"Yes, I'd like to see more of you too. That's actually why I'm here. I'd like you to come to dinner at my place on Saturday. Siham and Rizq are coming too. I want us to go back to having weekly dinners together. Every Saturday."

"Great idea. Yes, of course we'll be there."

"I also wanted to let you know that someone else will be there too."

"Someone else? You mean..." Her mother-in-law paused. "A man?"

"A who?! No, not a man, Auntie! Why would I...? Anyway, no. The someone else isn't a man. It's a girl actually. Her name is Shams, and she'll be living with me from now on. She's about Rizq's age."

"I don't understand. Why do you have a young girl living with you, Ayda?"

"Her mother died recently and, in her will, she specified that I be her daughter's guardian."

"Oh wow! So... her mother was a close friend of yours then?"

"You know I don't have any friends."

Ayda had always done her best not to smoke in front of her in-laws, but this time she simply couldn't control the urge. She pulled out a cigarette, lit it and took a deep drag. "The woman was Saef's other wife. Shams is Saef's daughter."

Their mouths fell open and they stared at Ayda.

"I wanted to let you know before you saw her—to prepare you."

"You mean... you mean Saef had a daughter?"

"Yes," Ayda replied simply, still smoking her cigarette.

When they remained silent, she felt the need to clarify. "He had a second wife, he cheated on me."

"He probably didn't see it like that," Sumayya replied abruptly. "He probably just wanted a family. I mean... he probably just wanted a child."

"Maybe. We'll never know what he was thinking. Anyway..." Ayda got up and gathered her purse. "We're expecting you on Saturday. She's excited to meet you. I know your love is going to make a difference with her. See you both then. Salaam."

Back in her car she lit another cigarette. "Of course she defended him," she said out loud. "He's her precious little baby who can do no wrong."

Ayda knew that, according to Islamic law, Saef had the right to take another wife. But she hated how he'd humiliated her. She hated that he had a completely separate life that she knew nothing about... and they were supposed to have been happily married! "If shit like this happens in happy marriages, then what kind of shit goes on in shitty marriages?"

As she pulled into her driveway, she saw Shams sitting on the front steps. "Damn it!" She stopped the car and opened the car door, but only stood up behind it. "Salaam, Shams. Come on, we've got an errand to run."

When Shams got in the car, Ayda said, "I thought I'd make it home before you. Have you been waiting long?"

"Just about ten minutes."

"Sorry. I went to see your grandparents. I invited them to dinner Saturday.

They're excited to get to know you."

"Thank you," she whispered.

"Tell me about your first day of school. How'd it go?"

Shams shrugged.

"That means nothing to me. Was it a good day or a bad day?"

"I don't know."

"Were there good moments?"

"Yeah," Shams replied. "There are a couple of girls who are nice to me. They let me sit with them at lunch. They seem cool."

"Good. So...were there any bad moments?"

"I heard a couple of guys say, 'Check out the new girl. Her hair's a ball of frizz, and her clothes don't even match.'"

"I'm sorry they hurt your feelings like that, but guys tend to be...moronic. You shouldn't pay any attention to those clowns. They like to make people laugh, but no one takes them seriously. So, were the good moments greater, or were the bad moments greater?"

Shams was quiet for a moment, thinking. "The good moments were greater. Even though it was my first day, I knew everything that was going on in all my classes. And my teachers seem nice. So yeah, the good moments were greater."

"Good. So you had a good day. *Alhamdulillah*."

They pulled into a plaza and got out of the car.

"Where are we going?" Shams asked.

"We're going to make you a copy of the house key, so you're not ever locked out again."

The next few days went by smoothly. Shams would arrive home from school, and Ayda would catch up with her about an hour later. They sat in the kitchen chatting about their day with Shams answering all of Ayda's questions but rarely volunteering any info on her own. The mood was relaxed, and they each enjoyed the company. Ayda hoped that in time, Shams would feel comfortable enough to open up to her without having to be probed.

After they'd had a snack—prepared by Marge—Shams said, "I'm going to go pray."

Ayda crossed her eyebrows. "Pray what?"

"*Dhuhr.*"

"What do you mean *dhuhr*? You're not Muslim."

Shams crossed her eyebrows in reply. "Yes, I am."

They stood there looking at each other for a moment.

"I didn't...I didn't realize your mom raised you Muslim. Was she?" Ayda asked.

"Yes, of course. So...do you want to pray together?"

Ayda looked down. "I'm not very uh...regular with my prayers. I mean, I only pray sometimes."

"My mom used to tell me that prayer—the most basic way we can connect with God—is the most important thing. I try to never miss a prayer."

"You should keep that up. Don't lose that. It's a good foundation."

Shams jumped down off her stool. Before she left the kitchen she tried once more. "Why don't you join me? We can make it a habit together."

Ayda stared at her, wondering how such a young girl could be so strong. "Maybe next time."

It would be hypocrisy, Ayda thought. *To pray and not be at peace. To pray and not feel that connection that Shams had mentioned. It was hypocrisy. But you can't gain that connection without putting in an effort,* she countered herself. *It's like any relationship; you can't get anything out of it without putting something in.* Still, she was not ready to commit. What was stopping her, she didn't know exactly, but she just couldn't.

At dinner, Ayda asked Shams if she was excited to meet her grandparents.

"I'm a little worried they won't like me."

Ayda laughed out loud. "Not like you? You're their son's daughter. They've prayed for you since the first day he and I were married. They're going to love you and pamper you. And my suggestion to you is: milk it! They're generous people; enjoy their time and all they do for you. It's all done out of love."

"Of course they'll love their grandchild, but what about *me*. What about my odd fashion sense and soft spokenness?"

"Is that how you feel about me?" Ayda asked.

"No. You...you give me confidence. I feel like you don't judge me, so I can be myself."

"You'll feel the same with them. And they're going to love your fashion sense. Anyone who loves colors will."

◆ ◆ ◆

Saturday finally rolled around. Ayda had asked Marge to stay to help serve dinner and clean up. She was busy in the kitchen, making last minute preparations and heating dinner. She'd already set the table. Everything was just about ready when the guests arrived. Siham and Rizq came first. Siham hugged Ayda and shook Shams's hand. "I'd like to hug you, if that's okay," she said to the girl.

Shams nodded, and Siham threw her arms around her and held her tightly. "I'm so glad to meet you, Shams."

"I'm glad to meet you, too."

"You've got your dad's eyes, *SubhanAllah*." She turned to Ayda and asked, "Do you see it?"

"I see it every time I look at her," Ayda said with a smile.

"*Allah yirhamu*, God have mercy on him," Siham said, and they all repeated the short supplication.

Rizq and Shams went into the living room and turned on the TV. Ayda and Siham went to help Marge in the kitchen; they could hear the kids laughing and joking.

"She seems like a good kid," Siham said.

"She's a great kid," Ayda said.

"And how're you dealing with everything?"

"I've doubled my cigarette intake, thank you. I consider that an achievement."

"Besides doubling your cigarette intake, are you okay?"

"I'm better than I expected I'd be, to be honest. But I'm still...angry as fuck. I'm doing my best not to show that because I know it's not her fault. And I love her. I really do. I didn't think I would. I thought I would resent everything about her. I agreed just so that...I wouldn't be giving up before I even tried, you know? But...I do love her. She's an innocent part of my life that I wish I could get back. And it's like, God gave it back to me. I don't know. I know I'm not really making any sense."

"You are," Siham said, putting her hand on her shoulder. "I get it."

"But I'm still angry as fuck."

"Yeah, that makes sense too."

They stopped talking when Marge came back into the kitchen, and Siham chatted with Marge for a bit. When the doorbell rang, Ayda went to answer. Her in-laws greeted the two women and Rizq, then they stood staring at Shams with wide smiles and tears in their eyes. After a moment of admiring their newfound granddaughter, Shams blushing the entire time, they hugged her and welcomed her into the family.

"*Alhamdulillah* that we have this opportunity to be a part of your life and for you to be a part of ours. *Alhamdulillah*," Shams's grandmother said, wiping her own tears and squeezing the girl tight.

"Oh, I brought you something. I don't know if you will like it." The older woman took out a box and handed it to the girl. Shams opened it and pulled out a silver necklace.

"It's beautiful," she said, putting it on. "Thank you." And she hugged her grandmother again.

Ayda was still in the kitchen when the rest of the family sat around the dining room table. Marge placed the last dish in the center then went back into the kitchen. Ayda breathed in deeply, preparing to go back out to her guests.

"Wish me luck, Marge."

"You don't need luck, Ms. Faisal. Your family is great. They won't call the cops and report the kidnapped girl." Marge smiled, and even though Ayda didn't, something about that exchange made Ayda ease up.

The dinner went exceptionally well. Ayda had expected a bit more awkwardness, but nobody seemed out of place at all. It was as though they'd been having those weekly dinners for years. Sumayya and Saleh asked Shams all kinds of questions and hung on her every word. Rizq cracked a few inappropriate jokes and got smacked on the back of the head by his mom. For the most part, Ayda sat quietly, observing the interactions.

"What should I call you guys?" Shams asked somewhere toward the beginning of the meal. It was Siham who spoke up. "You call them Sitto and Giddo. It's what Rizq calls them. And you call me Auntie Siham or Seema. And we call him Rizi, but he also goes by Clown or Dork, or anything you choose really."

"Or she can call me Cool Cuz. Right? That would be cool."

"I think I'll stick with Clown," Shams said, and the entire table exploded with laughter.

"Dude, we're supposed to stick together," Rizq whispered with a smile.

"This is the right thing," Ayda heard someone say. "This is how it should be." She looked up at Sumayya, but found her talking to Shams, and Siham was busy talking to Rizq about school. She couldn't tell where the voice had come from.

Sumayya and Saleh filled the evening telling Shams stories about her father. Among them was the story about how he had once climbed a tree to help the neighborhood cat get down.

"And as soon as he got to the branch she was on, that little animal climbed right back down. Saef said he swore he heard her say, 'sucker!' as she passed him."

"Then there was the time he and his friends skipped school and went to a movie. But when they got out of the theater, the mother of one of his friends caught them and drove them all back to school."

"Did you punish him when you found out?"

"We made him do the dishes for a week. But I told him I was more disappointed that he'd gotten caught than anything," Saleh said, howling. Shams joined his laughter. "But you two better never skip school. If I catch you..." he made a threatening gesture with his fingers then said, "I'd make sure...to take you out for sundaes after."

"Thanks for being such a great role model for our impressionable children, Baba," Siham said.

"Oh, boo," he replied, swatting her words away with his hand.

"We brought you some pictures of your dad, too. If you'd like to see them," Sumayya said.

"I'd love to. I have one family picture of us—my mom, my dad and me—I'm only about one in the picture. It's the only one I have of the three of us."

Sumayya pulled out an album from her oversized purse and sat beside Shams on the couch. She explained each picture to the girl, and they laughed together as Siham, Saleh, and Rizq looked over their shoulders. Ayda got up to check on the dishwasher; that was her excuse, anyway.

Marge had left just after dinner but not before loading the dishes and starting the machine. It was still going when Ayda went in, but she knew it would be. She grabbed her cigarettes and stepped out onto the back porch without anyone noticing. Sitting on the steps, inhaling the smoke, she pondered what her life had turned into. She enjoyed having Shams, and she really did love her, but that didn't change the fact that her very presence meant Saef's betrayal got shoved in her face every time she looked at the young girl. And what made it worse was the fact that Shams looked like him too. Ayda actually didn't know if that was the worst thing or the best thing. She was mad at him, but she loved him. Despite herself, she loved him.

"Hey," Siham said, startling Ayda as she sat down beside her on the steps.

"Are they finished going through the pictures?"

"They're taking it very slowly." Siham took the cigarette from Ayda and put it out. "You need to chill out with these."

"I don't want to."

"Yeah, I know. But you need to. It's not just about you anymore."

"I don't smoke in the house when she's home," she lied.

"It's not just that. What kind of an example do you set for her? I mean, she knows you smoke, and she knows how often. What message does that send to her?"

Ayda sighed. "You're right."

"Of course I am."

They sat quietly for a few moments, listening to the laugher filtering out to them from inside.

"This is great, by the way. What you're doing with her. I know it's hard, but God will reward you for it."

Ayda did a half-shrug. "I don't think I have a choice. I mean, I do enjoy her, I do love her and love having her here. But even if she were a little punk, I don't think I'd feel like I have a choice. It was like Saef was calling to me, asking me to do this for him. I could never say no."

Siham nodded and put her arm around Ayda's shoulders. "Come on, Didi. We should get back inside. We need to get going soon anyway."

Before they all left, Ayda made sure they were to come over every Saturday for dinner, without waiting for a weekly invitation.

"Do you want us to bring anything?" Sumayya offered.

"Dessert. Bring something chocolatey and rich in delicious calories."

When everyone had left, Shams helped Ayda tidy up.

"Sitto and Giddo invited me to go over there for a sleepover sometime."

"Oh, I think that's a great idea. I told you, they're gonna spoil you."

Shams smiled. "Why don't I go to the same school as Rizq?"

"He's in a different zone. Different neighborhoods go to different elementary and middle schools. There's only one high school in the city, so you'll end up together then. *In sha' Allah.*"

"He's funny."

"He's a riot. He gets that from me," Ayda said with a straight face.

Shams laughed out loud. "Yeah, I think you're right."

As she said good night to her that evening, Shams said, "Thank you. For today, for helping me get to know them. For...taking me in."

"You're a good kid, Shams. I think God sent you to me, not the other way around."

"You'll start to pray with me then?" the girl asked with a wide smile and a twinkle in her eye.

"Nice try."

"I'm learning. I do have a great teacher." Then she said good night and headed up to her room.

Chapter Eleven
SHAMS AND AYDA

One evening as they sat together in the living room, Shams said to Ayda, "You know, I don't really know a lot about you."

"What do you want to know?"

"Everything. Start with your parents."

"My parents were both Egyptian. They came to this country as children when they were each around ten years old. When they were in high school, they met at the local mosque. They'd seen each other before at the mosque during Eid and other events, but their first actual introduction was when they were sophomores or juniors. Then Mom went off to college and Dad started to work, but they sort of kept in touch through friends. During Mom's last year of college, Dad asked for Mom's hand in marriage. I think at that point she didn't mind either way. He was a good guy, but she didn't know him enough to love him. In any case, her parents refused; she was going to business school, and he wasn't even in college. A few months after she graduated, she married a doctor, but he turned out to be abusive. He used to hit her and take her money. Her parents pressured her to stay, but she wasn't having it.

"'No one will want to marry a divorced woman,' they said to her. But she told them she didn't care. She said she'd rather live alone with dignity than be married and live in fear and constant danger of being hurt or killed.

"Against their wishes, she got a divorce and moved into a tiny apartment not too far from her parents. When Dad found out, he went to ask her if she'd marry him. I guess he'd been in love with her for a while. 'Ask my parents,' she told him. 'They won't refuse this time.' So he did. They were married not too long after. They were happy. I have lots of pics of us as a family. They opened a bakery, and we did well.

"They used to encourage me in whatever I loved. They knew I was artsy, so they enrolled me in art classes. 'Do what you love and you will live a blessed life,' my mom used to say.

"When I was about twenty-two, Mom got sick. She didn't make it. Dad died a few weeks later of a broken heart. I miss them."

"*Allah yirhamhum*. They sound awesome," Shams said. "What happened to their bakery? That would be such a cool thing to run. We could have fresh bagels and croissants every day."

"It would be awesome. It used to be even better than awesome. My mom made the best homemade donuts ever. EVER. And she only gave me one when I did something good. So when I was a kid, I would make up different scenarios to try to squeeze a donut out of her. 'Today I gave my friend half my sandwich because she didn't have a lunch,' or 'I helped the teacher when all of her papers fell and scattered out all over the floor.' But my most imaginative reason for why I deserved a donut was because God had created me, and He created all things good." Shams and Ayda laughed.

"Did she give you a donut for that one?"

"She looked at me with one eyebrow cocked and a hand on her hip—" Ayda rose to imitate the posture— "and said, 'But that's not something *you* did. That's something God did. So...should I give Him the donut?'

"I said, 'yes,' and held out my hand. She crossed her arms and knitted both her eyebrows. I said, 'Didn't you teach me that God sends people to ask for things and when you feed them or clothe them, it's like you fed or clothed God? So give *me* the donut, and it'll be like you gave it to God.' Mom burst out laughing and gave me a huge hug. And the donut."

Ayda was quiet for a moment then she sighed and said, "Oh what I wouldn't give for one of her donuts."

"She never taught you how to make them?"

"She tried, but I was a pain in the ass. I never liked spending time in the kitchen."

"We could try to find a recipe online," Shams suggested.

Ayda agreed so Shams started researching. "Do you think the recipe had cinnamon in it?"

"Definitely had cinnamon," Ayda replied.

"What about condensed milk?"

"Definitely not. Mom never bought condensed milk."

"Okay...butter or oil?"

"How the hell am I supposed to know?! It was like thirty years ago!"

"You knew about the cinnamon and condensed milk!" Shams shouted back with a smile.

"Those are very specific, very unique ingredients. They stand out. But butter or oil...they're too similar."

"Well..." Shams thought. "Did the donuts taste rich or light?"

"I'm going to smack you."

When they finally decided on a recipe, Ayda held her head out the kitchen window to smoke a cigarette as Shams mixed the ingredients.

"Didn't you ever like cooking or baking?" the girl asked.

"No," Ayda answered flatly.

"Not even when my dad was here?"

"When your dad was here I cooked and baked. But I didn't necessarily like it—I did it out of a sense of duty."

"What was your favorite thing to make?"

"My favorite thing to make? Ummmm." Ayda thought for a moment as she finished her cigarette. "I make a really great chicken and broccoli soup."

"Will you make it for me sometime?"

"You won't like it."

"Yes I will."

"No, you won't."

"Why not?"

"Because you don't like broccoli."

"What? Yes, I do."

"Are you sure?"

"Of course I'm sure."

Ayda heaved a loud sigh. "Fiiiiiiine. I'll make it for you."

Shams laughed. "You never told me what happened to your parents' bakery."

"When they passed away, I sold it. I needed money to pay some hospital debts and funeral fees and some other loans we'd taken out. But the people who bought the bakery turned it into something else. I think a paint shop or something like that."

"That's too bad. It would be cool to own a bakery.

"I'm hoping to one day open an art company of some kind and have a small coffee shop inside where we'll make fresh pastries." Ayda paused for a minute. "Well, I won't make them. Maybe I'll hire Marge. Or you. Or I'll hire Marge, and you can be her underage slave...I mean, assistant."

"What kind of art company? Like an ad agency?"

"No," Ayda said. "I'm thinking an art gallery and a bookstore, in one. With a coffee shop."

"Customers can sip their coffee as they browse the art or read a book," Shams said, as the picture formed in her mind. "Then, they can buy whatever pieces of art appeal to them. I like it."

"Just be aware," Ayda said, "that this batch of donuts is your interview. If they come out good, you're hired. Otherwise..." Ayda shrugged and shook her head.

"Well, if this is my practical exam, stop talking to me so I can concentrate!"

"You're the one who keeps talking, you punk!"

Ayda tossed the kitchen towel at Shams, and they both giggled.

"So besides being Marge's underage slave in our art gallery/bookshop, what are your aspirations for the future?" Ayda asked.

"Is that a fancy way of asking what I want to be when I grow up?"

"That's exactly what it is."

"I don't really know. Lots of things appeal to me. I like the idea of being an architect and designing beautiful buildings. But I also like designing clothes. I'd like to have my own fashion line with my unique style."

"It seems you have a strong sense for art," Ayda said.

"I don't necessarily understand it. But I do enjoy art, and I like to make things, and draw, and paint, and stuff like that. I get it from Mom; she was an artist. She used to make pottery. She had her own online shop, and she did pretty well. She used to use different materials and designs and colors. She used to tell me to always acknowledge the beauty in things because God created everything with beauty. Her pieces always had tiny faults, faults that she intentionally left unfixed, attributing them to the individuality of things. She said there is beauty in everything, even in the breaks."

They were both quiet for a moment.

"Beauty in the breaks?" Ayda said doubtfully. "That's a lovely theory. Don't know how much truth there is to it, though."

Shams didn't reply as she continued making the donuts.

"You look like you're doing pretty well with that," Ayda said. "Was being a baker on the list of things you might like to be when you grow up?"

Shams giggled. "No."

"What about being a graphic designer? Do you have any interest in that?"

"I don't have any experience with it. I don't know."

"Well, one day when you come to work with me, you'll be able to check it out. Most of the people I work with are a bunch of clowns, but they're all talented. You'll enjoy hanging out with them, and I'm sure you'll learn a thing or two."

"Why won't I be able to hang out with you?"

"No, you will. It's just that I'm in a position now where I don't necessarily do any designing. I sign off on the ads and designs of the teams working under me. I help them with ideas, choosing colors, things like that, but they do the creating."

Shams nodded. "We do have a Take Your Child to Work Day. Even though I'm not your child..."

"I'd like that," Ayda interrupted. "I'd like that very much. But like we agreed before, you have to pretend you're that creepy ghost girl from all those horror movies. At least at first."

Shams laughed. "I'll walk in behind you with my hair pulled down over my face, wearing a white nightgown. And then proceed to torture your employees?"

"That's the plan! When is that Take Your Child to Work Day anyway?'"

"Next month. They'll send out an announcement a week or two before."

"So...it's basically a day off of school for you?"

"Well, except if you participate, then the next day you give an oral presentation on what you saw and learned. Anyone who doesn't want to participate—or can't for whatever reason—has to go to school that day."

Ayda nodded. "Is there a Bring Your Parent to School Day?"

"There's Career Day, when you can have any adult you know come in and talk to the class about what they do for a living and how they got to their current position."

"Everyone has to bring someone in?"

"No, usually for the whole class only three or four adults show up."

"Will you tell me when that day comes?"

"You really want to come?"

"I never miss an opportunity to warp young min...I mean, to inspire young minds." Ayda spoke as she lit a cigarette.

"But you know you won't be able to smoke?"

"What?! Come on! I was totally planning on passing out cigarettes to all the kids in class."

As usual, she spoke with a straight face, which only made Shams laugh even louder.

That night as they sat together eating Sham's donuts—which Ayda praised but said were not exactly like her mother's—Ayda said, "I told you about my parents. Now, tell me about your mom."

Of course, Ayda didn't really want to hear about the woman her husband had had an affair with. But she did want to hear about Shams...and to do that, to truly allow the young girl to be open with her, Ayda would have to hear about her mother. She suppressed the knot in her stomach and forced her face to be polite as she lit a cigarette. And she opened her ears and heart to listen.

"You know," Shams said, "you probably are killing me with those."

Ayda nodded, and put out the cigarette she'd only taken one puff from. "Only outside from now on. Now, go on."

Shams began telling Ayda baby stories her mother used to tell her. "She used to tell me I was the worst baby in the world."

"Yeah, I can see that."

"Hey!" Shams protested, tossing a throw pillow at Ayda. "She used to say that if I wasn't nursing, then I was crying. I didn't sleep at all my first month, apparently. And so Mom didn't sleep. She was like a zombie, she said, surviving on one cup of coffee a day. Even though the doctors said drinking coffee in moderation was okay, she thought that perhaps it was the caffeine making me such a pain in the ass, but she said she was 'running on fumes' so she couldn't go without it completely. When I got a bit older—two-ish I think—I would pull everything off the shelves, and once I almost pulled the bookcase on top of me. Dad grabbed it at the last second. I was in everything. Once she even found me in the dryer. But she was a really calm person. She never yelled or spanked me. It was always, 'Come Shams, sit. I'm not happy with your behavior. Do you know why it's wrong?' And she would explain why I shouldn't act in such a way and tell me the consequences if I were to do so again.

"She never forced me to do anything. I mean, I would end up doing whatever she wanted me to do, but somehow she always convinced me to do it, made me feel like it was my own choice. Like making my bed, for example. I remember not wanting to, and she let me not make it for a few days. Then the sheet started to come undone. I asked her to pull it back on, and in her calmest voice she said, 'I've been asking you to make your bed for days now, so no, I won't make it for you. I'll help you with it this time, but if it happens again, you're on your own.' And somehow I just knew that I needed to make my bed every day so it wouldn't get so messy that I couldn't handle it.

"She used to read to me every night before I fell asleep. Even after I was old enough to read to myself. Even after I could read as well as her, she would still read to me. I loved the sound of her voice, the way she tried to do some of the voices but never really could. There was something about those moments.... I don't know, everything was just perfect then."

Slow, soft tears began to trickle down her cheeks.

Ayda put her arm around Shams's shoulder and pulled the young girl toward her. They sat in the shared silence of loss for a while, hoping their individual pain could somehow be eased by their being together.

Then Shams spoke again. "Mom never remarried after Dad died. I asked her about it once, and she said she didn't trust herself. That really confused me. She explained that she didn't trust herself not to compare a new husband to Dad. She said somehow, she'd always be doing something wrong—either feeling like the new guy didn't match up, or enjoying things about him that she didn't about Dad. She felt like it was a sort of betrayal, I guess. Like she didn't want to betray Dad. I told her how could she think that when she'd been such a minor part of his life. But she said it wasn't about the quantity of time they spent together because the quality of their time together always made up for that. Do you think that's weird?"

Ayda was quiet for a minute. "I can understand it." But while she could understand it, she could not understand how or why *he* had betrayed *her*.

They had been happy, fulfilled. So how could he have done this to her? And what kind of a woman would agree to live the way Leah had, a secret who only got a few hours of his time every week? Why would she agree? It drove Ayda mad. But she realized that she would never know; the only people who could answer were both dead.

"I wish I could remember anything about Dad. I have no memories of him, not even those dream memories where you're not sure if it was a dream you had once or if it really happened."

"What do you want to know about him?"

Shams asked her all sorts of questions about Saef: what his job was like, what he did for fun, how they'd met, whether he remembered her birthday and their anniversary, how they celebrated 'Eid, what were his favorite color, meal, outfit.

Ayda talked about some of her favorite memories of Saef. "Your dad was one of those people that got along with everyone. He said what he wanted to without ever offending anyone. Clearly he didn't have my manners."

Shams laughed.

"He believed in treating everyone with kindness, even people he didn't quite care for. When we first got married, I was the one who encouraged him to pray and maintain a close connection with God."

Shams interrupted her. "Really?"

"Really. I was a different person then. My faith was stronger. And as we spent more time together, his faith increased. He became the one who encouraged me...to pray, to fast. He started reading more about Islam, reading Qur'an and *hadith*. When good things happened, he thanked God and praised Him. And when bad things happened, he thanked God and praised Him, and asked Him to alleviate his hardship. He tried to fast every Monday and Thursday, in the tradition of the Prophet, peace be upon him. He used to say, 'Prophet Muhammad's example was always love and kindness. If someone tells you something about Islam and it goes against love and kindness, that's a big red flag that it isn't from Islam.' He was extra good to his parents. They spoiled him, but he tried his best to always honor them, even if it meant he had less time to rest or relax.

"I remember once, we were planning on going away for a mini-vacation. It was just going to be a day trip, but we were both looking forward to it. We'd booked a private room on the beach, and the weather forecast was bright, sunny, warm—just perfect for our mini getaway. As we were finishing up some last minute packing on the morning of the trip, his mom calls and tells him his dad's car won't start. I hear him say, 'Can't he use your car for the next couple of days?' The next thing I know, he's saying, 'Ok, Mama. I'll be right over.' He hung up and turned to me and said, 'I'll be real quick. If I can't figure it out in a few minutes, I'll leave my car with them and you can just come pick me up.' We were still on schedule.

"But then he left and minutes turned to hours. One hour before our flight I called him and asked him if I should swing by and pick him up. He goes, 'No, Bill. My Dad's car is busted, so I won't be able to see you guys today.'

"I was pissed. First of all...Bill?! I mean, I'm his wife for God's sake. Why would he pretend to be speaking to someone else? And secondly, they were going to ruin our getaway. I was livid!

"He got home a few hours later. I had already unpacked our stuff. And I just ignored him. 'I'll make it up to you,' he said, 'I promise.'

"But I wasn't hearing it. The week went by..."

"You guys didn't talk all week?" Shams interrupted.

"No, we talked. But I kept it all really short—yes's and no's and doing my best to sort of avoid him."

"And he just stayed out of your way?"

"Are you kidding?" Ayda let out a giant laugh. "He could never stay out of my way. He would talk to me about things that otherwise he would've never even noticed, let alone mentioned. 'Do I put this in with the whites or colors?' he'd say, holding up a t-shirt or his beige pants. Normally he would have just thrown them somewhere in the vicinity of the laundry basket without a second thought.

"Anyway, so on Friday he showed up at my office at about two. 'Finish up and meet me downstairs,' he said. I didn't get it—why did he want to leave so early? And why hadn't he said anything about it that morning on our way to work. So, I finished up and met him downstairs in the parking lot. My first thought was that something was wrong. Either one of his parents had become sick or he'd had an argument at work. I expected it to be something bad. So we pulled out of the parking lot and he said, 'Are you ready?' I said, 'Ready for what?' 'Ready for our getaway?' he asked. I rolled my eyes and said, 'Our reservations were last week, Saef.'

"'Yeah,' he said, 'but then I called the hotel and rescheduled for this week and booked two nights instead of one.'

"My whole face lit up. 'I told you I'd make it up to you,' he said with this huge grin on his face.

"It was the best vacation ever. He put in a hundred and fifty percent. We had such a great time. On our way home, he said to me, 'Next time, trust that I'll make it up to you.' And I did. And he did make it up to me. Whether small or big, anytime he upset me, he'd always make it up to me."

Shams listened quietly, then after a short pause said, "I feel like he gave you all his goodness."

"Well, I was his wife."

"Mom was his wife too. But she didn't get any of that. He barely saw her."

"She did that to herself," Ayda almost said. She almost said, "Any woman who agrees to take a man from his wife deserves what she gets. Any woman who tries to ruin another's marriage ought to suffer." Instead of saying any of that, Ayda simply reached for a cigarette and lit it.

"It seems like you two were happy," Shams said. "So why did he marry my mom?"

The smile and laughter that had encompassed Ayda as she'd answered Shams's questions disappeared. In their place a heavy gloom set in, and her chest felt tight. "I don't know. The only people who can answer that question are no longer here."

"Well," Shams went on, oblivious to the change that had overcome Ayda, "How come you guys never had any kids?" Her eyes were set on Ayda in earnest.

"I...I ah...I can't have kids," Ayda replied, barely above a whisper.

Shams looked down at her hands in her lap. "I'm sorry I'm making you sad."

"You aren't making me sad. I like talking about your dad. I didn't. It had been too painful for me. But with you...I like it." She ruffled the girl's hair.

After a few moments went by in silence, Shams said, "Mom used to tell me that Dad found her just because of me. She used to say I was the glue that kept him with us. I didn't understand that until just now." After a short pause she continued, "I used to feel bad for Mom, knowing that even when Dad was alive, he was almost never around. She didn't even know all that stuff about him, like you do. I used to ask her, and she would just say things like, 'All I know is he loved you more than anything in the world.' Which isn't an answer to 'What's his favorite meal or what was his dream car.' But what do you tell your mom when she doesn't give you a straight answer? You maybe ask the same questions again, but eventually you stop, knowing that...well, she just doesn't know."

"Did that make you mad? Mad at her for not knowing? Mad at him because he never really gave her a chance to know?"

Shams thought for a moment, her eyebrows knitted. "Not mad. Sad. It made me feel like she was all alone even when he'd been around. She deserved better than that."

Ayda knew what she meant, yet a piece of her took it personally. "No. A woman who takes another woman's husband doesn't deserve better— she deserves all the pain the universe gives her." But she didn't say it. She kept quiet and reflected on what Shams had just shared with her. For the first time since she'd found out about Leah, she put herself in her shoes. Ayda imagined what it would have been like to have been kept a secret from Saef's family and friends. What it would have been like to have had only an hour or two of his time every week. And—if Ayda pretended to ignore the declaration of love Leah made in her letter and assumed that Saef had only married that woman to reproduce—what it would have been like to have been nothing more than a womb, a means to have a child. Ayda knew that she would not have tolerated such behavior. But it made her wonder what had happened to Leah for *her* to put up with it.

"Life is strange that way," Ayda finally said. "Lots of times, we don't get what we deserve."

They were quiet for a time, then Shams said, "But Mom used to tell me that God will make it up to us in Heaven."

Ayda looked at her and smiled. "She was right. So we have to always do the right thing."

They were quiet for a moment, then Ayda said, "Does this mean I have to stop swearing?"

Shams giggled and said, "You probably should."

"And give up cigarettes too, huh?"

"Yeah," Shams said.

Ayda dropped her head to her chest and fake cried.

"It's okay, Ayda," Shams said, rubbing her back. "I'll help you."

Chapter Twelve
SOME FIRSTS FOR SHAMS

Months passed, and Ayda and Shams easily fell into a routine. They were both comfortable and happy in their arrangement, and they continued to learn from each other.

One day, Ayda came home to find Shams curled up on the couch, crying, hugging the throw pillow.

She sat beside her. "What's wrong, Shams?" she asked in a soft voice. "What happened?"

The young girl sniffled, then she explained. "Those same kids that made fun of me on my first day, they do it every day. They call me 'frizz ball' and 'color explosion,' then they all burst into a laughing fit."

"Why do you care about what those kids say?"

"It hurts my feelings when they're mean to me."

"But my question is, why do you let it hurt your feelings? Do you not like your hair?"

"No, I like it."

"Do you think you dress poorly?"

Again, the girl shook her head. "No."

"Alright then. So why does their opinion matter to you? When those little shits say something to put you down, just tell them to fuck off."

Shams giggled through her tears. "I'd get suspended for saying that."

"Oh, well...I mean, you don't have to use those exact words. You can just say, 'I like my clothes, and your opinion doesn't mean anything.' Or 'I like myself this way, and if you don't, that doesn't bother me at all.'"

"But it does bother me. I want to be liked."

"Huh. I never had that problem." Ayda thought for a moment. "I think the question is, what do you want more: to keep dressing and acting in a way you like, in a way that makes you feel comfortable, or to be liked?"

"I want both."

"Then you keep being you. And you'll find someone who likes you the way you are. And the rest of those clowns, their opinions should wash past you, like air. Trust me, it's not these losers that you want to like you. You should only want people to like you for who you really are."

"You never wanted people to like you?" Shams asked.

"I never cared if they did. I like who I am. I like that I can draw well and I can manage teams. I like that I'm not shy. I like the colors I choose to dress in. I even like my slightly crooked teeth. I like me. If other people do too, that's cool. But if they don't, that doesn't bother me because I'm comfortable with who I am."

"There's nothing about you you don't like?"

"No, I have my flaws, and I know them very well. But just as I like myself despite my flaws, those who like me will continue to like me despite my flaws too."

"What's one of your flaws?"

"Swearing in front of kids, apparently."

Shams giggled. "What else?"

"I don't like that I have no desire to quit smoking. I know it's bad for me and it's a disgusting habit—but I don't want to quit."

They were quiet for a moment, then Ayda said, "Just so you know, I like your outfit."

Shams smiled and mumbled a thank you.

"But I stick with what I said: you shouldn't give a shit what anyone thinks of you."

Shams looked up at Ayda with a half-grin.

"What?" Ayda asked.

"You swore again."

"Did I?" She thought for a few seconds. "Oh, 'shit' isn't a swear."

Shams chuckled. Her mood had been lifted.

Each morning Ayda made sure Shams had her lunch before she got on the bus, and each morning, they'd have the same conversation.

"I don't need money today, Ayda. I've got my lunch."

"Just keep it with you. Maybe you'll want a chocolate chip ice-cream sandwich for dessert or something."

"Way to encourage me to eat healthy," the girl said with a giggle.

"Ok...maybe you'll want a healthy fruit salad for dessert. Is that better?"

"Why would I get a fruit salad if I can have an ice-cream sandwich?" Shams teased.

Ayda pursed her lips before playfully smacking the girl and handing her the money.

Ayda always took Shams shopping before her shoes had a chance to rip or her clothes had a chance to get too small.

"But I don't need anything," Shams would protest as they pulled into the mall parking lot.

"We'll walk around. We won't get anything."

Shams laughed. "You always say that then you end up buying me three or four items."

"Come on. Enough gabbing, let's go."

Ayda tried to be vigilant about being a responsible parent. In the evenings Shams did her homework in her room, so Ayda would pop in every once in a while and ask if she could help her with anything.

"Yeah, I have this math problem I can't figure out."

"Is Jack getting on the northbound train and Jill beginning on the southbound train and they're asking you to find out what time dinner's on at Grandma's? Cause if that's what it is, tell them Grandma always has dinner at five."

"Dinner at five," Shams said, pretending to write it down. "Got it."

They enjoyed each other's company, and Saturday dinners were one of their highlights, even for Ayda. Having her in-laws over and spending time with Siham and Rizq brought her back to a time when things were better, when life was good and made sense.

Shams's presence had improved all of their lives. Sumayya and Saleh had been yearning to talk to someone about their son, and Shams was the only one who could listen. It was medicine for them, and for her too.

One evening after they'd all gone home, Shams sat with Ayda on the back porch as she smoked a cigarette. They sat in silence for a few moments then Shams asked Ayda a question. "How old were you when you started smoking?"

Ayda thought for a minute. "Thirty-seven."

"Wow!"

"Wow what?"

"It just seems that at thirty-seven you should have known better."

"Totally." She took another puff of her cigarette.

After a short pause, Shams began again. "Can I try one?"

"No."

"Just one puff. I just want to taste what makes everyone love them so much."

"People know they taste like shit. They don't do it for the taste. It's something else, a feeling it gives you."

"Pleeeeeease."

"These things cause cancer. What kind of an adult would I be if I let you—a kid of only 12—try it? I'd be the worst guardian in the world."

"Better for me to try it here with you than with a bunch of kids at school."

Ayda turned to her. "You wouldn't."

Shams shrugged, a sly grin on her face. "Curiosity and peer pressure are a force to be reckoned with."

Ayda stared at her for a moment. "You're going to hate it."

"Good, I want to hate it. I just want to see what it's like."

Ayda handed the cigarette over and said, "Don't pull in too hard."

Shams's face lit up, and she took the cigarette quickly, before Ayda could change her mind.

"You get two puffs," Ayda said.

But Shams didn't need the second puff. As soon as she inhaled the smoke, she began coughing violently.

"I told you not to breathe in too deeply," Ayda said casually as the girl continued with her coughing fit.

When she had finally composed herself, Shams said, "They really do taste like shit."

"I told you."

"And they're...suffocating. I don't get why people are so addicted."

"Neither do we."

After Ayda finished the cigarette, they sat in the crisp outdoors for a while longer. The chirping of hidden crickets filled Ayda with a longing for days she knew could never return, days that had been filled with laughter but were painful to remember. When she had played in her parents' yard as a child, when she had sat on this same porch with Saef, his embrace protecting her from the chill of the outside world.

"Can I ask you something?" Shams asked after some time.

"You can ask me anything."

"Are you mad at my mom and dad?"

Ayda's stomach flipped. She continued to stare down at the ground beneath her feet. "Why do you ask?"

"It just seems like, whenever anyone mentions Dad, you clench your jaw and your face turns pink. It seems like you get really mad."

Ayda nodded slightly but remained silent. What was she supposed to say to this child? How could she tell her the truth without tainting the image of the young girl's parents...or of herself, for that matter? Surely Shams would not believe that Ayda had been a victim. Surely she would side with her parents and think less of Ayda for even implying that they had been anything short of honorable.

"It's okay," Shams said, breaking Ayda's trance. "You don't have to tell me." And she started to get up.

But Ayda put her hand on the girl's knees, motioning her to remain seated.

"I want to tell you. I just want to make sure I say it in a way you'll understand." She cleared her throat and began again. "Your father and I were happily married. Or...at least that's what I thought. I didn't know that he had...that he had married your mother until after he had died. I was hurt that he had betrayed me like that, and it hurt more because he wasn't around for me to ask all the questions that were—and still are—flying around my head, threatening to blow it up. I'm mad that your father cheated on me."

Shams was quiet for a while. "Yeah, I get that. But... you loved him, right?"

Ayda nodded.

"So, can't you forgive him? Mom once told me that if we wrong someone, God won't forgive us until that person does. And..." tears began filling her eyes and her voice began to shake. "I don't want God to be mad at Dad. Or Mom. So...can't you forgive them?"

The girl began to weep causing Ayda's tears to fall. She held Shams in her arms and squeezed her tight. They sat crying together for a few moments then Shams pulled away and said, "Please try, okay?"

Ayda nodded. But when Shams got up and went back inside, she said aloud, "I don't know how to forgive, Shams. My anger, my hurt, it's destroyed me. I don't know how to forgive. How do I let it go?" Forgiving someone was not as easy as saying the words, she knew that better than anyone. Forgiveness didn't come from the tongue; it came from the heart. But did she even still have a heart? She had gone hard and cold a long time ago, and she didn't know how to get back, how to let in the warmth and let go of the anger and resentment. She knew there was still goodness in her—

how else had she agreed to take in Shams? How else could she enjoy her company as she did? How else could she love her, for she was certain that she did? And now, for Shams if not for herself, she wanted so badly to let go of her anger. She wanted to forgive Saef for his betrayal. She just didn't know how.

That evening when Shams invited her to pray the evening prayer, Ayda agreed. They stood side-by-side and prayed, prostrating to God, asking for His blessings and His forgiveness. When they had finished, Ayda made a personal, silent supplication, asking God to heal her, to help her let go of the anger that had eaten her up for years. She kissed Shams goodnight and simply said to her, "I'm trying."

The young girl kissed her on the forehead and said, "I know."

That night Ayda's sleep was unrestful. She tossed in bed for hours before she fell asleep, and even then, sleep didn't last long; she was up again just two hours later. She turned on the lamp and went to grab her cigarettes, but on second thought, she got out of bed, washed up, and prayed. Her heart remained heavy, and she hated the feeling of being exhausted yet unable to sleep. Her mother's soft voice spoke to her from her memory, reminding her that whenever she had a hard time falling asleep, she should read Qur'an. "It will help you sleep," she'd always said. So Ayda took the Qur'an from her nightstand, dusted it off, and began to read. And sure enough, just a couple of pages in, she found her eyes closing and head drooping. She turned off the light and fell into a restful sleep.

But early the next morning, a blood curdling scream startled her awake.

Chapter Thirteen
MOTHERING AND RECONNECTING

Ayda ran into Shams's room.

"Something's wrong with me!" the girl yelled.

"What do you mean, Shams? What's wrong?" Ayda shrieked in alarm as she approached Shams's bed.

The girl pulled back the covers, and Ayda saw the stain.

"Oh." Ayda sighed in relief, the blood rushing back into her face and her heartbeat regulating again. "Oh my God, Shams. You scared the piss out of me."

"Why are you so calm?!"

"Well, it had to happen sometime, right?"

"What do you mean?" Shams replied, her face scrunched up and her voice trembling. "What had to happen? How is my bleeding...from down there!... normal?"

"Your mom never explained to you about getting your period?"

"I don't know what you mean."

"Okay," Ayda said in a calm voice. "Look, you're completely fine. What you're going through is totally normal, and all women go through it each month. It's an inevitable part of life, like death...and flat tires...and the donut shop being out of your favorite kind when you need it the most. And like the sun and stars. It's totally normal. It's just puberty."

"Puberty?"

"Don't you have health education in school?"

"Next year. What's puberty?"

"Puberty is when your body goes through changes to prepare you for adulthood—womanhood. The bleeding means your body is now capable of carrying a baby."

Please, please, thought Ayda, *don't ask me how a baby gets in there.*

"But how does a baby get in there?" Shams asked, as though on cue.

Shit! "Have you heard the word sex before?"

"Yeah, but I thought it was a swear."

"No, it's not a swear. Sex is what happens between a man and a woman. It's a special way they come together, and sometimes this union results in an embryo being formed, and that embryo grows to be a fetus and then a baby."

"But I don't want a baby!"

"Perfect! Then don't have sex."

"So I'm going to keep bleeding for the rest of my life?"

"No, no. Your period comes once a month. How long it lasts is different for each woman, but I'd say for most women it lasts between four to seven days."

"I'm going to ruin everything I touch! Or do I just stay locked up in the bathroom with you passing me my meals, like a prisoner?"

Ayda chuckled and got some sanitary napkins for Shams from the closet. "These stick right onto your underwear. You should change it every few hours, especially on days where the bleeding is heavy. Otherwise, you might bleed right through your clothes. It happens to the best of us, but it is one of the most embarrassing things in the world, so do your best to avoid it. Go on. Wash up and change your clothes. You'll feel better soon."

Shams did as she was told, and sometime later they met downstairs in the kitchen.

"You okay now?" Ayda asked with a smile.

"Better. But...would it be okay if I stayed home from school today. I just feel...I don't know...weird. Like everyone is going to know or something."

"You can stay home. But just remember, it's totally normal and every woman goes through it each month. I do, your teachers do, even some of your classmates do. There's nothing to be ashamed or embarrassed about. But stay home...so you can adjust."

"Will you stay with me?"

Ayda's eyebrows shot up, not expecting the request. "Sure, yes. Why not? I had stuff to take care of at the office, but I'll call and tell them what to do. Sure, spending a day together. It'll be fun. Anything specific you want to do?"

Ayda hoped her nervousness didn't sound like sarcasm, as it so often did. But Shams's calm reaction assured her a bit.

"No, just hang out."

After breakfast they took a walk around the neighborhood. Shams told Ayda that her mom used to go for a walk with her every day. "'You've got to remain connected to nature,' she'd say to me. I love being outside. I don't know if it's Mom's influence or just that we're born programmed to feel refreshed by nature. Don't you think?"

"I think lots of people may disagree with you, but I get what you're saying. I love breathing in the fresh air and taking in the view—the greens and blues—all the beauty. I just wish it came without flies and mosquitoes."

After their walk, they sat together in the living room. Ayda was working on some things for work and Shams was reading a novel.

"Is that for school?" Ayda asked her.

"No, I just like to read."

"The library is pretty close. We can walk there sometime. On a day when we haven't had our fill of the outdoors."

Shams laughed. "That would be fun."

At lunch time, Shams told Ayda she was going to prepare something for her. "I've seen Marge make these sandwiches, and they're totally awesome. But I don't think you've ever had one. So sit back, and enjoy the show."

Ayda watched Shams as she floated around the kitchen, pulling ingredients out of the fridge and arranging them delicately in their proper order on the plate. She even garnished it with a couple of pickles.

"Voila!" Shams handed one plate to Ayda and she took the other.

"This is impressive. If it tastes half as good as it looks, I'm getting rid of Marge and you can do the cooking from now on."

Shams pretended to hold her breath in anticipation as Ayda took a bite. Ayda chewed deliberately, exaggeratingly, savoring that first bite. "It's good. It's real good. But we can't get rid of Marge because she does the cleaning too. So unless you want to do toilets..."

"No, no, no. We keep Marge!" Shams said, playing along. "Actually, on a more serious note, I really like Marge."

"I do, too," Ayda said.

"She's been so nice to me since I got here. I'd like to do something nice for her. What do you think? Do you have any ideas?"

"Do you want to give her a raise? But it'll have to come from your allowance."

"Do I get an allowance?"

"You eat and sleep here don't you?"

"So...I'd have to pay her in food and...dreams?"

"Yes, you can give her a raise of food and dreams. I'm sure she would appreciate it," Ayda said with a straight face.

"That *does* sound appealing, but maybe we should come up with a few more ideas on the off chance we can think up something better. I mean, I know it'll be hard to top a raise of food and dreams, but let's see what we can do."

A couple of moments later, Shams said, "What if we invite her and her family over here for dinner, and *we* cook for *them*?"

"You really are gonna go with food?" Ayda said. "But... while I think that is a kind idea, it's possible they wouldn't really enjoy it. They might feel obligated to come, then hate every minute of it. But, we could get her a gift certificate to a nice restaurant, for her and her husband. And we can entertain her daughter while they go out. What do you think?"

"Wow, we really are going with food and dreams. Who'd a thunk?"

During the afternoon, after Ayda had called the office, Shams noticed that she seemed tense. "Is something wrong at work?"

"No," Ayda answered. "The CEO is a straight up ass. But that's not new. He was mad that I wasn't in today. Before this year I hadn't taken a personal day in close to ten years, and this dick is trying to give me a hard time about it. I'm just thinking of a way to repay his obnoxiousness."

"Are all the other people you work with equally obnoxious?"

Ayda lit a cigarette. "I don't know." She exhaled. "I don't talk to anyone about anything other than work. And in that area, I'm their boss so they have to listen. They do what I want and things are usually fine. But I don't chit chat with them."

"Why not?"

"I see no reason to. People, I've learned, will almost always disappoint you. It's best to do what you gotta do, be who you are despite everything, and not trust anyone too much."

"But I trust you?" Shams said.

Ayda stared straight ahead of her as she replied. "You probably shouldn't. You might wake up one day and find I've stolen all your food and dreams."

The young girl smiled at her. "Not possible."

"How can you be sure?"

"Because you're the one who made it possible for me to have those food and dreams to begin with. You are the source; you'd never hurt me."

Whether she was saying it to assure Ayda or herself, Ayda couldn't tell. "Sometimes people do shitty things. Often, they don't mean to hurt others, but it happens anyway."

"But if I understand someone's intention, then I won't get mad. Maybe I'll be sad that they hurt me, but I can't get mad. Sometimes, I think, people don't even try to figure each other out. I think that causes the most problems."

"I hope life doesn't jade you, Shams. I hope you can stay pure, because you are a peach."

"Hahaha! A peach?!"

Ayda smiled at Shams's laughter. "Yes, it means..."

"I know what you mean. Thank you."

"How're you feeling, by the way? Cramps?"

"Haven't noticed," Shams said.

"Yes, that is one secret of life: the busier you are, the harder it is to feel the pain. If you need anything, just let me know. I'll make sure I get pads enough for the both of us next time I go grocery shopping."

"I did want to ask you something." Shams's voice had gotten softer. She looked down and played with her fingers.

"You can ask me anything, always."

"This is a bit different. It's personal. Personal for you."

"I don't really understand, but I'm sticking with what I said—you should always feel like you can ask me anything."

"I heard Aunt Siham call you Didi. Can I call you Didi?"

Ayda's eyes went wide and she caught her breath.

"I'm sorry if I upset you," Shams said, quickly fumbling through her words. "Please forget I said anything."

"It was Saef who gave me that nickname. He never called me anything else. And when he was around, that's how I used to introduce myself. But when he died, when I found out about..." She paused. "I stopped being her. Siham is the only one who still calls me that because she's...she's my best friend. I guess she's just used to saying it. Or maybe...maybe she still sees her in me."

Shams sat quietly, unsure of whether she had caused Ayda pain, unsure if she had overstepped her bounds.

"But I liked Didi. I liked her more. So yeah, you can call me Didi."

Shams hugged Ayda tightly. "I think you're a Didi."

After she had left the room, Ayda said, "Yes, well, we all begin innocent. I thought I was a Didi too until I learned the truth."

Chapter Fourteen
DISCOVERING THE THIEF

Before going in to work the next morning, Ayda stopped by the bagel shop to grab some breakfast and coffee. She observed as the older gentleman in front of her placed his order. Something about him was familiar, but Ayda couldn't place it. A boisterous toddler zipped through the place, diverting Ayda's attention away from the customer in front of her.

"Hi!" said the little boy, waving up at Ayda as he danced around.

"Hello there, young man," Ayda said, smiling. "You look like you're happy you're about to get some breakfast."

"Yeah...donuts are gooooood."

Ayda laughed. "What will you have with the donut?"

"Chocolate."

"My kind of breakfast."

She smiled at his parents who stood behind her, and looked up just in time to see the man in front of her hand the cashier his money. Her eyes fixated on the mark she saw on the back of his hand. Even when the man smiled at Ayda and moved over, making room for her to approach the counter and order, she remained frozen in place. Her stare shifted upwards leaving the man's hand to refocus on his face.

"You?" She spoke aloud, not even realizing it.

Just then the young boy knocked over a display. The noise and confusion snapped Ayda out of her trance, and she left the shop.

Lying low in her car, Ayda waited for the man to appear. When he finally drove off, she was right behind him.

"He's heavier. And mostly bald. That's not how I remember him," she said to herself, "but there is no mistaking that third eye."

A tornado of emotions hit her. She'd been searching for this man her entire adult life, and to finally find him completely by accident caused her to break out into tearful laughter.

"Let's see where you've been hiding, Ghazi."

A few minutes later, she pulled over to the side of the road as his Audi turned into the driveway of a grand Victorian house with a freshly groomed lawn. Ayda saw there was also a black Mercedes parked in the driveway.

"Thieving has done you well, Ghazi Dabbour."

As she sat there, envisioning his break down when all his assets would be torn from his greedy little grip and he'd be thrown out onto the streets with nothing but a bag of his clothes, Ayda saw a young woman in her mid-twenties come out onto the porch.

"You like them young, you little fuck."

But a moment later, Ayda saw an older woman walk out and wrap her arms around the younger one.

"He's got a family. Ghazi Dabbour has a family."

And just like that, her images of victory crumbled.

She went to work, closed the door of her office and pulled down the blinds. Since her parents' death, Ayda had been contriving a plan for that thief. He had disappeared with her parents' money, and she was intent on getting it back, plus profit. It was her right. And she knew her actions would affect his life. She'd make sure that if what he owed her didn't break his back, the lawyer fees certainly would. But she had never figured in his having a family. It was one thing to destroy a man who deserved it—it was quite another to destroy his family.

"But he did this," she said to herself. "You are just taking back what's rightfully yours."

But if I take back what's mine at the expense of innocent people, is that right? How will God judge me?

And suddenly she had the urge to pray. She knew it would not bring an immediate answer—might never bring any answer—but she hoped that by taking that step towards God, He would guide her to do what was right.

She went to the ladies' room to make ablution. When someone walked in as she was washing her feet in the sink, puddles of water all around her, she smiled wide and continued rubbing her feet under the running faucet. When she finished, she wiped up the puddles she'd made on the floor and counter.

Back in her office, Ayda pulled out the prayer mat and prayer gown from her desk drawer, where they had remained untouched for years. After aligning herself in the appropriate direction, she began.

And, as sure as she expected, three seconds later Colette knocked softly on the door and entered. Ayda's assistant had never seen her praying before. Actually, no one in the office even knew that Ayda was Muslim. Colette stood staring for a few seconds, then shut the door behind her and ran to tell her co-workers. Before Ayda had finished her prayer, word had spread throughout the entire office that she was Muslim. Not only that, but there were even rumors that now she was going to be coming to work in hijab. Someone had gone so far as to claim they'd heard her once discussing how to make a bomb, which clearly made her a member of ISIS as well.

All of this took place right outside her office, while she sat inside, asking God to guide her to make the right decision. She asked Him to make her path to reclaiming her rights easy if it was the right thing to do, and to make it difficult if it was not. Her prayer took about seven minutes. When she finished, she put away her prayer mat and gown, opened the door to her office, and called in Colette.

"What did you want?" she asked, lighting a cigarette.

"Um...no...I ah... I figured it out," Colette stuttered.

"Then go."

Ayda was still caught up in thoughts about how to proceed with the man who'd swindled her parents; she was oblivious to the commotion her prayer had caused throughout the office.

Siham called her a short while later.

"Remember I told you that when my parents were still alive, they'd gone into business with a man who ended up taking their money and disappearing?"

"Yeah?"

"I saw him today. Ran into him at the bagel shop."

"Seriously? You're sure?"

"Yes. He's older, fatter, more bald and grey, but it's him."

"Wow. This is great! You can finally make him pay you back."

"But he has a family," Ayda said, a hesitation in her voice.

"What's that got to do with anything?" Siham asked. "You're not going to off him; you're just taking back what's yours."

"I don't want innocent people hurt by this. What if I end up taking all their money? And what about just the scandal it will cause? How are they going to feel knowing their father is a crook? Or was a crook?"

"Why is that your problem, Didi? This man stole from your parents, from you. You still have the contract that specifies the terms of their deal. He did not uphold his end. You told me he disappeared right when your mom was sick and needed money for treatment. He cheated you, and now it's time he pays you back. If this is going to affect him, then he should have thought of that before.

"This isn't revenge, Didi. He didn't do you wrong so now you're going to do him wrong. This is a matter of theft: he stole something from you, and now you're going to take it back. It's your right. And you should never forgo your rights; it cheapens you and allows others to step all over you. You know that better than anyone. I'm surprised that you need me to say any of this. This second guessing yourself is not you."

Ayda took a long drag on her cigarette. "You're right. You're absolutely right."

"Of course I'm right. I just don't get why you're so hesitant. It's not like you. What gives?"

"I'm not entirely sure," Ayda said. "I think having Shams around...She reminds me to pray, she encourages me to do good. I was worried I'd do something against God. She's such a bad influence."

Siham understood. "But this isn't going against God, Didi. God encourages us to take what is rightfully ours. That's all you're doing."

"Yes. Absolutely. You're right. I'm going to call the lawyer in the morning and have him get started."

When Frederick Williams walked into Ayda's office the following day, she showed him the contract that had existed between Ghazi Dabbour and her parents. He sat quietly for more than a few minutes studying it while Ayda smoked her cigarette.

"You know, you really shouldn't smoke indoors."

Ayda made no indication that she'd heard him. "What do you think?" she asked, pointing her cigarette toward the papers in the lawyer's hand.

"You've definitely got a case. Let me study this. How did you find him? This address?"

"I saw him one day on the street and followed him home."

The lawyer nodded. "He looks the same now—all these years later—that you'd recognize him right away?"

"He has a distinct birthmark on the back of his hand, on his fingers. It looks like an eye."

Williams nodded.

"The contract states that in case of breach of contract, the losing party will pay all attorney fees, did I understand that section correctly?" Ayda asked.

"Yes, there is a fee shifting provision in case of breach," Williams said.

"And we are going to win, right?"

Williams looked up at her. "If everything you've told me is correct, there's no reason we won't."

"Good. Then make sure you charge a shitload."

When the lawyer left, Ayda pulled out another cigarette and made a silent prayer that her plan was sound and that she'd win the case.

"Please God," she said, her cigarette dangling from her fingers, "guide me to do what's right and help me to retrieve what is rightfully mine."

◆ ◆ ◆

Ayda finished her cigarette and went to refresh her coffee in the office kitchenette. From a distance, she could hear whispers and laughter. When she approached a bit, she heard snippets like "rule us by *shari'a* law" and "convert" and "recruited by ISIS." Her favorite was "put a bomb in the CEO's office." She walked up to the group gossiping around the coffee maker and stretched her hand through their huddle to get to the coffee pot. Everyone stared at her, frozen in place, faces red. As soon as she made eye contact with each of them, they turned their gaze down to their feet. She poured her coffee, staring at each member of the group, then returned the pot without changing her line of sight. When she spoke, everyone held their breath.

"I declined working with ISIS as I like to take sole credit for my work." She took two steps away then turned back again to the group. "If they do find the 'firecracker' in Derek's office before it goes off, you'll know who put it there."

Then she walked away.

You so shouldn't have done that! she said to herself.

Yeah, but I realized it too late.

You might as well have threatened to kill them all. This is exactly the type of shit that gets innocent people locked up!

Shut up!

The following day, Colette again walked in on Ayda while she was praying. Later, when Ayda called her in to discuss the business at hand, Ayda told Colette she wouldn't be in the office the following day. *It's just a little white lie*, Ayda rationalized.

"Ok, I'll let HR know. Hope everything is okay?" Colette said, a hint of concern in her voice.

Ayda cocked one eyebrow and gave a half grin, the look in her eyes spitting venom. "Everything is perfect. So perfect, I'm bursting! Exploding!"

When Ayda got to work the following day, Colette and four other department employees, Derek and two HR employees were all out sick. Ayda stood in the center of the cubicles and laughed out loud.

"Alice?" she yelled.

Hearing her name, the secretary stood holding a pen and pad. "You've been promoted to assistant, effective immediately. Let them know in HR, and also let them know that my plans changed so I am present today. Cynthia?"

Jolted by hearing her name, Cynthia stood abruptly, knocking over her coffee mug, spilling the liquid all over her desk.

"Once you clean up that mess," Ayda continued, "you're the leader of the High Profile case. Choose your team from those who are here today. The rest of you get a bonus equal to one day's pay. Alice, take care of that with HR.

"You've got balls, people! I admire that!"

She went back to her office and lit a cigarette. Some businesses did retreats to build team spirit. Some did workshops. That wasn't Ayda's style. What she had just done was far more effective than any retreat or workshop.

Alice came in an hour later with the papers from HR for Ayda to sign. "Do you want me to continue with my secretarial duties, Ms. Faisal?"

"Of course not. You're an assistant. Have HR hire someone. The job description should be 'secretary to work for a member of ISIS.'"

Alice took the papers Ayda had signed and said, "I'm not going to say that."

"And why the hell not?" Ayda asked, incredulously.

"Because then ISIS'll be pissed you're not undercover anymore." She left and shut the door behind her.

"I think I just met my new best friend," Ayda said, staring at the closed door.

The following day the buzz in the office was all about how Ayda had given a day's bonus to everyone who had been present the previous day and how Alice and Cynthia had been promoted, despite their junior experience. Colette wasn't sure if she was out of a job or had been demoted or what.

She went into Ayda's office, dragging her feet and wringing her hands. "Um...Ms. Faisal...I...Uh..."

"Spit it out, Colette. What?"

"I just... I know that Alice was promoted to assistant, so I was wondering... where that leaves me?"

"Why didn't you come to work yesterday, Colette?"

Ayda's eyes were boring into hers, the woman's face growing redder and redder, but unable to tear her gaze away.

"I wasn't feeling well," she finally answered.

"Oh come on, don't lie! I hate people who lie," Ayda exclaimed. Then in a regular tone she continued, "You are right where you were before, Colette. You and Alice will share responsibilities. Now go."

Colette opened the door, and just as she was about to step out, Ayda said, "Oh, and Colette. You've been my assistant for almost ten years now. You probably know, better than anyone else here, how hard I work my ass off. If I were planning to blow up the company, do you really think I'd give this place all my time and energy?"

The two women stared at each other for a few more seconds before Ayda waved her hand, shooing Colette away.

The environment in the agency returned to normal as the talk of ISIS and bombs dwindled. But what happened the following week had everyone on their guard again.

Chapter Fifteen
MAKING AMENDS

Shams noticed that Ayda had been spending lots of time on the phone, and she usually had a serious look on her face as she took the calls into another room. Actually, Ayda always had a serious look on her face, but these days it was even more intense. Her eyebrows had grown a crease between them. Once when Ayda got off the phone, Shams asked her if anything was wrong.

"No," Ayda said, "just trying to figure out some stuff. And my accountant isn't the brightest, so it's taking longer than it should."

"Things for work?" Shams asked.

"No."

But she did not give any further explanation, and Shams understood she should drop the subject.

The following Wednesday, Shams had a half-day. She was surprised to see Ayda's car in the driveway when she got home.

"Salaam. What's going on? Why are you here?" Shams asked.

"This *is* my house, you know. I can't very well go spend my day off at the neighbor's; they'd think I was crazy. Well, even more crazy than I actually am."

"You know what I mean," Shams giggled. "Why did you take the day off?"

"I didn't. I took a half-day."

"Ugh!" Shams screamed with a smile. "Why did you take a half-day?"

"No need to get all hissy with me, young lady. You should have said what you meant the first time." Ayda's voice was cool, but, as usual, she was holding back her smile. "I took a half-day because we have an important errand to run. Come on, get ready." Ayda grabbed her keys and waited for Shams in the car. When it took her a couple of minutes, Ayda beeped twice.

"I was in the bathroom," Shams said a few moments later as she climbed in.

"Oh, did I make you rush? Did you not wash your ass? You better not have sat yourself down in this car without washing your ass."

"I washed my ass, but I didn't wash my hands!" Shams retorted as she proceeded to rub her hands all over Ayda's sleeve, Ayda wriggling away and screaming in disgust. Shams's laughter filled the car.

"So, where are we going?"

"To the bank," Ayda said.

"But why do you need me there?"

"You'll see."

When they arrived, Ayda walked straight into one of the customer service offices without waiting to be shown in. Shams followed her.

"Hello, Ms. Faisal," the man said, standing to greet her. "And this must be Shams. Hello, I'm Sam. Nice to meet you."

Shams shook his hand and sat down next to Ayda with no expectations.

"I can tell you're not sure why you're here, Shams. Let me explain." Then Sam proceeded to tell Shams that her dad had left behind a good amount of money. When his assets had been dispersed, it had not been known that he had a child, so his wealth went to his wife and his parents. But now that Shams was in the picture, Ayda wanted her to get her rightful amount.

"I should have done it a long time ago. I don't want God to punish me for something as foolish as money. Do you forgive me?"

Shams was still confused. "I don't understand. Dad left me money?"

"Yes. And it should have gone to you a long time ago. But better late than never?" Ayda looked expectantly at the young girl.

"But can I even have my own bank account?"

"Yes," Sam said. "But since you're a minor, you won't be able to take the money out. Your guardian," he said, pointing to Ayda, "can help you with that if need be."

"I was going to keep it in a bond so that neither of us could get to it before you turned eighteen, but then I thought there might be something you'd need. So this way, you can get to your money...you just have to go through me first."

Ayda gave her a wide, fake smile, and finally, Shams's eyebrows relaxed and a grin came over her face.

"And once you're eighteen," Sam continued, "you'll automatically be the sole beneficiary, and you'll have full access to your account."

"Cool. So when I'm eighteen I can blow my fortune on a Mercedes?"

Ayda cocked one eyebrow and looked closely at the girl.

"A BMW?"

Ayda pretended to smack her on the back of the head.

"Go ahead, Sam. Maybe I'll use all her money on a trip to Hawaii before she gets to be eighteen, so we won't have to worry about her blowing it."

Shams laughed and Sam smiled as he finished up the paperwork and had them sign in all the appropriate places.

"Congratulations, Shams. You now have your own bank account. Use it wisely," Sam said.

"So, how much money are we talking about anyway? A few thousand dollars?" Shams stood up as she spoke, preparing to leave.

Sam chuckled. "A little more than that. Two hundred thousand dollars. Good luck. Oh, and if you ever buy that BMW, do look me up...I'd love a ride!"

Sam bid them goodbye, taking the paperwork to be processed somewhere out of sight. Shams was still trying to lift her chin from the ground.

"A lady never drools," Ayda said. "Come on, Shams. We're all done here."

The young girl, unable to snap out of her daze, followed Ayda out of the bank and into the car.

"Wow. When you said we were going to the bank, I didn't expect this."

"Once it's in your hands, you need to use it wisely. Promise me you will."

"I promise."

"Good. Now, we should go celebrate that you're rich."

They had lunch at a local restaurant and walked around a couple of department stores. They returned home a few hours later carrying baked pretzels and wearing smiles and laughing. That evening at dinner, Shams asked if she could get a weekly allowance. "You can give it to me from the money in the bank."

"Didn't I just finish telling you not to waste that money?!"

"But you give me pocket money anyway. Now that I have my own money, you can give it to me from there."

"No. No one is touching the money in the bank. End of story. You want something, let me know. Just like we've been doing it. Hasn't this been working?"

"Yes, but I just..."

"No buts. End of story."

Every few weeks, Shams went to her grandparents or to Siham's for the weekend, and Ayda was left in the big empty house all alone. She often thought of calling Shams to check in on her, but always decided against it at the last minute.

"You should do something for yourself when Shams goes away for the weekend," Siham had told her.

"I do. I relax."

"You should do something you wouldn't otherwise do. Go out. Have fun!"

"I should go to a bar and pick up men?" Ayda questioned, with her usual straight face.

Siham smacked her shoulder. "I'm serious."

"Honestly, Seema, you know me better than that. A warm cup of coffee and a good movie or book win over anything else. You know that."

"But it's not good for you to be locked away like this!"

"I am not locked away. I go to work every day, thank you very much. And I rather enjoy being home with Shams. Don't tell me to go out just because that's what society says I should do. I have no desire to go out. I'm perfectly fine here."

"But if you went out, you'd have a chance..."

"A chance of what? Of meeting someone? Oh, come on, Siham, I have no desire to enter any relationship at this stage in my life. And like you should talk!"

"I stay single because you are."

"What?!" Ayda screamed.

"When you're an old lady, Shams off on her own, and you're all alone, you're gonna need some company. That's where I come in. If I get married now, I'll have to deal with his shit. This way, I only have to deal with yours."

"Thank you for your compassion and generosity, but I can deal with my own shit all alone."

Siham shrugged.

"How's work going?" Ayda asked.

"Good. I have this one client. He's an older man—probably as old as Mom and Dad—and he's got this furniture business, a few branches all over the country. He's been using conventional ads for the last ten or fifteen years, and he wants to change things up so he's looking for something really special. I'm having fun with it even though it should be stressing me out. Good ol' Mr. Azid Ghobor."

"That's great."

"I still want you on board," Siham said. "And this is a perfect chance to join us, with this new account."

"I have a lot going on at work now, Seema. We'll see."

Chapter Sixteen
LIKE ALL FAMILIES

Shams wasn't her usual self when she came home from school that day. She wasn't smiling, and she answered all of Ayda's questions with short yes's and no's. She stayed in her room most of the afternoon, and when she came down for dinner, her eyes were red and puffy. After taking only a few bites, she told Ayda she had no appetite, and she went back up to her room. Ayda cleared the table and did the dishes, then went up and knocked on Shams's door.

When she went in, she found Shams holding a picture frame and crying into her pillow. Ayda sat on the edge of the bed and with a slow hesitation, placed her hand on Shams's back. She rubbed her back for a few minutes as Shams continued to cry into her pillow.

A moment later, the young girl looked up and said, "I miss my mom," between sobs.

Ayda continued to rub her back. She said softly, "Of course you do. Even I still miss my parents. The special people in our lives, we don't ever stop missing them."

Sham's cries subsided to sniffles, and after a few minutes, she began, "One of the girls in my class came in to school crying today. When we asked her what was wrong, she said her mom was very sick. She said she was going to need chemo and radiation. And when she said that I started to remember when my mom first began to get sick. I told her to go see a doctor, but she was afraid. Anyway, she eventually went, and they found a tumor in her breast. But it wasn't just the one tumor; the cancer had spread to her lymph nodes, her lungs, it was all over. And she…"

The memories overwhelmed her, and Shams cried harder. Ayda kept her arms around the young girl and squeezed tight. A moment later, Shams continued, "She wouldn't fight it. The doctors told her the chemo would weaken her and cause all sorts of side effects. Mom asked how much more time the chemo would give her, and the doctors said they couldn't know for sure but probably only a few months. So she refused the treatment.

"'You have to try, Mom,' I told her. 'You have to fight.'

"But she didn't believe treatment was the way to fight. People die from chemo more than they do from cancer, she told me. And no matter what I said, she wouldn't change her mind.

"Those two years, she had lots of good days. She had some bad days too when the pain was really bad. But she had more good days when we laughed together and went out and just enjoyed being together. It was during that time that she started talking about you more.

"Anyway, when that girl in school told us about her mom, it just...it upset me. That other lady's gonna do chemo and radiation. Maybe if Mom had agreed, maybe those two years would have been two and a half. Or three. Or who knows...God can make anything happen. I just got angry remembering that she didn't even try."

Ayda sat quietly with Shams. She had no words of comfort or of wisdom; she simply stayed with her and held her, not rushing her tears, not telling her to stop crying. Just being there for her, the only way she could.

Eventually, Shams fell asleep, and Ayda pulled the covers over her. She took the picture from Shams's hands, turned off the light, and pulled the door behind her, leaving it open just an inch.

The next morning as Shams and Ayda sat eating breakfast, Ayda asked her if she was okay to go to school.

"Yeah, I'm okay. Thanks for sitting with me last night."

"That's what family does."

Shams looked up at her. "Are we family? Because you have to take care of me?"

"Of course we're family. And not because I *have* to take care of you. We're family because you are a piece of your dad, and he was...." She hesitated before continuing, not sure if she could be that honest with herself. But her pause lasted only a second. "He was my whole world. And I feel like you could have been my daughter. Like you should have been. I'm not taking anything from your mom—she will always be your mom. But I feel like it was God's plan to bring you to me, to help me see lots of things I was blind to before."

Shams smiled and gathered her bag just as the bus beeped. "A simple, 'Yes, we are family' would have done just fine. Looks like you're starting to go soft on me, Didi."

Ayda threw the kitchen towel at her, just hitting her bag. "Punk!"

As the door closed, Ayda heard a muffled, "I love you, too."

Ayda finished up breakfast then took out the framed picture that Shams had been clinging to the night before. She stared at it intently. Shams looked just the same in it, smiling her widest, hugging her mother. Leah was fair skinned with a rosy complexion and big hazel eyes. She looked about thirty in the picture, which meant she had been very young when she'd married Saef. Ayda tried to feel rage as she looked at this woman, but she could not. She felt pain and a tightness in her chest which made it difficult for her to breathe. She took the hammer and a nail from the tool box under the kitchen sink. About halfway down on the wall of the staircase, she hammered the nail at about eye level and hung the photo. And there it was, for all the world to see: her husband's other wife and their daughter. Her husband, the man she'd loved, the man she had always believed had loved her, had betrayed her, had lived a completely separate life that she'd known nothing about. And in that life he'd fathered a daughter, a beautiful, well mannered, smart girl... who was a daily reminder of her husband's unfaithfulness.

But that photo of Shams and Leah represented something bigger as well. It served as a reminder to Ayda that good can come from pain. Shams had been with her only a few months now, yet already there was a brightness to Ayda's life, a brightness that would not have existed had Saef never married Leah. Yes, goodness can come from pain, just as the pains of childbirth lead to miracles. She could not have a child naturally, but these were *her* labor pains.

Just before Ayda left for work, Marge arrived. After their usual greetings, Marge asked how things were going with Shams.

"Well. Thank you, Marge."

"Seems like she's brought some color into your life."

"Yes, I believe she has. I'm blessed to have her here."

"Good thing she found a family in you. Such a shame to be so young and without a family."

Until that moment, Ayda hadn't thought for a second about the aunt who had dropped Shams off a few months before or about the possibility that she had other family out there somewhere, family that, perhaps, would want to be a part of Shams's life. The idea of having to share her—or worse, of losing her to someone else—sent shivers down her spine.

Ayda's car wasn't in the driveway when Shams got home from school. As she ran up the stairs to her room, she caught site of the picture of her and her mother hanging on the wall. She froze in place. She vaguely remembered taking it out the night before, but how had it gotten to the wall?

"Marge," she called out, "did you hang this picture here?"

"No, dear. It must have been Ms. Faisal."

About an hour later, Ayda walked in the door. Shams greeted her by throwing her arms around her, and Ayda could tell there were tears in her eyes.

"Are you okay, Shams? Did something happen at school today?"

Shams shook her head without pulling away. "I just wanted to show you how much I appreciate what you did."

Ayda hugged Shams in return but was still confused. "What did I do?"

"You hung up the picture of Mom and me."

And suddenly Ayda remembered, and her stomach flipped at the realization that she'd be faced with the image of her husband's other wife every day, several times a day. She swallowed and said, "Everyone has pictures of their family up on their walls. It's only normal."

Shams pulled away, and her face lit up. "So can we put up more? You must have pictures of you and Dad that you can hang up?"

Despite herself, and despite her smile, Ayda's eyes began to fill with tears. "I don't think I'm ready for that quite yet," she said softly. And Shams hugged her again, more tightly this time.

The following weekend Shams's grandparents invited her to spend the weekend with them. She was more than happy to get a dose of spoiling from them. Once Shams left, the house felt hauntingly empty. Ayda had lived alone for years; she had enjoyed her independence and her solitary, but Shams's arrival in her life had changed that. Ayda enjoyed the time she spent with Shams, their talks, even the quiet times spent sitting watching a movie. Shams had filled the empty space and brought life back into Ayda's home.

And back into Sumayya's and Saleh's lives as well. Shams's appearance had resurrected their son. They saw his face in hers and felt they could speak about him without the pain. Shams soaked up every word about what her dad had been like as a child and teenager. She listened to stories of how he used to steal the car while his parents were out. Or how he and his friends used to play soccer in the street by the light of the lamp posts. "And we'd hear those boys cheering from across the neighborhood 'Goooooooooooal!' Or sometimes it was 'Noooooo!' It was always the world cup finals in our neighborhood. And your dad was the most valuable player."

Their eyes shone bright when they told their stories, and the three of them would fill the house with laughter.

"Oh, and you should have seen him as a toddler, afraid of the water. Sumayya, pull out those pictures of him in the pool. See, Shams, see the terror in his face. He'd cry like that the entire time we stayed in the water. It was meant to be fun, we wanted him to enjoy it, but he just screamed his head off the entire time. I'd tell your grandmother to let him get out, but she'd say, 'No. He just needs to get used to it.' And he'd cling to her the way a baby monkey clings to his mama, wrapping his skinny little arms around her neck."

"Then after a while," Sumayya took over, "he stopped crying. He'd still cling to me for dear life, but he wouldn't wail. And eventually, he learned to enjoy it, even if he was in there on his own, without me. It's like everything: it just takes getting used to."

As they grabbed some popcorn from the coffee table and Saleh adjusted the TV so they could watch the movie, Sumayya said, "Speaking of getting used to, how're things with Ayda?"

Saleh sat back on the couch, and he and Sumayya stared at Shams intently.

"Good," she said.

"So, you don't have any problems with her?" her grandfather asked.

"No. She's kind."

The grandparents exchanged a look, then Sumayya said, "We just...we were thinking, if you're not comfortable there, we'd be happy to have you live here with us."

"Thank you. But no. I'm happy with Didi."

"Didi?" Saleh said. "She doesn't like to be called Didi."

"She said it would be okay if I called her that. She just seems more like a Didi than an Ayda, you know?"

The elderly couple sat quietly for a moment. "She didn't always used to be so tough," Saleh said. "She was Didi all while Saef was here. She doted after him. She was funny..."

"She's still super funny," Shams defended.

"Yes," Sumayya continued, "but now it's a dry humor, a sarcastic humor. Before she enjoyed laughing. Saef's death really destroyed her."

They sat quietly for a while, then Shams spoke up. "I don't think it was Dad's death that changed Didi."

"What do you mean?" Saleh asked.

"I mean, I think she...I think she found out about me and Mom then. I think that's what did it."

"What do you mean she found about you and Mom? How?"

Shams shrugged.

"You mean she's known about you all these years and she never told us?!" Sumayya had gone from bright and amusing to dark and fuming in just seconds.

She got up from the couch and started pacing, Shams staring at her. Saleh asked, "Shams, are you sure?"

The girl nodded, her wide, wondering eyes expressing the confusion she'd been thrown into.

"How dare she keep this from us?! We had a right to know. We could have been a part of your life. If she didn't want to be, that was her problem. But we could have been!" The elderly woman paced back and forth, huffing, her face and ears glowing red.

Saleh sat quietly on the couch beside Shams, watching, waiting, knowing his wife was planning something. A moment later she said, "Grab your coats. Hurry up!"

She took her keys from the rack and headed out toward the car as Saleh and Shams watched with wide eyes.

"Don't do this, Sumayya," her husband whispered.

"I don't want to cause Didi trouble," Shams said, her voice shaking. "She's been only good to me. I don't want to make problems for her. Please."

"Your grandmother's bark is worse than her bite, trust me. But if she doesn't go now, she'll go later, without us. If we go with her now, we can at least try to control things. Come on. It'll be fine, don't worry."

But her grandfather's words were empty comfort. Shams sat in the back of the car as Sumayya sped through town. She stopped the car with a screech in Ayda's driveway and ran to the front door, Saleh and Shams close behind. She banged on the door and rang the bell several times.

Ayda answered with her robe half on, her face white as chalk. "What's wrong? Is Shams okay? What's happened?!" Her panic settled then turned to confusion when Shams ran in and wrapped her arms around her.

"How could you keep this from us?!" Sumayya yelled, still standing on the doorstep.

"Keep your voice down," her husband said calmly.

Ayda, her arm still around Shams, took a few steps backwards into the house to make room for them to enter. She closed the door behind them and asked, "What did I keep from you?"

"You knew about Shams for all these years, and you never said anything. It was our right to know about her."

"I'm sorry," Shams whispered. "I'm so sorry."

Holding the girl tighter and rubbing her back, Ayda stood her ground. Her face, which had been a ghost white only moments before, was now crimson. "I told you about her when the time was right."

"Ten years?! Ten years after you found out?! During that time, there was never a right time?!"

"Shams was two when Saef died. And he was with her mother for at least a year before that. That's three years your son could have told you about them. Three years he led a secret life. But it was *his* life. If he'd wanted you to know, he would have told you. But he didn't. And as it was *his* life, I didn't feel it was my place to intrude. I became involved when Leah involved me, and not a day before, because this had nothing to do with me. It had to do with him. And if he had wanted you to know, he would have told you."

"Humph! Speaking with you is like talking to a brick wall! You knew we were mourning him, looking to hang on to anything of his that remained. You could have done us the courtesy of telling us he had a daughter!" Sumayya yelled.

"And he could have done me the courtesy of staying faithful. But life is not kind to us no matter how much we give."

Her mother-in-law waved her hand and stormed out of the house. Her father-in-law took a step towards Ayda. When Ayda saw the pain in the man's eyes, her face relaxed, but she did not smile. Saleh pulled her gently by the shoulders and kissed her forehead. Then he turned to leave and motioned for Shams to join him. The girl simply shook her head, holding on tighter to Ayda's waist.

Ayda led Shams to the couch, and the young girl began to apologize. "Hahaha," Ayda said sarcastically. "You think you did this? No, my young friend. This was all part of my master plan."

"Your master plan?"

"The house is like a haunted house without you. I can't even smoke in the living room without hearing you go, 'Tut tut tut. You know you're slowly killing me.' So this was a plan to get you back. And look how well it worked. I'm quite impressed with myself."

"Yeah." Shams giggled softly through her tears. "Me too."

"You shouldn't be though. I have completely awesome powers. You'll see them one day."

"I look forward to it."

The following Saturday dinner started off with some tension. Her in-laws entered the house with soft smiles and hugged Ayda as they always did, but Ayda stood rigid, her face stiff. They tried to joke and laugh, but Ayda did not even pretend to be amused. She refused to meet Sumayya in the eyes and kept her gaze down during the meal. Siham could feel the tension in the air, but she did not understand where it had come from.

"What's going on?" she whispered to Ayda. But Ayda simply shook her head.

A few minutes later, Sumayya said aloud, "Ayda, I ...I just wanted to say...." Ayda looked up at her then, and saw her mother-in-law's weak smile, tears welling in her eyes.

"I..."

Sumayya's pause, which lasted no more than a couple of seconds, was long enough for a hundred thoughts to fly through Ayda's mind. She remembered long ago days, when, on a rare occasion, Sumayya had sided with her in an argument she was having with Saef. She remembered how, at the time of Saef's death, despite her being broken and overcome with grief, the older woman had tried to console her. She remembered that she was Saef's mother.

"You really like the roast, Auntie. I know," Ayda said. "Marge is a great cook. But it's Shams's slave work that really adds flavor to the meal." She nodded at Sumayya, accepting her unspoken apology, and just like that, they'd cleared the air.

The rest of the evening was spent laughing and joking. When it came time to leave, Ayda's father-in-law asked if they could take Shams for the night. "You'll have to ask her. If it's up to me...I mean...she's so smelly." Ayda plugged her nose and wrinkled her face.

"Maybe next week, Giddo. Okay?" Shams said.

And Sumayya and Saleh knew that they hadn't completely blown their chances of spending time with Shams.

"What was that today?" Siham asked again before she left.

"Just...nothing. Forget about it. It's done now."

Siham shrugged and kissed Shams and Ayda, and Rizq said his goodbyes as well.

That evening as they sat together in the living room, Ayda reading and Shams knitting, Ayda said, "You know you could have gone with your grandparents if you wanted to. I wouldn't have been upset or angry. You know that, right?"

"Yeah, I know. But then you'd smoke all over the house, and we don't want that. I simply can't trust you to be left alone."

"I am liable to get into trouble. Better keep an eye on me."

A while later, Ayda said, "I'm glad you stayed."

"I know." Shams said it without looking up.

Ayda tossed a throw pillow at her. "But you are getting better."

"I know," Shams replied. "Pretty soon I'll be smoking and sleeping with one eye open too."

"I do not sleep with one eye open!" Ayda slammed her book closed.

"If you say so."

With a huff, Ayda opened her book again, but she kept catching Shams staring at her out of the corner of her eye. "Stop doing that," Ayda said.

"I can't stop. It's too fun." Shams smiled widely as she continued with her knitting.

"Ugh. I know." A moment later she said, "I'm Frankenstein, and you're the monster."

Chapter Seventeen
A KIDNAPPING

A few minutes after Ayda had settled into her office, the elevator doors slid open and out walked a young girl with hands smeared in blood and dirt, her bare feet peering out from a long formerly-white nightgown. Her long hair fell forward, obscuring her face. She stopped just outside of the elevator and continued to stand there, without speaking or moving. It took a few moments for people to start to notice her.

"Hey, what's that?" someone whispered.

"It's a ghost," someone yelled.

"Don't be ridiculous, there is no such thing as…" and before he could say the word, the apparition began to float up as she spread her arms out. When a brave soul tried to approach, she hissed and made unintelligible noises. Everyone moved back, away from her into a huddle. The commotion caused Ayda to come out of her office. When she saw the ghost, she yelled out in a commanding tone, "No…No!" She stood on top of the nearest desk. Spreading her hands out before her she said, "By Allah, I command you to leave. You may take no sacrifices from here!" She began to recite words in Arabic that no one understood. When she finished she yelled, "Allahu Akbar!" The apparition immediately crumbled to the floor. A few seconds of silence passed, then Alice began to laugh and clap. "Good show! Good show!"

Shams stood up and bowed while Ayda stepped down off the desk.

"Alice, why did you interrupt?" she asked her. "We could have kept going."

"Yeah, I know. But poor Chuck over here already pissed his pants."

Ayda walked over and kissed Shams. "Wonderful show, young lady.

Wonderful."

"And you were great," Shams replied. "You didn't even hesitate for a second. It was like we had rehearsed it!"

"Honey, with two great minds like ours, who needs rehearsals?"

Colette took a few steps forward and asked, "Ms. Faisal, who's the young lady?"

"She's the girl I kidnapped a couple of months ago." Then Ayda and Shams went into Ayda's office and shut the door.

"Marge and I did a great job with your makeup."

"Yeah, I totally love it. Your using *Ayatul Kursi*—that was brilliant! Not like they'll get it though. But that final 'Allahu akbar!' Totally awesome! I wish we could do it again! We totally should have recorded it."

Ayda asked Alice to show Shams around and introduce her to all the teams.

"You scared the shit out of us," one of the guys said to her. "I felt like I'd been transported into a horror movie. All that was missing was the music."

"We actually thought of that, but we couldn't figure out how to make it happen." Shams sat with some of the employees and watched as they worked. She saw the storyboards for a few different campaigns and even made a couple of suggestions.

"But how did you get to be with Ayda?" they asked.

"Didn't you hear?" she answered. "She kidnapped me."

Most of them laughed, but Shams did not notice the look of fright that came over one of the team members; she simply went on with the tour and enjoyed the office atmosphere. When it came time to go, Ayda collected her from the group. They went into the elevator, and as the doors slid shut, Shams's eyes grew wide and her body shivered, the blood draining from her face. "Help me!" she said in a loud whisper, throwing out her hands as though grabbing for a safety ring.

"We really should cool it with this whole kidnapping thing. Not all of these people will get it."

"You're probably right," Shams said. "But it's so fun."

As soon as they arrived home, Shams showered and washed the make-up from her face and arms. Then, Ayda and Shams dined on the turkey dinner Marge had prepared for them. Afterwards, when Shams sat doing her homework in the living room, Ayda pulled out a book and began to read. The house was perfectly quiet, and they were each engrossed in their work. When the doorbell rang, breaking the peaceful silence, they both jumped. Shams stood behind Ayda when she looked out the window to find a couple of cops standing on the doorstep.

"Good evening. Are you Ms. Faisal?"

"Yes," Ayda said.

"Sorry to bother you, ma'am, but we're investigating a possible kidnapping."

"Shit," she muttered.

"Excuse me?"

"What exactly do you want, officer? You want to search the house?"

"No, we'd just like to ask you a few questions. May we come in?"

"No. We can speak here. What would you like to know?"

"There have been reports that a young lady has been living with you lately." He pointed behind Ayda at Shams.

"Yes."

"Well, can you tell us who she is?"

"She can tell you herself." Ayda put one arm around Shams and motioned with the other for her to speak. After Shams introduced herself, the cop asked her how she'd come to live with Ayda.

"My mom died. In her will, she named Ayda as my guardian."

"Oh," the cop said, putting away his pad. "Sorry for your loss. So, you're family?"

"Sort of," Shams replied.

"Yes, officer, we're family. Shams is my late husband's daughter. Any more questions?"

"I don't understand why the people you work with would think you'd kidnapped her."

"I don't tend to go spreading my personal affairs left and right. And most of the people I work with don't understand my humor. Can we help you with anything else?"

"No, ma'am. Sorry to have disturbed you."

"Who made this claim, Officer?"

"It was an anonymous call. They just said they work with you."

Of course it was anonymous. They're too cowardly to have given a name, and they knew it was a joke!

Ayda shut the door behind them. "Now we have to do something even better to get those clowns back!"

"It's not really their fault. You did say you kidnapped me. And I went along with it."

"What kidnapper admits to their crime?!"

Shams shrugged. "The kind that thinks no one will believe her."

"I wouldn't be surprised if those clowns reported this 'kidnapping' to the media. Next thing we know the phone will be ringing with news stations wanting to interview the kidnapped girl."

She hadn't finished the sentence when the phone rang.

"Whoa! You really do have some kind of magical powers, huh?"

Ayda gave her a half grin as she answered. But it wasn't the news looking to interview Shams; it was the lawyer giving Ayda some bad news.

Chapter Eighteen
VISIT WITH ANN

"What do you mean they want to see me?" Shams asked.

"Mr. Williams said they contacted him and asked him to set it up. Your aunt wants to spend time with you."

"I stayed with her for a few days after Mom died; even then, she didn't want to spend time with me. They've never been interested in being a part of my life."

"Well, maybe they realize they were wrong. All people make mistakes—the best people are those who try to fix their mistakes. Maybe that's what this is."

"I don't trust them," Shams said. "If they wanted to fix their mistake, they could have started on the day Mom died."

Ayda had the same reservations, but for Shams's sake, she hoped her instincts were wrong.

"They want you to spend the weekend with them."

"I don't want to."

Ayda paused for a moment. When she spoke again her tone was softer, her words slower. She wanted to calm not only her own but also Shams's anxiety. "What about a short time on Sunday then?"

"Will you be there?"

"That wasn't the plan..."

"I won't go if you're not going to be there."

"Okay," Ayda said determinedly. "I'll be there then."

They were quiet for some time, then Ayda asked, "Were you this anxious about meeting me for the first time?"

"No, not at all," Shams said, shrugging.

"Why not?"

"Because Mom's the one who sent me to you. And even though I didn't know you, I knew Mom would only send me to someone she trusted."

Ayda looked down and grabbed a cigarette.

"It's part of the reason I don't trust them," Shams said. "If Mom trusted them, she would have sent me to them. But she didn't. She trusted you more than her own sister."

The words were like a hug wrapped in fire, like the warmth of love surrounded by an unavoidable sheath of poisoned spears. She continued to smoke her cigarette as she wrapped her arms around Shams's shoulder.

They sat together in the thickness of apprehension and smoke for some time. Then Shams said, "Will you fight for me? If they try to take me away, will you fight for me?"

Ayda drew the girl even closer. "I'll rip their fu.... I mean, of course I'll fight for you. No one's going to take you from me. You're my under-aged slave, and anyone who wants to take you will have to deal with my crazy. I made Chuck piss his pants just for fun—imagine what I could do if someone really crossed me."

Somehow life had thrown them together. And somehow, against all expectations and all norms of society, they had become family.

The following Saturday dinner was at Ayda's in-laws'. Shams told them about the aunt that suddenly wanted to spend time with her.

"Well, family is family, sweetie. It makes you richer."

"Not always, Sitto. These people weren't there for me when I needed someone the most, when I didn't have anyone. Why are they trying to make room for themselves in my life now?"

"Maybe it was just hard for them before. We all deal with grief differently. Maybe it was too hard for them to be there with you, when your mom had just passed."

"I don't know. Maybe," Shams said.

"Always give people the benefit of the doubt. Always," her grandmother told her.

"I totally agree with that," Siham said. "But if you give someone the benefit of the doubt once and they prove unworthy, then you don't give them a second chance. Meet with them, Shams, and see how it goes. But remember, your instincts will be right almost every single time. If you start to feel iffy about it, even if you can't put your finger on a concrete reason why, then you give it up, you go back to how it was before: one holiday card a year and that's all."

Shams nodded. "But what do I say if that's how I feel? They'll ask for an explanation."

"Don't you worry about that," Ayda said. "I'll take care of it."

Again, the girl simply nodded. "I'm nervous."

"That's understandable," her grandmother said. "But *In sha' Allah*, everything will be fine."

That evening around midnight, Ayda awoke to find Shams standing beside her bed.

"Are you okay?" Ayda croaked.

"I'm just...can I sleep next to you?"

"Are you feeling sick?" Ayda sat up in bed.

"No, I'm fine. I'm just scared. About how tomorrow will go."

Ayda nodded, pulled down the covers and tapped the bed, motioning for Shams to climb in. When the young girl had crawled in and curled up against her, Ayda put her arm around her and closed her eyes, but sleep had disappeared. This was the first time since Saef's death that she had slept next to anyone. And it was the first time in her life to sleep next to someone other than her husband. It made her remember how he used to wrap her in his arms, how she loved feeling his warm breath on her neck. The feeling came back and enveloped her, and Ayda fell asleep dreaming of the one person she would rather be with, completely unaware of the trouble waiting for her on the other side of her dreams.

The next morning, Ayda and Shams ate breakfast in silence. Shams was too nervous to speak, and Ayda respected her need for quiet. They got into the car just before noon and headed toward Shams's aunt's house, directed by the GPS on Ayda's phone.

"You have nothing to be nervous about," Ayda said as they drove. "They make you feel comfortable, you enjoy their company, great. It's more family you get to spend time with, to learn from, to love and be loved by. If you don't get that feeling, that's cool too—no one will force you to see them again."

Shams nodded, still uneasy.

A few moments later, they pulled into the driveway of a pale green, ranch-style house. The paint was chipping in many places, and a few of the roof tiles were dangling down. The shudders were painted a deep brown, but many of them were covered in cracks. The yard was yellow from neglect. There was an old burgundy hatchback in the driveway with its muffler resting on the ground. Ayda thought perhaps the entire neighborhood was in the same state, but when she looked at other houses on the street, their lawns green, paint fresh and bright, and windows sparkling, she knew the eyesore before them wasn't a matter of neighborhood or even age of the house.

Ayda took a deep breath and tapped Shams on the knee. "Ready?" she asked with a smile.

"Not really," Shams replied, swallowing hard and wringing her hands.

Ayda relaxed in her seat and looked straight ahead, the smile disappearing from her face. "Want a cigarette?"

Shams smiled and shook her head, then without a word, she opened the car door. Ayda followed suit.

Before they had a chance to ring the doorbell, Ann swung open the door. "Oh, Shams! You've grown so much these past few months!" The lady threw her arms around her as Shams stood frozen, her eyebrows knitted with confusion.

"And Ayda, so good to see you again!" She moved as if to hug her, but Ayda put up her hand and said, "No." Ann's confusion lasted no more than a second, then she led them inside.

"Please don't mind the mess," she said, picking up a few items of clothing and something that looked like a dog's chew toy from the floor. She moved rather quickly, trying to tidy up the place. But the mess was simply too far gone for her efforts to make any sort of impact. She put the pile of things on a beat-up armchair in the living room, cleared the couch of the clothes and pizza boxes, potato chip bags, socks, shoes and some other items Ayda could not quite decipher, and told them to have a seat. "Can I get you something to drink?" she offered, but both Ayda and Shams declined.

"So Shams, how have you been these last few months?"

"Fine."

"How's school? I'll bet you do real well. Your mom was real smart."

"I do okay."

"She does better than okay. She's on the honor roll," Ayda said proudly. "She's just humble." Ayda winked at Shams.

"Wow," Ann said, "that's great. Good for you, Shams!"

After a long, awkward silence, Shams spoke up. "Where are the boys?"

"After church their dad took them to the park. Did you two go to church this morning?"

"Aunt Ann, you know I'm Muslim, just like Mom was. So is Ayda."

"Moslem? Really? No, I didn't know."

"That's why we read Qur'an at the funeral and the sheikh was the one who officiated the ceremony.'"

"I knew there was some speech in some 'mother language.' I didn't know it was the Koran."

Shams and the two women sat there, staring at each other, a wide, insincere smile plastered on Ann's face.

"I hope the boys get back soon so you can see them." Turning to Ayda she continued, "They're great, very friendly and loving. Let me get you something to nibble on till they get back." She got up and went over to the kitchen.

Shams looked over at Ayda who was, unlike her usual self, managing to control her facial expression and wearing a convincing smile. "You're doing great," Ayda whispered.

Shams replied with a shrug.

Ann came back into the living room carrying a tray of chips, crackers, and dip. Ayda helped herself, and Shams grabbed a couple of crackers as well. As Ann sat down, she said, "I think you should come to church with us sometime. I think you'd really like it. The peace, the spirituality. It's wonderful being in a room with people who believe in God and want nothing more than to please Him."

Ayda did not even try to control herself; she cocked her eyebrows and stared at the woman. "You know, we 'Moslems' worship God, too."

"You do? I thought you didn't believe in Jesus?"

"We believe that God is the Creator, and that Jesus was a prophet—one of God's creations—as were Moses, Noah, and Muhammad, just to name a few. They were all men sent by God to guide people to worship God."

"Oh." Disbelief covered Ann's raised eyebrows and wide eyes. A moment later she plastered a wide smile on her face and turned to Shams. "So tell me, what do you like to do for fun? Do you have any hobbies?"

"I like to read and knit. I hope to have my own line of clothes one day."

"Oh, that's a wonderful goal! Good for you. I'd like to see some of your work sometime."

Shams nodded.

"It's important not to give up on your goals," her aunt continued. "I used to be a model, believe it or not. But then I got married and had kids." She shrugged.

Ayda looked at her closely, and for the first time, she saw that Ann's eyes were gray. Her dark brown hair with its wide curls that fell below her shoulders could have indeed been the hair of a model—just not one wearing the stretched-out, stained, torn housedress that now hung sloppily on Ann's body.

Ayda and Shams did not stay long. They each ate a few crackers, then Ayda said they should get going.

"Oh, I had hoped Shams would stick around to see the boys. They do miss you!"

"Maybe another time," Ayda replied, standing up and putting her sunglasses on. "Thank you for today," she said as she made her way to the door. Shams was right behind her.

"Thank you for coming. I'm so glad we got to spend time together, Shams. I hope that next time we'll have a longer visit, and you can spend some time with your cousins."

Shams only replied with a goodbye hug.

After they had driven for a minute or two, Ayda asked Shams, "How do you think it went?"

"It was totally weird. I'm so glad it's over."

Ayda nodded. A moment later, Shams said, "She kept talking about next time, next time. I don't think I want there to be a next time."

"That's normal. Most families are like that. But, if you want my opinion...do you want my opinion?"

Shams nodded emphatically. "Yes."

"Well, I think that anyone of your family who does you good and asks for your time, then they deserve it. It's like this fee you pay for being in a certain club—even if you don't really want to be a member of the club. Or you can think of it as a tax. As long as they're good to you, then you repay them with kindness and give them some of your time. If at any point they stop being good to you, then you stop paying that tax."

"But they weren't good to me before."

"Yeah, but they're trying. They keep trying, you pay that tax. They stop trying, you stop paying that tax."

Shams was quiet for a moment. Then she looked out the window and said, "I hope they stop trying."

Ayda looked over at her. "But what do I know. Some insanely rich people get away with not paying their taxes; maybe that's the way to go."

That evening Shams's grandparents called to check how the visit had gone. When she told them about the awkwardness, the messy house that hadn't been tidied since she'd last been there, months ago, Saleh said, "Well, it was good of you to go. They probably won't ask for a repeat visit anytime soon."

Siham also called in the evening.

"It was a pigsty," Ayda told her. "Their house looked like it was falling apart, but not from age, from neglect. I just had a bad feeling about it all."

"Did you tell Shams?"

"I can't tell her. Maybe I'm wrong. I don't want to be the reason she loses contact with the only biological family she has left on her mother's side."

"But your instincts are never wrong, Didi."

"Yeah, I know. That's what scares me."

Chapter Nineteen
CROOKS AND BIRTHDAYS

Days turned to weeks, and Ayda was relieved Ann hadn't called again. One Friday afternoon, as Ayda packed up her things to leave work, her secretary informed her that Mr. Fred Williams was waiting to see her.

"Show him in."

She continued arranging her things, and when the lawyer entered, Ayda said, "Give it to me quick, Mr. Williams; I was on my way out."

"You should sit down for this, Ms. Faisal."

She stopped short and looked him in the face. He'd never looked so serious before, not even when she had first seen him, when he had come to tell her that she was appointed guardian of a young girl she'd never met. Even then, he didn't look as serious as he looked now.

She sat down in her chair silently, and the lawyer sat across from her.

"This morning I was informed that Ann Fraco, Sham's aunt, is going to file for sole custody of Shams. Since she is her biological aunt, she does have a case."

Ayda stared at him for a long moment. "But the mother's will is crystal clear."

"Yes. I'm not saying they have an easy case, but they do have a case."

"And Shams and I are the same religion. I'll raise her in the same culture of her parents; Ann won't. Doesn't that count for anything? And..." She took the cigarette pack from her desk and lit a cigarette, blowing smoke directly at Fred. "Where were these people before? They are her biological family—so what took them so long to show interest? She stayed with them for a few days after her mother's passing; why didn't they show this kind of concern, this kind of interest then?"

The lawyer sat quietly, giving Ayda a chance to spit out all the words that were making her sick.

When she had finished, he said, "And we'll say all that at the hearing. We will also want to show them that you care for her better than they will..."

"That'll be easy. They live like animals."

"And that her mental and emotional health are not compromised by living with her father's wife."

"It was her mother that chose me!"

"Yes, but we'll still have to show that you're the better caregiver."

"Whatever you need to do, do it. And whatever I need to do, I'll do it. Just tell me what you need from me."

"I will. Okay, so that was some of the bad news. There's more. The man you followed, the one you believe is Ghazi Dabbour, is actually Azid Ghobor. He's the owner of a furniture franchise."

"No, that's not possible. I know Ghazi Dabbour. It's not possible that two different men have that exact same birthmark in the exact same spot. I'm sure it's him."

"When I remembered how you had recognized him, that occurred to me as well. So I did some research...

"Ghazi Dabbour went bankrupt in 1996..."

"The year Mom died."

"Yes. And after he went bankrupt, he seemed to disappear. Azid Ghobor showed up on the scene then. With a little digging, I found that the two men are really one and the same. After he went bankrupt, Ghazi Dabbour moved away for a time, then returned with a different name. I assume he was hoping to escape his past and start fresh. And it seems to have worked; his current business is thriving, worth millions."

"But if he went bankrupt the year Mom died, does that mean... does that mean..."

"It means he'll claim that his current business was funded from other sources. That, like any business, there was a certain percentage of risk in the venture your parents entered into with him, and that it simply failed."

Ayda sat still, taking in what the lawyer was saying. "You can't possibly be saying that that's it. That after all these years, that after I finally found this prick, that he's going to just get away with stealing my parents' money?"

"We are going to continue with the lawsuit, Ms. Faisal. I just wanted you to know exactly what we're up against."

When he left, Ayda lit another cigarette and thought of the hell she had been reeled into. When she had bumped into Ghazi Dabbour, an intense hope had ignited in her. She was so close to taking back what was rightfully hers that she could taste it. She had pictured herself celebrating the return of her parents' money, she had pictured herself investing it in her own project. She had dreamed, with full conviction, that it would soon come true. Now, it was slipping away before she even had a chance to touch it. And that was just one problem. She also had to deal with Shams's irritating aunt.

"Did you say his alias is Azid Ghobor?" Siham asked when Ayda met with her for lunch later that day.

"Yeah. I feel like I've heard that name before too. But I can't put my finger on it," Ayda replied.

"You feel like you've heard that name before because I mentioned it before. Remember when I told you I had a new client, a huge account? That's him! Azid Ghobor."

The two women stared at each other with wide eyes, each trying to figure out what to do next, how they could turn this to their advantage. As the moments passed, their hope waned.

"If we don't come up with anything, I'll just decline his account," Siham said.

"It seems like my life is getting more fucked up by the second. First this prick Ghazi and now Ann."

"I don't think you should tell Shams about her aunt," Siham said. "It may all blow over without her ever having to know. Save her the anxiety."

Ayda blew a puff of smoke up into the crisp air of the outdoor café.

"How're things going with her anyway? You both seem well adjusted...but sometimes things aren't what they seem?"

"You know me better than that, Seema. With me, things are *always* as they seem."

"Yeah," her sister-in-law said. "But you never know."

"I thought it would suck. Or maybe not so much that it would suck as much as I was just worried about how it would go, how I'd be able to look at this person who is the embodiment of the cause of my greatest pain, and treat her kindly. But with Shams, it comes easily. She's so unique. I love that she has her own style, her own personality. She goes the way she wants despite the taunts and jests. Yeah, she needs a bit of toughening up so those little punks don't get to her, but generally, she's great. And I wonder...maybe I had to go through that pain, I had to be hurt like that to be blessed with her in my life. I don't know.

"And I don't think it was too difficult for her to adjust to me either. She was a bit reserved in the beginning, but I think my openness gives her comfort. I think," she blew out another puff of smoke, "sometimes she feels like she's got to take care of me. And ...I know it's selfish, but I like that feeling."

Siham was quiet for a minute, then she said, "I admire how you are with her. I think you're doing a great job. It takes balls to raise a child whose face is living proof of your husband's betrayal. It takes balls."

"Thank you," Ayda said. "I do have a nice pair of balls."

Siham laughed as Ayda continued puffing on her cigarette.

Although the time with her sister-in-law had allowed her to vent, Ayda was still undecided about whether to tell Shams about her aunt's lawsuit. After dinner that evening, Ayda sat on the couch pretending to read as Shams knitted away.

"What are you making anyway?" Ayda asked.

"A sweater and matching cap. I made the cap already, but I'm just starting on the sweater."

"When're you going to make something for me?"

Shams lowered her arms and looked up at Ayda. "I didn't know you wanted anything. What would you like?"

"A car."

"What?"

"A cigarette."

"Huh?"

"A phone case."

"I can do that."

"A book cover."

"Okay."

"Socks. But socks that actually work, ones that actually keep your feet warm, not just any ol' pair of knitted socks."

"No problem."

"Cool."

"Cool."

Ayda held the book up to her face for another few minutes then closed it and put it down.

"You had mentioned to me that before your mom passed away, you only had contact with your aunt once a year."

Shams nodded. "A birthday card."

"So, since you came here, she hasn't tried to contact you at all...I mean, besides when we visited?"

"Just the birthday card. They don't even write a full line, just 'Dear Shams' at the top and 'Love Aunt Ann and Family' at the bottom. I always send a thank you card anyway and tell them a bit about what's going on in my life, but they never write back."

"What kind of stuff did you tell them this time?"

"I told them about Sitto and Giddo and spending time with Rizq and Aunt Siham. I told them about my inheritance from Dad, and about Marge and how I'm her under-aged slave."

She giggled as Ayda whacked her with a throw pillow. But their chat had shed light on something important, and Ayda now understood Ann's recent interest in becoming Shams's guardian. She also realized something else.

"Wait a minute. When was that? I mean, when did you send them that thank you card?"

"Remember when that envelope came in the mail addressed to me?"

"I assumed you'd tell me about it. Then when you didn't, I assumed you didn't want to. So...that was your birthday card from them?"

"Yeah," Shams said.

"That was a couple of weeks ago. When was your birthday?"

"A couple of weeks ago," Shams said matter-of-factly.

"And you didn't tell me?!"

Shams shrugged but didn't look up from her knitting. "It's not a big deal. Mom and Dad never celebrated our birthdays. Plus, I thought you knew."

"You thought I knew?! You thought I would know and not at least recognize it?" Her voice was layered in disappointment, sadness, and surprise.

But Shams didn't seem to notice. "I told you, Mom and Dad never celebrated birthdays."

"But I'll bet they at least acknowledged them? They at least woke up that morning and said, 'Happy Birthday, Shams. I'm so glad God blessed us with you.'"

For the first time, Shams stopped her knitting and lowered her hands to her lap. "That's actually exactly what Mom used to say. How'd you know that?"

"Because it was what your dad used to say to me. I can't believe you didn't tell me! Well, come on. Get up off that couch! We are going to celebrate."

"But we don't celebrate birthdays."

"It isn't really a celebration if it's two weeks late. It's more of a... 'glad you're alive' commemoration."

"How's that different?"

But Ayda had already gone upstairs. "I'll be ready in fifteen minutes," she called down, prompting Shams to get up and get ready.

Twenty minutes later they sat in the car, Ayda driving and smoking a cigarette.

"Where are we going?" Excitement made Shams's voice higher, her eyes brighter.

"A bar."

"A what?"

"A club."

"Huh?"

"The library."

Shams chuckled.

"I always see ads for this place, and they always mention birthday parties. So we'll check it out."

"It isn't a McDonald's is it? 'Cause I think I've outgrown their birthday parties."

"Don't be ridiculous," Ayda said. "It's a Burger King."

Shams burst out laughing, bringing a smile to Ayda's face.

When they finally pulled into the parking lot of the trampoline park, Shams squealed. "I've always wanted to come here! Thank you so much, Didi."

Shams gave Ayda a big hug, and Ayda kissed her forehead. "I hope you enjoy it."

"I will, but only if you jump with me."

"No."

"Come on!"

"Hell no!"

"It's my birthday and I won't have a good time unless you jump with me."

"We don't celebrate birthdays."

"Diiiiidiiiiiii! Come on! Pleeeeeeease!"

"Um...no. I will watch you and take pictures and everything else, but I will not jump."

"Then we aren't going in."

"Come on, Shams. Let's go."

"I'm serious. I won't go in if you're not going to jump with me."

"Fine, then put your seatbelt back on," Ayda said.

Shams reached over and buckled up, her laughter replaced with a grimace.

"Don't be stubborn, Shams. You're only hurting yourself."

"You're the one who's being stubborn. And you're the one who's ruining this, not me."

They sat in the parking lot for a few more minutes.

"Start the car," Shams said. "We're only wasting time."

With a loud, "Humph! Fine!" Ayda took the key from the ignition, grabbed her purse and got out of the car.

"Yes!" Shams exclaimed, following her into the building.

At the information desk, Ayda said, "This young lady has kidnapped me and brought me here against my will."

The man behind the desk looked at Shams and winked. "This is a really great place to bring kidnapped parents."

After they had locked their shoes and belongings in the locker, Shams ran onto the trampoline and started jumping.

Ayda stood at the entrance staring at her. "Come on in!" Shams shouted. "The water's perfect."

"But I don't know how to swim," Ayda said.

"You'll never learn without getting wet!"

And with that, Shams jumped over to Ayda, grabbed her by the hand, and dragged her into the arena. A moment later, Ayda was jumping, getting higher and higher, her laughter getting louder and louder. They jump-raced, jumped off the trampoline walls, and played trampoline basketball. They even joined a dodgeball game. Ayda was the last one left on her team because she'd been running away from the ball the entire game. When it was finally her versus two teenage boys, she caught the ball mid-air, outing the larger boy, and immediately flung it at the shorter one, knocking him in the leg and winning the game. Shams cheered for her as though she'd just won an Olympic gold medal. "You were totally awesome! I wish I could have recorded it. I could see the moment you transformed, from the scared-of-the-ball old lady, to the take-no-prisoners warrior, out for blood! And then their faces when they lost! It was priceless!"

"That's one secret of life, my sweet Shams. Never reveal your true power too soon. Let the element of surprise always be in your favor."

They laughed together, enjoying the victory. Ayda felt great. Well, not exactly great. Her legs were sore, and her lower back was in more pain than she'd known in months. But emotionally, she felt refreshed. They sat down in the dining area and had pizza. Once they'd finished, the lights dimmed, and a sort of drumming sound filled the air. When Shams looked up, she saw the entire staff walking toward her, their leader carrying a chocolate cupcake with one candle lit. They were singing Happy Birthday.

Shams covered her face in her hands. Ayda smiled watching her. After Shams blew out the candle and the staff walked away, she began eating her cupcake. As she took the final bite, Ayda said to her, "Happy Birthday, sweetie. I'm so glad God blessed me with you."

And as she melted into the young girl's embrace, Ayda knew she had to deal with that crazy aunt without Shams finding out.

At work the following morning, Ayda called the banker. After reminding him of herself and Shams, she asked, "What happens to Shams's money if, for any reason, I'm not her guardian?"

"Do you mean after your passing?"

"Yes...and no. Just generally, what if someone else is legally assigned to be her guardian?"

"Well then they'll be in charge of the account, they'll have access to it the same way you do."

"How can I make it so that no one can access it but her?"

"Put it in a bond. That'll freeze it so she can't get to it before her eighteenth birthday. But you didn't want to do that, if I recall. You said you wanted it to be accessible in case she needed it."

"That's right. I just...it just occurred to me that...well, I won't live forever, and if someone else is appointed her guardian, I worry they might take advantage of her."

"Unless you put the money in a bond, there's no guarantee that won't happen."

"Thank you," Ayda said, and hung up without hearing Sam's reply.

With a cigarette at her lips, she stood looking out her office window. She was almost certain that Ann had only filed that custody case for the money. Why else would she appear now in the girl's life? Why the sudden interest?

Like it or not, Ann was Shams's biological family. Ayda didn't want Shams to know of her aunt's deceptive ways, she didn't want her to think worse of her than she already did. But she couldn't let that woman have access to Sham's money either. She called Fred Williams to ask if there was any way to secure Shams's money, but he gave her the same answer as the banker. "So what can I do to secure this money, to make sure that, if Ann gets guardianship, she can't touch that money?"

"I hate to say this, Ms. Faisal, but if Ann is really after Shams's money, you can probably make this whole lawsuit disappear."

She hung up without saying goodbye. He'd said out loud what she'd been thinking. But how much money would it take for these leeches to go away? And what if she turned out to be wrong—they would use it against her in the case for sure.

"Your instincts are never wrong." Siham's words came echoing back, as though someone had said them aloud. Ayda grabbed her purse and pack of cigarettes and was about to step out of the door when Derek stopped her.

"We need to talk."

Chapter Twenty
DOORS CLOSING...AND OPENING

"We have a potential client looking to produce a huge ad campaign for his newest products. He wants content for every media outlet—from TV to social media. We've never worked with him before, but he said, and I quote, 'Money is not an issue.'"

"Sounds good. Why are you wasting my time with this?"

"His name is Azid Ghobor. And he says the only way I'd get his business is if we let you go."

"What do you mean 'let me go'? 'Let me go' where?"

"You're not stupid, Ayda."

"No, but it seems *you* are. I still have those videos of you sexually harassing your employees..."

"You're forgetting, Ayda, that I got a divorce last year. So that won't matter at all to my personal life. I can fuck whoever I want."

"But it will affect your work here. You think they just let sexual harassers keep their jobs?"

"The president of our beautiful country has sexual harassment allegations against him, and he's still in office. I'm not too worried."

Ayda stared at him, her face flushed with hatred and her eyes spitting fire. "This department runs on my sweat and blood. It's what makes this company money."

"Your team does great work."

"They're the best."

"I think we'll be fine."

"They're the best, but they still need direction."

"I think we'll be fine," he repeated.

Ayda's mind raced with an appropriate reply. She wanted her words to slap him, not just to get back at him for firing her, but because of everything he represented: the middle-aged man who always got away with abusing others simply because he had a dick. She wanted to maim him with the appropriate words. But as the words wouldn't come, she kneed him in the groin instead. As Derek wailed in pain on the floor, she grabbed all her things. At the door she looked back and said, "I'm taking my clients with me. You're going to regret this moment for the rest of your life."

On her way home, she called Siham. "That little fuck got me fired!"

"Which little fuck?"

"Ghazi Dabbour...or Azid Ghobor, whatever the fuck his name is. After you declined to work with him, he offered Derek his business with a blank check provided he got rid of me."

"That little fuck."

"I'm going to rip through that bastard. Before it was just taking back what is rightfully mine. Now it's revenge."

When Derek had entered her office, she'd been on her way out with a very specific agenda. But now, now that she was out of a job, she didn't know if she could go through with her original plan. She stopped at the green light trying to decide if she should turn right to go home or left to proceed with her plan. The honking from the car behind her didn't faze her. Even as the car passed her and the driver asked if she needed help, she didn't seem to notice. She simply sat there staring straight out in front of her, gripping the wheel so tightly that her knuckles turned white. The light turned red, and she was still undecided.

"Please God, guide me to do what's right."

And when the light turned green, she made the turn.

◆◆◆

"Come in," Ann said. "I'm sorry, I wasn't expecting company." She ran around picking clothes up off the floor and furniture, and throwing empty bags of potato chips and cookies into a trash bin. "Can I get you something to drink?" she offered, still standing up.

"Sit down, Ann. We have something important to discuss, and I can't stay long."

When Ann sat down, Ayda stared at her silently, trying to read her, trying to figure out why someone who seemed lost and naïve could be so heartless.

"Why are you filing for custody of Shams?"

Ann lowered her gaze to her lap where she was wringing her hands. "She's family. I just want to make sure she's taken care of."

"You can't even take care of yourself. You're living in a dump."

Ann raised her eyes to Ayda for just a split second, her face blushing. "I'm not good with cleaning up, but I take care of my family."

"Perhaps. But Shams already has someone to take care of her. She is doing well with me. Her grades are good, she's well adjusted. She's happy with me. Why do you want to change that?"

"She's my sister's daughter, for God's sake. I have a right to be in her life."

"Why now? You weren't in her life before her mother died. You weren't even in her life *when* her mother died. You didn't even try to take care of her then. What made you wait all this time?"

Ann continued to look down, and wring her hands, but she didn't answer.

"Who put you up to this?"

"What are you talking about?" the woman whispered.

"Who told you you'd get her money? Because you won't. That money is frozen in an account you can't get access to. Only she can access it when she's eighteen."

"I thought her guardian could withdraw from it in the meantime?" Ann said, looking up at Ayda in earnest.

Ayda nodded. "I see."

A moment of uneasy silence passed between them.

"So how much? How much to make this lawsuit go away?"

"I'm not after her money," Ann said. "I want my niece in my life."

"You can still be part of her life without being her guardian. So how much?"

The answer came from a low-pitched, male voice, somewhere beyond the walls of the living room. "Fifty thousand."

Ayda's lips turned up with disgust, and her eyes became tight slits. Until that moment, Ayda had held onto the thread of possibility that her gut had been wrong, that Ann really did want to take care of Shams. But Ann's red face, and that unapologetic, bass voice she'd just heard, proved to her that, as always, her instincts had been correct.

A man with broad shoulders and a four-day stubble emerged. His ribbed tank undershirt, torn at the side, was half tucked into his flannel pajama pants.

Ayda looked at him as though he'd been in the room the entire time.

"I just lost my job. I don't have fifty thousand to spare. I can give you ten."

He laughed out loud and sat on the couch beside his wife. "You think we don't know what kind of money you have? We know you're rich. You can afford it."

"I will not give you fifty thousand dollars. If you want to continue with this case, you'll lose. You won't just lose the money you're after, you'll also lose any and all visitation with Shams. It's your choice."

She looked from Ann to her husband, waiting for a reply, but when one didn't come, Ayda grabbed her purse and rose. "Fine. You've made your decision. I'll see you in court. But like I said, you will lose. And it will be the biggest loss of your life." She started off towards the door.

"Wait," the man said.

She stopped walking but did not turn around.

"Thirty thousand," he said.

Ayda turned around and stepped right up to him as he and his wife remained seated on the couch. "Twenty. And I won't negotiate again. If the next word out of your mouth is anything other than 'fine,' I walk, and you'll get jack."

He looked at his wife, but she was still staring at her hands in her lap. He sighed heavily. After a short pause he whispered, "Fine."

Ayda sat down and took out her checkbook. "I'll give you ten thousand now and ten after you've dropped the case. I'll also have you sign a notarized contract that states you will never again fight me for custody of Shams. This is the kind of shit you do once; you pull it again, I'll make sure you're the ones who pay." She signed the check and held it out to them.

The husband took it and stared at it.

"I'll send my lawyer to you with the contract and remaining money once he informs me that you've dropped the case." She got up and walked to the door. With her hand on the knob, she turned to Ann and said, "Shams doesn't know anything about your filing for custody, and I want to keep it that way. I don't want her to find out about any of this, not about the case or the money. And I don't want you to disappear from her life either. There must be something good about you she can learn from. And if not, she still deserves to know her family."

Without waiting for a reply or saying goodbye, Ayda left. She had wanted to be wrong about them, but she felt relieved. Perhaps this was for the best. This way she could avoid the possibility of losing Shams, especially to people who only wanted to take advantage of her. "*Alhamdulillah,*" she repeated as she drove back home.

Ayda still had to tell Shams about losing her job, but the issue with Ann had been a much bigger burden.

When she pulled in, Marge was still in the house, and Shams hadn't arrived from school yet. "What brings you back home so early, Ms. Faisal? I hope everything's okay?"

Ayda rubbed her arm as she smiled meekly at Marge. "Thank you, Marge. I praise God for the good moments and the bad. And right now, I am having both."

"Sorry to hear that. But you're one of the toughest, smartest women I know, Ms. Faisal. I'm sure you'll be fine."

Ayda nodded half-heartedly at the words of encouragement. "I lost my job today, Marge. I've been at that company for almost twenty years, and today, at the request of a rich client who has a personal vendetta against me, they let me go."

Marge stood there with her mouth agape and her eyes wide with disbelief. Ayda sensed her concern.

"I won't be offended if you search for another job, Marge. But, for now, you do still have one here." She patted the woman on the shoulder then climbed the stairs to her room. After a long warm shower, she stepped into her house clothes. She was about to leave her room when, out of the corner of her eye, she spotted the prayer rug. Sliding her prayer gown on over her clothes, she spread out the rug and prayed. After she finished, she remained seated, raised her hands, and began to supplicate. She thanked God for His blessings, asked Him to forgive her parents and husband for their shortcomings and to grant them Heaven, and to bless her in-laws, Siham, Rizq and Shams with health and happiness and strength of faith. "Guide me to do what's right always, God. Please...let me keep You close so that You can guide me."

As she put away the rug and her prayer gown, Ayda heard the front door close and knew it was Shams returning from school. The young girl's quick steps up the stairs caught up with Ayda before she could leave her room. After greeting her and giving her a hug, Shams plopped down on Ayda's bed. "Why're you home so early?"

Ayda sat down next to her. "They fired me today."

Shams sat up straight, her eyes wide. "No way!"

"Yes way."

"But...but...you run that place!"

"But Ghazi Dabbour offered them a blank check for his business if they got rid of me. To them, it's all about the money."

"But I thought the CEO liked you?"

"No one at work likes me."

"You know what I mean. I thought he valued your work?"

"No, Derek wanted to fire me years ago, but I have info on him that could ruin his personal and professional life. That's why he's stayed away from me."

Shams sat in her bewilderment for a moment then hugged Ayda.

"This is obviously an emergency—you should take some money from my account."

"What? No! Shams, that is *your* money for when you grow up."

"Just enough to get us by for now, until you find another job."

"I have enough savings to keep us alive for a while. Don't you worry about it, sweetie. We're going to be fine."

"*In sha' Allah*," Shams whispered.

And Ayda repeated it even louder.

"But what are you going to do? I mean, to find a job?"

"Now may be the perfect time to open that art gallery/bookstore we talked about. It's possible this is my blessing in disguise. So I am saying *Alhamdulillah*...even though I just spent my entire car ride home cursing Ghazi Dabbour. But, now that my mind is clearer and the initial shock has faded, I say *Alhamdulillah*, and let's see where this opportunity will take us." Ayda's eyes were sparkling when she spoke, and her voice was higher pitched than usual.

"I know you're strong. You're probably the strongest person I know. But you can be real with me. I won't think any less of you."

Ayda looked at her and gave her a half-grin, then she reached out and wrapped her arms around her. "Where would I be without you, Shams?"

"Enjoying a Hawaiian vacation, I think."

"Totally. You're ruining all my fun."

After dinner, as they sat in the living room, Shams overheard most of Ayda's conversation with Siham. "Yeah, I'll start checking out locations right away. I'll think of that when the time comes. I know we need a set plan, but I just don't want to get bogged down with the details just yet. Fine, I'll sleep on it and give you a definite business structure tomorrow. Your money's ready, right? Good. And I'm going to contact my clients, have them get in touch with you. I know, but I'm hoping my strongest team will be willing to join your firm. No, of course people aren't going to leave their positions for lower pay. But it may be an opportunity. I mean, they may see it like that. Yes, if the clients agree, I'll work with you till the project launches. Well, in that case there's nothing to be done really. I'll just focus on my project. Isn't it too soon for that now? Ok. I'll be in touch tomorrow. Salaam."

She hung up and lit a cigarette.

"What's it too soon for?" Shams asked.

"Huh?" Ayda had dazed off.

"Aunt Siham said something then you said, 'Isn't it too soon for that now?' What is it too soon for?"

"She was asking me about staff to run the place. Like how many it would take in the beginning."

They were quiet for a while, Ayda smoking her cigarette and Shams knitting. Then Ayda said, "How're you coming on my phone case/book cover/socks?"

"Almost done. You'll have them in a couple of days."

"Good. You'd better finish them before we open this place—I'm going to need all the underage slave labor I can get."

"Really? Are you really gonna let me help out with it?"

Ayda looked at her with crossed eyebrows. "Your donuts weren't *exactly* like my mom's, but they were pretty good. So, yeah, you get the job!"

The next couple of days were busy for Ayda. She met with the lawyer and explained what had transpired with Ann. He took the check for the remaining amount from Ayda and drew up a contract stating that upon receipt of the money, they would never again attempt to gain custody of Shams. Mr. Williams also used the meeting to inform her of their progress with the Ghazi Dabbour case. At the end of his briefing, Ayda added, "And yesterday Ghazi bribed my boss to fire me. And he did."

"Good."

"Excuse you?"

"This helps your case. Not only can we now ask for punitive damages, but it's proof that he is a dangerous businessman, one who uses entrapment to get what he wants. Do you want to bring your company into this? File for wrongful termination?"

"No. I want Derek to suffer on a completely different level. Still thinking that one up."

"But if you don't fight it, you'll lose your pension. You've been at this place for how long?"

"Nearly twenty years."

"That's not something you should give up without a fight. Think about it."

Ayda considered the lawyer's words. She knew there was a truth to them. But she simply didn't want to deal with the politics of it anymore. She wanted to be done with all of that and saw this as an opportunity. "I'll keep you updated," she said.

After she finished her meeting with Fred Williams, she met with a real estate agent. She explained to the woman the type of business she was planning on opening, how much space she'd need, and the type of location she was interested in. "And I'm starting this business as I've just lost a job, so I'm looking for something affordable." The agent assured her they would be able to find something that fit her criteria and told her to expect a call in a couple of days.

Ayda's next stop was Siham's agency. Sitting at Siham's desk, she lit a cigarette and began calling her biggest clients.

"I wanted to inform you that I've left the firm and am now working with Siham Tawwab at On the Mark. After discussing your account with her, she's agreed to produce your ad for ten percent less than what you were originally going to pay. Yes, I realize there is a punitive clause for terminating the contract, but even with the amount you've already paid, this is still a smarter deal." But Ayda wasn't successful in convincing her former client in something she herself didn't totally believe. With the next client, she took a different approach.

"They accepted a high paying account in exchange for my termination. I had been with the company for nearly twenty years, but that didn't mean anything to them. You're right, business is business, but if they're willing to get rid of the department head, then they won't care too much about swapping out clients—they could sell your material to the highest paying competitor. Of course not, but clearly ethics and appropriate business dealings don't seem to matter too much to them. Look, I know you've already paid a significant percentage and that if you pull out now, you'll lose that money. But we'll take on your account at On the Mark for the balance remaining. No, it's not a loss for us. It's less profit financially, but we're gaining you as a client here at On the Mark, and that's important to us."

She only secured one of the three clients, but Ayda still considered it a win.

"But isn't their content copyright protected?" Siham asked.

"It hasn't gone to production yet, so no. I'm going to use the exact same content...it's going to kill Derek. I'm only disappointed that I won't be there to watch."

Ayda stuck around for the rest of the afternoon, meeting Siham's team and familiarizing herself with the place and the people. She left feeling relieved that she had a plan and was determined to make it work. "Please God. Please bless this new stage in my life."

She felt like she was making progress in every aspect of her life. The only order of business that she hadn't figured out was how to deal with that lowlife Derek.

"Why don't you do what that lawyer guy Fred says and sue for wrongful termination?" Shams asked her that evening.

"I'm just...tired of the judicial system, everything taking forever. And the fees. And the overall hassle of it. And let's say I do file the suit and win— then what? Whatever they pay me won't be enough to get that bloodsucker back."

She smoked her cigarette in silence, staring at the space before her, her eyes squinted in concentration on something that was not there. "I want to humiliate him by using his own despicable past to do so. I'm this close to figuring out how. Just need a few more days to ruminate on it."

"Well, if you need me to play ghost-girl again, I'm totally up for it."

Ayda smiled at her. Then, her smile began to disappear and her eyes grew wide, her back straightened. The energy from her idea continued to mount until Ayda was standing. "Shams, you my dear girl, are a genius."

"Yeah, I know."

Shams's remark had sparked a domino effect in Ayda's mind which formulated a plan. But for her plan to work, she would need an inside accomplice. Who could Ayda recruit to help in the downfall of that slimy CEO? And just as suddenly as the plan had come to her, she knew exactly who her co-conspirator should be. Checking the time on her wristwatch, she realized it was too late to call; everyone would have already gone home. The morning was soon enough; it was just a couple of hours before she would be able to begin her final project for the company that had taken so much of her talent and hard work.

Chapter Twenty-One
RECRUITING HELP

Fred Williams called Ayda the following day to tell her that Shams's aunt had withdrawn the lawsuit. "I'll go over there tomorrow with the check and the contract."

"Good."

"And things are moving along with the Ghazi Dabbour case. We're scheduled for court in a few weeks. Like I said before, it won't be an easy trial, but I do have hope."

"Hope? I need more than hope, Mr. Williams."

"All we can do is our best, and hope, Ms. Faisal. Have you considered what I told you, about wrongful termination?"

"Still thinking it over. I'll let you know."

Ayda knew it would not be easy to recruit Alice, her assistant. After all, Derek was the CEO of the company Alice worked for; she would not risk her job lightly. Ayda called Alice and asked her to meet her at a restaurant near the office. When Alice agreed, Ayda added, "But don't tell anyone you'll be meeting me."

When they met a few hours later, Ayda wasted no time. She lit a cigarette and began. "You know this last client that Derek took on, Ghazi...I mean Azid Ghobor? His one stipulation for commissioning the agency was that Derek get rid of me. I want to do something to get back at both those bastards, but I'll need your help."

Ayda explained her plan to Alice and told her it would require that she recruit at least one other team member.

"And if it doesn't work," Ayda warned, "I can't guarantee that you both won't lose your jobs. But in that case, I *can* guarantee you positions at On the Mark Agency."

Alice's eyebrows were knitted and her face unsmiling as she listened to Ayda's plan. At one point, she even took the cigarette from Ayda's hand and began to smoke it herself.

"What do you think? Are you in?"

Alice finished off the cigarette and looked down as she snubbed it in the ashtray. "That son of a bitch has harassed me so many times. At first it was inappropriate words, remarks about my clothes. Then it became worse and more frequent. He actually grabbed my ass once and said, 'When are you going to give me a piece of that.' I wanted to cut his dick off. I wanted to go to the police. But he's the CEO." She lifted her head. "And I need my job."

"I can't guarantee you the same salary you're getting there, but I can guarantee that you'll have a job."

"Do you know that I got up the nerve to report him to HR once?" Alice continued. "The guy in that department looked me up and down and said, 'With that outfit on, isn't that the response you were going for?'"

Ayda listened as Alice confided other instances where Derek had harassed her or one of their other female colleagues. "Whether you accept my proposal or not, I will stand behind you if you want to report him to the police. He used to pull this shit with me a long time ago, before I tied him up naked to a bedpost and blackmailed him into giving me the promotion I deserved. And I still have the videos of him harassing other women in the office."

"You should have just cut it off right then."

They remained quiet for a few moments.

Finally, Alice spoke. "What do you need me to do?"

Chapter Twenty-Two
ART & BOOKS

The realtor called Ayda and set up an appointment to show her three properties. They met on Sunday morning at the parking lot of the first location.

"This place is bustling during the week, but lots of the local businesses take Sunday off, as you know."

The outside of the building was nondescript. Nothing about it appealed to Ayda. Even the neighborhood itself didn't seem the right fit for an art bookstore.

"Is that a liquor shop next door?"

"Yes, they've been around for nearly fifteen years, as has the pizzeria on the other side. I know it doesn't seem impressive from the outside, but wait till you see inside." They stepped into the building as the realtor continued. "What you couldn't see from the outside was that the lot is riverside, and the back wall is completely glass, so all patrons get a beautiful view of the running water, and the small patch of green. It would be great for outdoor tables."

Ayda stood, staring at the inside of the place. It was much larger than it appeared from the outside, able to host the café, the bookshop and the art gallery, even if they were to be three different entities. The back room wasn't a kitchen but could easily be transformed to cater fresh pastries and hot drinks. Ayda stood in the center of the main section and closed her eyes. She could see the baristas bouncing between tables, art hanging from the walls, patrons sitting in chairs throughout the place, reading and chatting softly. She could see it. The only problem was the location. Sighing heavily, she said, "What else have you got?"

The agent drove her to a nearby plaza which hosted a gaming store, a couple of restaurants, and a few boutiques. It was already quite commercial. "Shops here do open on Sundays, but a bit later. This place has a lot of traffic—all the locals come here to shop and dine." She opened the door of the empty shop, but nothing in it impressed Ayda. The agent kept talking, glamorizing its selling points, but Ayda tuned her out. It was not as spacious as the previous place, nor did it have the same feel. The backroom was tiny, probably unable to fit a proper sized oven. Again, Ayda stood in the middle of the place and closed her eyes. She tried to force the images of art lining the walls, and customers cuddled up on armchairs reading books off the shelves—but the images would not come. She opened her eyes and asked the agent to show her the last property.

Twenty minutes later, they pulled up to an isolated building located just across the street from a local park. The two-story building was wide and had its own private parking lot. Up the street were the high school and a local ice-cream shop. "This area is very family friendly. The rent is higher than the other two options, and it isn't as commercial as the last place, but anyone going to or from the high school passes by here. It should be easy to get the word out about your establishment." She kept talking as she opened the door and showed Ayda around inside. The walls had been freshly painted and the floors newly waxed. There was no backroom, but the bathroom, although not exactly what Ayda would've picked, was decent enough to remain as it was, which would cut down on some of the money she'd need to spend on renovations. The upstairs had a sort of partitioned off area that looked like it actually had been a kitchen in a past life. As the realtor kept talking, Ayda stood in the center of the top floor. Immediately she could visualize customers pulling up chairs at the café, ordering croissants and latte's from behind the counter. She saw college-aged kids standing before the art on the walls, examining it, searching for its meaning, extracting inspiration. She saw the story lady huddled in one corner, surrounded by a dozen children, all leaning in to hear her better. She saw herself, standing in the corner, her arm around Shams, smiling at her.

Ayda gave another deep sigh and asked the agent once again to go over the rental fees for each establishment. She asked about the contract durations and about local contractors to do some repairs. She typed everything the real estate agent said into her phone.

Although Ayda had seen only three properties, and although the one definitely had its drawbacks and would still require some work, she had already made up her mind.

On her drive home, she thanked God that He had made it so easy to find a place. Years ago, when Ayda and Siham had begun this same journey, they had spent months searching for a place, and in the end, they'd been unsuccessful. *SubhanAllah*, she thought, *things only happen when God wills. Alhamdulillah.*

When Saturday arrived, Ayda woke Shams up earlier than the weekend-usual and told her to get dressed. "I want to show you something."

After they'd had breakfast, they got in the car and drove to the place Ayda had chosen. "This is it," Ayda said, pulling into the parking lot.

"This is what?"

"This is your future first job."

"Huh?"

"I'm opening my art bookstore here. This is it."

"Really?!" Shams rushed out of the car and ran all around the perimeter of the building. "This is such a great place. We've driven by here before, and every time, I wonder what kind of place it used to be. But now, I won't wonder anymore, because I know what it has grown into! Congratulations!" She hugged Ayda and gave her a kiss.

"But I'm going to need your help setting it up and getting it running."

"Totally!"

"I know it doesn't look like much on the outside..."

"All it needs is a coat of paint and some minor fixes here and there."

"Yes. And the inside is beautiful."

"When will it be yours?"

"I'm only renting, but we should have the key in just a couple of days."

"It's so beautiful, Didi. Congratulations."

"Thanks sweetie."

Something about sharing that moment with Shams made it even more precious. They stood side by side, Ayda's arm around Shams's shoulder, taking in the beautiful building, imagining all the different ways they could make it look.

"What color are you going to paint it?"

Ayda shook her head. "I was thinking a deep red. But then I worried it would look odd. What do you think?"

"Well," Shams began, walking in closer to the building, "we've got lots of things to our advantage. The view out the back, for one. The river and the grass help promote a nature-based theme, sticking to browns and reds. At the same time, it's an art bookstore, and art represents culture, and culture is often a symbol of modernity. So we could go with a more modern look, something that sticks out, like orange or yellow. I think a deep purple with black trim along the shudders and doorways and all that, I think it would be really cool."

Ayda stared at the building for a moment, then she closed her eyes and breathed in. A moment later she exhaled slowly and said, "Purple with black it is then."

"Awesome!"

"And we'll try to stick to that color scheme on the inside as well—tables and chairs and table covers, boards and bookcases, even our plates."

"This is going to be so cool."

Ayda nodded. "Yes. It is going to be so cool."

Once the contracts were signed and the key was in hand, it was time to start shopping. First, Ayda hired painters to take care of the exterior. Then she, Siham, and Shams, occasionally accompanied by Rizq, went shopping for everything they'd need to make the art bookstore not only functional, but chic too. Mr. Williams, the lawyer, was taking care of the licensing and other legal matters to open the business. He assured Ayda it would be a smooth process. "You should be ready to open in less than a month."

Shams helped Ayda choose curtains and blinds for the beautiful circumferential windows. Shams also chose the plates, cups, and silverware. Together, they decided on large black bookcases to line the store and black tables of similar design for the café. Tablecloths of various shades of purple were purchased to match the curtains and the building's new facade. The chairs were a bit trickier—the fancy ones were not comfortable, and the comfortable ones were rather ugly.

"Online," Shams said. "We should be able to find something good online."

They continued to shop and prepare the store for business. Ayda had contracted book distributors and had made an announcement at the local art museum and the high school, letting them know not only about the grand opening, but also inviting any artists to collaborate with her, so that their work could be displayed. She even contacted the nearest school of art, and although they were more than an hour's drive away, she received so many contacts of interest that she decided her original plan of alternating the art every month was not a quick enough rotation and decided to do it every two weeks instead.

She prepared systems for contacting collaborators, and selling books. She searched for a couple of employees to run the café and cash register. Shams was involved in every step. It was a lot of work, and each evening they collapsed with exhaustion. But their excitement and pride at bringing this dream to fruition far outweighed their physical fatigue.

It took them a month of non-stop work, but finally opening day arrived. It was early May, and the weather was perfect—the sun was warm, and a soft breeze billowed the leaves in the trees. Soft music played throughout the shop, and patrons began to walk in. The first customer was so delighted by her complimentary coffee that she bought three books. People started meandering in, and soon, the scene that Ayda had imagined just a month before became a reality. Mothers chased their children through the children's book section. Intellectuals wearing glasses and intrigued expressions traversed the walls, admiring the art. The employees served coffee and pastries with bright smiles. Shams took a group of children into a corner and began reading to them, inflecting her voice to personify each character. Soon the children's laughter bounced off the walls. Siham and Rizq were there, enjoying the victory with Ayda.

"You made it happen, Didi. I'm so proud of you," Siham told her.

Ayda hugged her friend. "I didn't make it happen. If I hadn't lost my job I wouldn't be here now. This is all God's doing. He made it so easy. *Alhamdulillah.*"

They ordered coffee from the kitchen upstairs then went outside onto the grass. Holding their mugs, they looked at the beautiful flowing river with birds dipping into it for their breakfast and turtles hiding from them under rocks. For the first time since Saef's death, Ayda felt at ease.

Mr. Williams arrived just then and joined them out back. "Congratulations, Ms. Faisal. Looks great."

"Thanks, but I borrowed a shit-load of money to open this place, Mr. Williams. We need to win that case against Ghazi."

"Our trial's set for next week. It shouldn't be long now. Oh, and everything's been taken care of with Ann and her husband. They signed the contract and I gave them the check."

"*Alhamdulillah.*"

Sumayya and Saleh showed up at the opening with a bouquet of flowers for Ayda. "You're doing a great job with everything, Didi. Saef would have been so proud of you. We're all so proud of you."

Ayda took the flowers and thanked them, then she excused herself, saying she needed to go check on the kitchen and mingle with the patrons. Instead, she locked herself in the bathroom of her office. She sat on the closed toilet with her face in her hands and tears flowing down her cheeks. She wasn't exactly sure why she was so emotional or what had brought it on, but suddenly, she missed Saef. She missed her parents. They would have loved to see her here. They would have been so proud. Her heart ached that she could not share this moment with them. She allowed herself a few minutes to cry, then washed her face and straightened her clothes before going back out. She visited the kitchen, where the pastry chef and her assistant were managing well and supplies were under control. Patrons sitting in the upstairs café congratulated her and said they looked forward to returning on a weekly basis. She stopped by a few guests admiring the art and mentioned that all artwork was for sale.

"This is a great idea," one guest said. "Combining books and art. It's like heaven."

Ayda smiled at the lady, thanked her, and said she'd hope to see her again.

"Oh, you will! And often."

When it was time to close, they had to practically shove the last customers out the door. The employees cleaned up, and Ayda thanked them for their work. "You're welcome to the leftover pastries."

They each grabbed a muffin or bagel, and as they left, Ayda reminded them not to be late the next day.

Sumayya, Saleh, Siham, Rizq and Shams stood waiting in the parking lot as Ayda made sure the back doors were locked, then came out and locked the front door.

"Come on, Didi. We're taking you for a dinner celebration," Saleh said.

"Thank you, Uncle, but I'm so tired. I just want to go home and..."

"Oh, come on Didi," Rizq interrupted. "How often do we *go out* as a whole family? We want to celebrate with you."

Shams added, "Stop being an ass, Didi. Let's go."

Ayda looked at Shams in quasi-disbelief. "I'm pretty sure you shouldn't be talking to me like that."

"You may be right, but you taught me to say what I mean."

Ayda ruffled Shams's hair. "So you're saying that you learned how to be a punk from me?"

"You *are* the best teacher."

Ayda laughed as she pretended to smack Shams upside the head. "Ok, so where are we going?"

They went to a seafood restaurant, and Ayda ordered lobster. "Lobster is my celebratory food," she announced. "Hope someone brought a credit card because I'm maxed out for the rest of my life."

Saleh insisted on treating, and they all even ordered dessert. Before the meal arrived, he made a short prayer. "May God bless us all, and all our endeavors, and increase us without decreasing us." When the food arrived, they all said "*Bismillah*" and dug in.

Everyone was worn out from such a long day, so the conversation was scarce, but they were all smiling, enjoying the food, company, and occasion.

On the ride home, Shams was still bursting with excitement. Although Ayda was exhausted, she enjoyed Shams's brightness. It was a great feeling to be surrounded by people who were happy for her happiness and success.

"It was such a great day! Everything came out great. Did you see, we already sold four pieces of art. That's so awesome. Do you think you'll want to put your work up there sometime?"

"I don't know. I hadn't thought of it. I had wanted the artwork to encourage local artists and to get their names circulating, give them a push and a pat on the back. I never thought about displaying my own stuff."

"I think people liked the plates and cups, don't you?"

"They were the best part of the whole place!"

Shams chuckled. "I really like story time. Do you think I can do that every day?"

"You've got school."

"After school."

"I think it will be more special if we do it once a week. You can even advertise on our announcement board."

"Can I pick the book and make a little poster for it?"

"Who did you think was going to do that?"

"Yes!" Shams's enthusiasm was medicine to Ayda's soul. Seeing her happy made Ayda's cares disappear. She could forget about Ghazi Dabbour and Derek. She could forget that she'd lost her job unjustly. She could forget about all the pain, and just enjoy Shams's presence.

◆ ◆ ◆

The following Sunday, Ayda sat drinking her coffee after breakfast. "Shams, hurry up," she called. "We're already late."

"I'll be down in a sec."

Ayda placed the empty mug in the sink. When she turned around, Shams was standing there, holding out a gift-wrapped package.

"What's this?"

"It's a present. For you. Happy Mother's Day."

Shams kept holding out the gift, but Ayda stood frozen in place, staring from the present to Shams's smiling face. "But...but...." Tears began to well up in her eyes. "But I'm...not...."

"Mom called you my second mom. Even though you didn't give birth to me, you're still a mom to me."

A tear had slid down Ayda's cheek.

"Mom told me love only makes things better. I love you. And you love me. And that's what a mother does."

Ayda hugged the young girl and kissed the top of her head. After a moment, she loosened her grip and stepped back, taking the present from Shams's extended hand.

"It's really not a big gift. Don't get your hopes up."

Ayda sat down in the nearest chair, and Shams sat beside her. She unwrapped the gift slowly. When she had removed all the wrapping paper, a framed photo of her and Shams stared back at her. They were both smiling, probably even laughing. The image made the tears flow freely from Ayda's eyes.

"I thought we could hang it next to the one already on the staircase, of me and Mom. I mean, if you want."

Ayda hugged Shams again. "This is the most perfect gift, Shams. Thank you." After staring at it for a moment, Ayda took out the hammer and nails and hung the picture beside the other above the staircase.

Standing a few steps back, admiring the photos, Ayda said, "They fit here perfectly. I can't even remember what this wall looked like before. It's like these pictures have always been here." Ayda ruffled Shams's hair.

"You're not going to go all soft on me now, are you?" Shams said through a chuckle.

"Of course not. Go get my purse and keys, under-aged slave!"

"That's more like it." Shams laughed as she ran off to do what she was told.

Ayda made a silent prayer that Shams would always be kept safe. "Please protect her from all evil, God. Help her to remain good and kind and compassionate. Help her to always keep You in her sight. Ameen."

But no matter how sincerely Ayda prayed for Shams, she could not change the young girl's fate.

Chapter Twenty-Three
VINDICATION

The following week was the trial against Ghazi Dabbour. Ayda wore a pair of knee-high black boots, a short black skirt and a bright red button-down blouse with a blazer.

"You never wear red lipstick," Shams remarked.

"I know. I heard a sermon once comparing it to biting into raw flesh."

"That's so disgusting!"

"Totally. But today I think I want to look like I could bite someone's head off."

"Makes sense. You look great, though."

"Thanks sweetie."

"Do you want me there with you?"

"You know...I really do. But I need you at the store. Siham will be there, but I need you to keep an eye on things for me. She's coming by to pick you up soon, so go get ready."

"I already am. And my homework's in my bag so I can get it done there."

"Good." Ayda sprayed some perfume on her neck and wrists, then stood up and gave Shams a quick kiss. "I'll see you in a bit."

"*In sha' Allah*. I'll pray for you!" Shams called behind her.

On the steps of the courthouse, Ayda took in the last few puffs of her cigarette then stomped it out on the ground. As she entered the courtroom, she made a silent plea, "Please, God. Please help me win. For the sake of my parents."

She took her seat beside Fred Williams, and the proceedings began just a few minutes later. She avoided looking at Ghazi the entire time; she didn't trust herself not to jump up and strangle him.

The other lawyer kept drilling home the idea that Azid Ghobor made his current fortune after he had officially gone bankrupt. Even without taking into consideration that he changed his name to have a fresh start, claimed the lawyer, his bankruptcy meant he was no longer legally nor financially liable for any business transactions he entered as Ghazi Dabbour.

After both sides stated their case, court adjourned for a short recess, and Ayda got up to leave.

"Don't go too far," Mr. Williams said. "This might not take long."

"Is that a good thing or a bad thing?"

The lawyer shrugged his shoulders. "I've done my best, Ms. Faisal. I've shown the proof that he swindled your folks, proof that he got you fired and is thus an immoral businessman. I've played the emotional card as well, relating how your mother couldn't afford the treatment she needed because Dabbour didn't return the money. I have done all I can do. But I honestly don't know how this will go."

Ayda nodded and headed out. She leaned against one of the pillars in front of the building, lit a cigarette, and took out her cell to call Siham.

"Salaam, Didi. How's it going?"

"*Alhamdulillah.* We're on recess now for the judge to deliberate. But Mr. Williams seems to think it could go either way. We'll just have to wait and see."

"Just don't do anything stupid, Ayda."

Siham never called her Ayda.

"What do you mean, 'don't do anything stupid'?"

"Don't punch him. Don't give him a flat tire. Don't stalk his wife and kids. It'll be over soon, so just...don't do anything stupid."

"I am not the type of woman to bring innocent bystanders into things."

"Maybe. But you *are* the type to cause all sorts of problems. Just resist the urge. Resist it!"

Ayda shook her head and said, "You don't know me at all, Seema. After all these years. I'm disappointed." She sighed heavily before continuing. "Is everything okay at the shop?"

"Yes. Shams and I have everything under control."

"Good. And thank you. I'll be there as soon as this is over."

After they hung up, Ayda took a stroll through the parking lot. She hadn't gotten very far when Mr. Williams called her, saying they were ready to announce the verdict. On her way back to the building, she spotted Ghazi Dabbour's car. She stood there for a moment, considering. Then rushed over and let the air out of both tires on the driver's side. "I totally blame Siham for that. Such a great idea."

Back in the courtroom, Ayda settled in just before the judge entered. Mr. Williams whispered, "If you believe in prayer, this is the time."

Before delivering his verdict, the judge spoke for a few minutes. He talked about the amount of time that had passed, about the fact that bankruptcy can, in many instances, provide the debtor with a clean slate.

"But," Ayda heard the judge say, "there are also instances, when a person abuses the system. And as this is the *judicial* system, it is my obligation to provide a *just* verdict.

"If this had been a failed business deal, where the import business the Faisals entered into with Mr. Dabbour had floundered, then this trial would be a waste of my time. But I don't think that's what we're looking at here. For that reason, I find in favor of Ms. Ayda Faisal."

Ayda let out a sigh of relief and praised God as the judge continued.

"Azid Ghobor will pay to Ms. Ayda Faisal the original thirty thousand dollars that her parents had lent him, as well as an approximation of the profit these funds should have accrued, an amount calculated at five hundred thousand dollars."

Ayda was speechless. She had never imagined that the court would award her so much. Her eyes teared up, and Mr. Williams put his hand on her shoulder. She was so ecstatic that she didn't even bother saying all the things she'd planned to say to that crook Ghazi; she didn't even notice him leave the courtroom.

As soon as she got in her car, she called Siham.

"Are we celebrating?" Siham said as she picked up the phone.

"You bet your ass we're celebrating!"

"Woohoo!" Siham screamed, surprising some of the customers in the shop.

"Half a million dollars!" Ayda screamed. "They awarded me half a million dollars!"

Siham was silent.

"Hello? Seema, you there? Did the line go dead?"

"I'm here," came a whisper on the other end of the line. "I'm here. I just... did you really say half a million dollars?"

"Yes!" Ayda was laughing and crying as she shared the news with her friend. "Don't tell Shams. Did she hear you?"

"No, she's upstairs."

"Good, just tell her that we won. Don't say how much we get. I want to surprise her. I'm going to run a quick errand. I'll see you guys in a bit."

Ayda pulled into the cemetery and walked over to her parents' graves. After she recited the customary verses from the Qur'an and made a supplication, she shared the good news of her victory with them. "I know it comes too late, and that it means nothing to you now. But at least I fought for what is rightfully ours, and, by God's Grace, the court awarded us a half million dollars. And I already know how I'm going to spend at least some of it. *In sha' Allah*, this money will help us all benefit." She said a final supplication for her parents then headed to the bookstore.

As soon as she walked in, her head low, her pace slow, Shams ran up to her. "What's wrong?" the girl asked. "Aunt Siham said you won the case? Didn't you win?"

Ayda put her arm around Shams and continued walking slowly. "Yeah, I won."

"Then what's wrong then?"

"They didn't award me the amount I expected."

"Oh," Shams said. "How much did you get?"

Ayda didn't say anything.

"Is it really that small?"

Ayda stuck out her bottom lip and nodded her head slowly. "They awarded me... half a million dollars!" she screamed, bouncing with excitement. And just as with Siham, Shams stood frozen in place, unable to speak or breathe.

"Is she okay?" one of the customers said.

"Yes," Ayda replied. "This is her being happy."

Ayda walked over to the cashier and pulled the microphone toward her, activating the intercom. "Ladies and gentlemen, boys and girls, may I have your attention please. For those of you who don't know me, my name is Ayda Faisal; I'm the owner of Art & Books. Today I had a bit of good fortune, praise God, and to share that with you, I'm announcing our first promotion: for today only, each of you will be gifted one free book with your purchase of books or art. Thank you for your business, and I hope to see all of you again."

Everyone in the store cheered. Siham came up to Ayda and put her arm around her. Smiling she said, "Shouldn't you hold off on the philanthropy until the money makes it to your account?"

"Probably. But I'm in a great mood, and I want everyone around me to be in a great mood too."

◆◆◆

That evening, as Ayda and Shams sat in the yard, Ayda asked how she thought they should spend the money.

"Well," the girl said, "you have to give a portion to charity before you do anything else."

Ayda smiled widely hearing Shams say what she had already planned to do.

"What?" the young girl said, smiling self-consciously.

"I wish I could take the credit for you, Shams. Your mom did a great job. She would be so proud of you—just like I am."

Ayda pulled out a cigarette and went on, "Okay, after the charity..."

"Before anything else, we said we're going to quit smoking." Shams snatched the cigarette from her.

"Did we say that?"

"Yes," the girl replied.

"Are you sure? Because I don't think..."

"I'm sure. I know you'll still do it when I'm not around, but at least stop smoking when you're with me. It can be a first step. Okay?"

"Do I have a choice?"

"Not really. And after we give the money to charity, then we have to pay off Aunt Siham for the money you borrowed for the bookstore."

"Check."

"Once that's done, we need to give Marge a bonus. And a raise."

"Yes, Marge puts up with all your crap, she totally deserves a bonus and raise. I wonder if she'd like to work at the store."

"I don't think so, but we can ask."

"Why don't you think so?"

Shams shrugged. "I think Marge enjoys the quiet of the house. We're not around most of the time, so she basically moves around as though this is her place. I think she likes it. But we can ask her anyway."

"Ok, so once we give charity, pay back Siham, give Marge a bonus and a raise, what do we do with the rest of the money?"

On her own, Ayda had gotten as far as Shams had, but she had no further ideas. She was interested in hearing the girl's thoughts.

"Well, I was thinking we could make Art & Books a chain. We wait for a year or two, then if things continue to go well, we open another branch."

"Another branch. That's a great idea."

The days turned into weeks, and soon Ghazi Dabbour had paid her compensation. Ayda used some of the money to install a water fountain in a mosque located in the less developed part of town. She did this in her parents' names, with the intention that every drop of water from the fountain used to quench someone's thirst be written in her parents' scales of good deeds. She donated another percentage to organizations that helped refugees get on their feet and reconnect with family. Another percentage she gave to local half-way houses and shelters. When people thanked her, she said, "Just say a prayer for my parents."

She paid Siham back every penny she had borrowed to start up the shop. "Does this mean you no longer want my help with the bookstore?"

"No longer want your help? I'm going on a yearlong vacation—who do you think I'm leaving in charge?"

Siham chuckled. "I'm serious, Didi."

"So am I. Well, not about going on vacation, but about keeping you in charge. I'm still going to need your help with lots of different things. You won't get rid of me that easily."

Lastly, Ayda added a hefty sum to Shams's bank account without telling her. If anything were to happen to her, Ayda wanted Shams to be as financially comfortable as possible.

◆◆◆

A few weeks later, Ayda was walking the aisles of the bookstore when she got a call from Alice.

"The ads are live. He's paid a lot of money for a wide reach, so even if he pulls them in an hour, thousands of people will still have seen them. I've emailed you a direct link. Cynthia and I have quit, and we'll be at On the Mark in the morning."

Before she even saw the ads, Ayda knew Alice and Cynthia had done a good thing.

"Thank you for helping me with this, Alice."

"We did it for all of us, for everyone that man has ever taken advantage of. He had it coming."

Ayda darted to her office and flipped open her laptop. Clicking eagerly on the link she said, "Let's see that new ad of yours Mr. I'ma-claim-bankruptcy-and-steal-all-your-money."

Seconds later the ad appeared. It took a few moments for Ayda's eyes to adjust to the image. There was Ghazi, wearing nothing more than a pair of briefs laying on top of an exhausted, naked Derek on a bed. The text read, "Ghobor Furniture: We pride ourselves on comfort and durability!"

Ayda's laughter rang out throughout the entire store.

Chapter Twenty-Four
IT'S NOT SAFE TO BE YOU

Art & Books continued to thrive. And five years later, they had bought the building housing their original location and opened another branch thirty miles away. Shams and Rizq worked after school and on weekends, and Ayda split her time between the two branches. Shams kept her flare for colors as she outgrew the awkward stages of adolescence and entered young womanhood with a more mature style of eye-catching outfits. She'd gotten her driver's license and had begged Ayda to let her withdraw some money from her account to buy a car.

"No."

"Not a new car, a used, beat up one! It won't cost more than a couple thousand dollars."

"That's a couple thousand dollars you'll need for college."

"Please, Didi. If I have a car, I can help out more at the shop."

Ayda, who now had a few more laugh lines framing her mouth and crow's feet dancing around her eyes, smiled and took Shams by the shoulders.

"You know I don't like to say no to anything you ask for. I let you go on that trip to Greece and Turkey last year even though I spent the entire twelve days in constant anxiety. I didn't get up off the prayer mat while you were away, but I let you go because I knew it would be a wonderful experience for you. But this is different. Please don't ask me again because I truly hate to say no to you, but this time, I just have to."

Shams dropped her head in defeat and nodded. Ayda kissed her on the top of the head. "Don't worry about helping me out more at the shop— your time will come."

Shams's disappointment was obvious, but the girl didn't talk back or act out. She and Didi had remained close over the years, Shams never going through that withdrawal phase most teens experience when they distance themselves from their families. Perhaps Shams felt more comfortable because Didi was not her biological mother. She talked to her about everything. When a boy at school had started to take interest in her, Shams told Didi, and Didi listened.

"He pays attention to me. He notices when I wear something new or do my hair different. When he asks for my advice about something, he usually takes it. And he's just...nice. He's not a troublemaker or anyone who seeks attention. He kind of lays low in our class, but when he answers a question or makes a point, he's usually right."

"Have you gone out with him? Outside of school?"

"Once. After school we walked around the mall. He bought me an iced coffee. Then he drove me to the shop. He usually swings by on the days I work."

"He sounds like a good guy."

"Yeah, he is. But..."

"But what?" Ayda smiled warmly at the girl, anticipating her question.

"How do I know if I love him?"

"Do you need to know?"

"Don't I?"

Ayda shrugged. "Love is a beautiful, warm, complicated mystery. We know why we love most of the people in our lives. Our family, friends who've stuck by us. Lots of our loves make sense. But then there are loves that make no sense: like when you meet someone and you don't know them very well, yet you wonder about them, worry about them, even pray for them. Or when we continue to love people who've harmed us or broken our heart.

"But the romantic love that you're wondering about, while it remains a beautiful emotion, is worthless without action. And by action I don't mean buying you chocolates or gifts. True action comes from fulfilling one's responsibilities and commitment. And you and this young man—at this age, at this point in your lives—neither of you is ready for a commitment.

"So whether it is love or not, it doesn't really matter. You're not going to run off and marry him. Just...don't do anything that would force you into a commitment; that's no way to start a real relationship whether or not love is involved."

"You don't mind that I'm sort of seeing him?"

"I want you to be able to share anything and everything with me, Shams. As your guardian, and your friend, I have to tell you that too much time with someone—with anyone—causes attachment. And often that attachment can lead us astray. You have helped me to get closer to God—don't do anything that will push *you* further from Him. As you've told me plenty of times, your relationship with Him is *the* most important relationship."

"Speaking of our relationship with God..." Shams began, an obvious hesitation in her manner, "there's something I want to talk to you about."

"Of course. Let's go grab some ice-cream, and we can talk about it while we're out. Come on get dressed. Your treat."

Ayda got up as Shams threw a throw pillow at her.

Twenty minutes later, they were sitting in a booth in a local ice-cream shop. Ayda munched on French fries as she waited for her strawberry shortcake with chocolate ice-cream and Shams for her French vanilla banana split.

"Why French fries?" Shams asked.

"What do you mean 'why'?"

"I mean, we're here to have ice-cream. So, why the fries?"

"Fries are the perfect appetizer to ice-cream. Have I taught you nothing of importance?!"

"Must have missed that lesson," Shams said, chuckling. "I don't know how, but you never cease to amaze me, Didi."

"I know. That's just me being completely awesome."

Again, Shams chuckled.

"Can I ask you something? How come you never remarried?"

Ayda stopped chewing and furrowed her eyebrows at Shams. "Where did that come from?"

"From how awesome you are. I would think you'd have met lots of men who noticed your awesomeness and wanted a piece of it. So how come you never shared it with anyone?"

"I share it with you. You get lots of your awesome from me."

Shams laughed. "I know. But I mean...really. Seriously. How come?"

Ayda thought for a minute as the waitress placed their sundaes on the table. "I had a great marriage once, then it..." She paused and reworded it. "In any relationship there has to be give and take. And I do all my giving to you, Siham and Rizq, your grandparents, and the store. I have no desire to give in any other direction."

They sat eating their sundaes for a few minutes, then Shams said, "There is a direction I feel like I want to give in, but I want to give you a heads up first."

"Shoot."

Shams took a deep breath, put her spoon down, and looked directly at Ayda. "I'm going to start wearing hijab."

Shams's words knocked from Ayda the ability to speak, blink and chew. She sat frozen, holding her spoon suspended in mid-air. "What?" she finally managed to whisper.

"I've decided to start wearing hijab. After winter break."

Ayda put her spoon down and stared at Shams so intensely that the young woman's face flushed, and she looked down at her plate.

"You can't," Ayda said. "You just can't."

"Why not?"

"Because it isn't safe. We live in a world where people die because of the color of their skin and because of their faith. No, you can't. It isn't safe."

Shams was silent for a moment. When she looked up, her face was soft, and her lips curved gently into a small smile, but her voice was firm. "Didi, this is more than a childhood desire or passing whim. I want to do this. I know this will help me get closer to God. I want to be close to Him."

"But you can't be close to Him if you're always in danger."

Shams smiled wider. "But if I do this, and my intention is to be closer to Him, then anything that happens to me, He will guide me through it."

"That's not the way it works, Shams. Do you think that all the people who die of starvation or cancer or car accidents every day, do you think that none of those people were close to God? Some were, for sure, but in the end, their fate was the same as those who were not."

"What we see happening in the physical world may not be what is actually happening in the spiritual world. The truth is, we're all going to die someday, right? But even though deaths may appear to us to be the same, I don't believe they are. They can't be, because God tells us He will be there for those who are patient and are constant in their prayers. And I believe Him."

"But God doesn't want you to do something that puts you in danger, Shams."

"I won't be in danger."

"Yes! You will. Tolerance of Muslims is a rare commodity these days."

Shams took Ayda's hand in her own. "Then imagine how much prouder of me God will be if I do something for Him despite it putting me in danger."

"His being proud of you won't save you from this world."

"Nothing's going to save me from this world. But I do believe in the Hereafter, and I want to do what I can to be sent to the good place."

"But wearing hijab…"

"Please, Didi. Please just be happy for me. Please just be happy that I choose God's pleasure over anything else."

Ayda stared at her for a long moment. "Of course I'm happy you choose God's pleasure. Of course I'm proud of you. You're my daugh…" She gulped and looked down at her plate. "If I had a daughter, I wouldn't be more proud of her than I am of you. I just worry about you."

Shams went around to Ayda's side of the booth and sat beside her, putting her arm around her. "You don't have to worry about me. I've got two powerhouses on my side: God…and you."

Ayda hugged her tightly, but the knot in her chest did not loosen.

As she'd intended, Shams went to school after winter break wearing hijab. Ayda held her breath as the girl boarded the bus in the morning. She took comfort in knowing that Rizq treated Shams like his younger sister, and he would be there to help if trouble found her.

Throughout the day, Ayda resisted the urge to call Shams on her cell and check up on her.

"She's going to be fine," Siham said, trying to comfort her.

"What if she isn't? What if someone tries to bully her or pull it off or push her down the stairs or..."

"Shams is capable of defending herself. She's been under your wing for more than five years now. She's got it covered."

"No one has it covered, Siham. They can gang up on her. They can wait for her to be alone, and ..."

"Stop! Didi, you've got to stop this! So what, now you're going to go around following her, making sure no one says or does anything to bother her? You can't do that, Didi. None of us can. We raise them the best we can, but the time comes when we have to let them go. And yes, our worry isn't so much with how they'll do but how the world will do to them. Still, we can only sit, wait and watch. And give them our advice. And pray for them. Besides that, there is nothing in our power to do to protect them. We have to let them live their lives."

Ayda stared at Siham for a moment. When she finally spoke, she said, "I need a cigarette," and she turned to leave.

"You haven't smoked in three years!"

Ayda waved Siham's words away with her hand and continued walking. She pulled out of her purse the solitary cigarette she kept with her, in case of an "emergency," and stepped out back. With the cigarette at her lips, she stared at the blank screen of her cell phone, wondering how much longer she had to wait before calling Shams. Suddenly, the screen lit up. An image of Shams popped up, and Ayda anxiously clicked open the line. "Salaam, sweetie. How are you? How did today go?"

The sound on the other end was muffled, and Ayda's heart sank. Her knees became weak and the blood drained from her face. "Shams! Shams, what's the matter? What happened?"

"Sorry, Didi," came the reply. "Rizq told me the funniest joke just as I was calling you."

Ayda sat on the nearby rock, closed her eyes, and tried to slow her heartbeat. "*Alhamdulillah*," she whispered inaudibly.

"I just wanted to let you know that I'm headed to the bookstore with Rizq. I wasn't scheduled for today, but I don't have a lot of studying, so I might as well make use of my time, right?"

"Right. I'll see you soon then."

Ayda put out her cigarette and dropped the phone into her pocket. Shams was fine. For today. But how would the rest of her days go? Ayda raised her hands in supplication and asked God to bless Shams always and to keep her safe. "I place her in Your trust, God. I place her in Your trust."

And although the words had only verbalized the way she knew she should feel, something about actually uttering them helped Ayda to let go. She knew this did not mean that nothing bad would happen to Shams. She knew it did not mean that Shams would live a life free of hardship or danger or grief. But it did mean that she believed God would help her through whatever lies before them. And this admission helped ease her heart. She recited one of her favorite verses from the Qur'an: "And put your trust in God, and sufficient is God as your guardian."

Later that night, Ayda asked Shams how her first day as a hijabi went.

"Fine. The same. Oh, wait, no. Actually, this girl came up to me—I've seen her around before but she's not a junior—she told me she's Muslim too. I was like, 'I thought Rizq and I were the only ones.' And she was like, 'I thought I was the only one until I saw you in hijab!' She seems nice enough. We exchanged numbers."

"That's great. A nice surprise." Ayda was quiet for a minute then asked, "What about the not-so-nice surprises? Any of those today?"

Shams kissed Ayda on the cheek. "Nothing bad happened. I promise."

"But that's just one day," Ayda whispered.

"But all we have is one day, Didi. Today is all we have. And if it was a good day, then that's success."

But not all of Shams's days were good. The following week Shams heard someone scream down the corridor, "Go home, towelhead!" She turned on her heels to catch the culprit, but the group of laughing senior boys betrayed none of their members. "Bunch of jackasses," she said aloud to herself. And although she hadn't meant for anyone else to hear, a girl beside her said, "That's not very nice."

"Excuse me?" Shams said, looking at her with knitted eyebrows. "Didn't you hear what they said to me?"

"Jackasses are actually pretty smart," the girl said. "I'm sure they'd be offended to be compared to a group of degenerates like that."

And again, somehow, what could have been a bad situation, a bad moment, turned into one where Shams made a new friend.

The following month, however, even Shams couldn't find the silver lining to the fear she experienced.

Chapter Twenty-Five
NOWHERE TO RUN

During her free period, Shams sat outside in the school courtyard and worked on a report that was due soon. The courtyard was empty, but after ten or fifteen minutes, a guy from her grade came out and sat beside her on the ground. They weren't in any classes together, but Shams knew who he was. He had a bad reputation as a druggie, and Shams became acutely aware that he was sitting too close. She stood and casually started gathering her things, when he grabbed her arm.

"I can rip that sheet right off your head."

Shams yanked her arm away. "That would be harassment, Brett. And you wouldn't get away with it."

"You know how many girls I've fucked? Most of them kept screaming, 'No, no!' But I always do what *I* want."

He took a step closer.

"Get out of my way!" Shams screamed.

"I won't let you go until I get what I want. Either you take that thing off your head, or you let me feel you up. Your choice."

Only he didn't have a chance to say the word 'choice.' Shams kneed him in the groin with all her might. As he writhed in pain on the ground, she ran to the principal's office. The secretary called Ayda to come pick up Shams.

Shams was nervous and upset, but she remained composed.

"Where is this little shit? I'm going to tear his..."

"I took care of him, Didi."

"What about the next time, huh? What if he corners you again...or has a group of his goons gang up on you? What then?"

"We're suspending him, Ms. Faisal, and he will be under surveillance once he comes back to school."

"Under surveillance? You won't be able to monitor his every move. And what if he finds out where we live? Or where she works?"

"Ms. Faisal, Brett is not a very promising student, and he'll probably drop out soon, but he's not a criminal."

"The hell he isn't! He boasted about raping girls! And all you're going to do is suspend him?!"

"If you'd like to report this to the police..."

"I wasn't waiting for your permission! Of course I'm going to report this. I had just hoped that you would have shown more concern about the safety of your students.

"Come on, Shams. Let's go." Ayda stomped out of the school with her arm around a slightly dazed Shams.

They sat silently in the car for a few minutes without Ayda turning on the ignition. "Are you okay?" Ayda had calmed down a bit, her voice was soft.

Shams, staring out the window with wide unmoving eyes, only nodded. A minute later, she closed her eyes and shook her head, as though to wipe away a thought. "I'm fine, Didi. Let's go home."

"We're going to the police station first."

"It won't make a difference. If he wants to hurt me, he won't care about any police report."

"Maybe. But we have to do our part. Never let anyone intimidate you from exercising your rights or from standing up for yourself. Never. It takes courage to do it, but you've got to brace yourself and just do it, because if you don't, your regret will haunt you."

Shams was unusually quiet that evening as they ate dinner. Ayda tried to get her to open up; she asked her about her friends, subjects at school, how things in the shop were going, and what books she had planned for story time. Shams replied, but her voice was barely above a whisper and her answers were brief. Finally, she said, "I'm not going to change my mind about the hijab. I know you think this has made me doubt my decision, but it hasn't."

"I know," Ayda said.

When she didn't pursue the matter further, Shams asked, "That's it? You're not going to try to convince me?"

"What did I tell you today? Don't let anyone intimidate you from exercising your rights. And it is your right to wear hijab. Plus…" Ayda took another bite and chewed slowly. "I'm totally impressed by your knee to the groin technique. Hopefully it did permanent damage."

Shams smiled.

"I'm very proud of you, Shams," Ayda said suddenly, looking earnestly at the young woman. "Very proud." She got up and kissed the girl on her forehead.

A week went by, and Ayda could tell that Shams was nervous to go to school on the day her assailant was due to return.

"Do you want to stay home?" Ayda offered.

"No," Shams said, but her face remained long, her eyes cast over with worry.

"You're going to be fine, Shams. Don't even think about it."

Shams nodded and tried to take Ayda's advice. She tried to forget about it, to pretend that today was a day just like any other. And she almost succeeded, until fifth period.

The bell rang and the halls buzzed with students on their way to their next classes. Shams grabbed some books from her locker, but when she slammed it shut, her harasser appeared, standing about three feet from her. Shams froze in place, unable to move, unable to speak. The students were thinning out of the halls, and in thirty seconds, there would be no one around except for her and that predator.

He took a step forward and said, "You can go to the cops all you want, you little whore, but I will take what I want from you."

The blood drained from her face as he took another step closer.

Chapter Twenty-Six
GOOD FROM BAD

Suddenly Shams felt someone's arm wrap around her shoulders. She jumped, turning her head to see Rizq standing beside her. Out of nowhere, two guys Shams only knew as being on the football team put themselves between her and her assailant.

"You had best watch your step there, Brett," one of the guys said. "If you ever bother Shams again, you'll be heading to the emergency room with a lot more than a pair of throbbing balls. If you so much as look sideways at Shams—or at any girl in this school—we will be there, and we won't leave until we're absolutely sure you're no longer a threat. I know you're not the sharpest tool, but I think you understand. Or would you like a visual demonstration?"

Brett looked from the guys to Shams and back again, then he shook his head, waved their words away with his hand, turned and left.

When Brett was out of sight, the player who had spoken went up to Shams and put out his fist. "I was supposed to walk you to your next class, but I totally blanked. My bad. But we've got your back, sweet pea. As salaamu aleykum."

She bumped her fist to his, and the two guys left.

"You okay?" Rizq asked her.

She nodded. "What if you guys aren't around next time? What if he manages to get me alone? What if..."

"Shh. Shams, the entire football team—JV and varsity—are looking out for you. And they have all their friends looking out for you. And the teachers, too. You've got your own undercover bodyguards. You have nothing to worry about."

Shams nodded, but she didn't believe him.

As she gathered her things at the end of the next period, a couple of her friends stood beside her desk. "We'll walk with you."

"Thanks you guys. But your classes are on the other side of the building. You'll never make it back on time."

"Oh, Shams, Shams, Shams. You should know us well enough by now to know we never go to Calc!" The girls' laughter eased her worry and put her in a positive mood.

For the next week Shams's friends and schoolmates made sure she was never alone in the hallways.

On Friday afternoon, a girl she'd seen around but didn't know very well came up to her after last period and walked with her to her locker. "You know," she said, "I think what you did—reporting him to the cops and everything—is really cool. I wish I'd been that strong when he..."

Shams looked at her classmate in disbelief.

"Thank you for doing what I couldn't. Now at least people know about him; they'll be warned."

◆◆◆

"Now aren't you glad we reported it?" Ayda asked that evening when Shams told her about the conversation she'd had at school.

"How can someone like him just be left out in the world, free to harass and terrorize everyone?"

"Unfortunately, that's the way of the world—too many enjoying freedoms they abuse. But it's up to the rest of us to put them in their place."

"We won't always be able to stop catastrophes before they happen, though."

Ayda nodded. "True. But we must always try."

It seemed so backwards to Shams, that doing right, maintaining a positive outlook, believing in the good of people was so difficult. "Why is wrong easy and right so difficult?"

"To test us. To see who is true and who is not. To separate the good—the truly good, those who are good because good is right not because it is easy—from the bad. Because the truly good, they get the best reward in the end."

Shams knew that, but it still seemed unfair.

Before she went to bed that night, she called Rizq. "I can't go around for the rest of my life with bodyguards and escorts."

"Why not?" Rizq replied. "Famous people do it all the time."

"I'm not famous."

"You are just as good as those people; don't let anyone tell you otherwise," he joked.

"I'm serious, Rizq."

"It's not for the rest of your life. And it's not just you. The student council is proposing to institute an 'escort pass,' so students can be a few minutes late to class if they were walking other students to their classes. The idea is that no one is left in the halls alone."

She was quiet for a long time.

"Shams, you still there?"

"Yeah, I'm still here. I just...I hate this."

"Me too. But it'll pass. And the school will be safer with the escort pass system, so there is a good side to all of this."

"*Alhamdulillah*," Shams said. "Thanks, Rizq. You're a great big brother who is actually three weeks younger than me."

Rizq laughed. "And you're a great little older sister."

After Shams got off the phone, she prayed *Isha* and got into bed. Maybe there was a good side to what had happened to her. And it wasn't just the escort system at school. It was her renewed dedication, to herself, to her faith. *Haters are always going to hate*, she thought. *I can only be me.*

But she also made a very important decision about her life that night. Sharing that decision with Ayda? She was sure that would be another test.

Chapter Twenty-Seven
IN THE BLINK OF AN EYE

Shams enjoyed working at the bookshop. She liked helping customers find the titles they were looking for. She enjoyed explaining the art to patrons. Being there didn't seem like work to her, but Ayda made sure she and Rizq clocked in and out and got paid the same as the other employees.

"A bit of nepotism isn't so bad, Aunt Didi. I mean, even the former president put his kids and their spouses in positions they weren't qualified for," Rizq said, trying to weasel a higher pay rate from his boss.

"First of all, that clown was incompetent, so we can't take anything he said or did as a model. And second, nepotism is for rich brats who can't get their own foot in the door but need their dad or mom to pull favors for them. Are you a rich brat who fits those criteria?"

"Not yet, but I could be if you'd give me a little preferential treatment."

Ayda smacked Rizq on the back of the head, and they all laughed it off.

"Now that your junior year is more than half-way over, Rizq, do you know what the hell you're going to do about college?"

"Community college. Business administration. And when I'm rich and famous, I'm not going to hold all this against you, Aunt Didi. I'm gonna let you run one of my multi-national, billion dollar businesses."

"Thank you. I look forward to it."

"No problem."

"What about you, Shams?" Rizq asked. "Do you know where you're going to apply for college?"

"I...uh...I'm still researching." She gave Rizq a death stare but made sure Didi hadn't seen.

"I thought you had decided on art school. Wasn't that your decision?" Didi asked, oblivious to the exchange that had taken place between the cousins.

"Well...I...I'm still going over everything, you know. I still have the summer and fall to figure it out. Oh, by the way, that new artist called earlier. He wanted to speak with you about displaying his art here." She handed Ayda a piece of paper with a name and number scribbled on it, and, just as Shams had intended, the older woman went immediately to the phone and dialed the number.

"What's going on?" Rizq whispered to Shams when Ayda was out of earshot.

"I'm thinking of deferring for a year. And when I do go to school, it probably won't be art school. But I don't know what she'll do when I tell her."

The weeks went by, and soon it was Shams's birthday. Ayda told her she had a surprise for her. "But in order to get it, you have to come to the second branch."

"See, now if you'd let me get a car, I'd be there right away. But since you won't, I have to waste time finding a ride."

"Rizq's coming; he'll bring you. Nice one though."

"Hey, I had to try."

As the last few customers were checking out, Shams and Rizq arrived and sat down in the café area. A few minutes later, Didi entered carrying a birthday cake, followed by Sumayya, Saleh, and Siham. They were all singing happy birthday to Shams. The cake was made of cupcakes, all of Shams's favorite kinds.

"And I'm going to eat one of each!"

Her grandparents gave her a card with money in it. "I wanted to get you clothes, but your grandfather wouldn't let me. He said, 'Let her pick out what she wants.' So get yourself something nice."

"Thank you, guys." Shams kissed them both.

Siham gave her niece a gift certificate to the arts and crafts store.

"This is awesome. I'm going to buy some yarn and make Rizq an ugly sweater that he'll have to wear to show how much he appreciates my gift. But I'll make you something nice, Auntie."

As they sat eating cake, Siham asked, "Where's your gift, Didi?"

"I think, having you all here, and these delicious cupcakes, this's the best gift Didi could give me," Shams said.

"I'm pretty sure you're going to like my present more than you like cupcakes," Ayda replied.

She finished the last bite of her cupcake, then fiddled in her purse and pulled out a card. "Happy birthday, sweetie," Ayda said, kissing Shams on the forehead.

As soon as the girl opened the card, a key fell out and clinked as it hit the floor. Shams picked it up and opened the card again.

"It's the red Toyota sitting in the parking lot."

Shams's mouth fell open. She looked from the card to Ayda, and back again. "But you said I couldn't have a car?!"

"I said no such thing. I said you couldn't use your money to buy a car. There's a difference. That's your money for college and all that."

Shams jumped up and threw her arms around Ayda, hugging her more intensely than she'd hugged anyone, ever. Ayda, too, held her tightly. Whether it was knowing that soon Shams would be off to school and they wouldn't be seeing much of each other, or simply because Shams's parents were both gone and she and Ayda felt like they were lucky to have each other, it wasn't clear. But tears filled their eyes, and their embrace lasted for a long moment. It had taken a series of painful and traumatizing events, but they had found each other, and in their relationship, they had the unconditional love they each needed. They found the compassion and sincerity they each craved.

Ayda finally patted Shams on the back and said, "Go on. I know you're dying to see it."

Shams kissed Ayda on the cheek and ran out to see her new car, Rizq right on her heels.

It was the most expensive, biggest, best present Shams had ever gotten, and she knew she'd never get a gift as valuable again. It was brand new and had that new-car smell. Shams climbed into the driver's seat and ran her hand over the smooth gray leather of the seats and the dashboard. She gripped the steering wheel and opened all the pockets and pouches she found. The following morning, before Ayda left for work, she explained some basics about car mechanics to Shams. She showed her how to check the oil and where to add it if the need arose. She showed her where the windshield fluid went and taught her a little about spark plugs.

"The car is brand new, Didi. I don't need to know this stuff."

"Now the car is brand new, but one day it won't be. And you need to be able to depend on yourself if something goes wrong. Obviously some things are major and require a mechanic, but you need to know the basics." She showed Shams how to get the spare out of the trunk and how to change the tire, even making the girl get down on her knees and go through all the steps.

"You ever seen a girl standing by the side of the road, needing help because of a flat tire? I don't ever want that to be you. Keep a fresh outfit in the car in case you end up getting your clothes greasy while you're on your way to a job interview or something. You can always find a bathroom to change in. Just don't ever be that helpless girl standing by the side of the road if the problem is something you can fix yourself."

Shams was grateful to Ayda for so many reasons. For the car and showing her some basic mechanics...but mostly for the love and support she'd showered on her over the past six years. She wanted to make her proud, figuring that would somehow repay Ayda for everything. But Shams knew that there was one decision she had made that would disappoint Ayda, and it made her nauseous thinking that she would soon have to break it to her.

◆ ◆ ◆

One early fall morning, as Marge made breakfast and the sun shone brightly, Ayda and Shams sat on the porch enjoying the birds' chorus. "*SubhanAllah*. It's all so beautiful, this great world. And yet, to some, it's so small. They travel from one end to the other, admiring God's creation, learning from His Majesty, praying on different soils of the same wide earth as though they're just taking a trip into the city." Ayda closed her eyes and concentrated on the sounds of nature all around.

"Do you know? Did Rizq tell you?" Shams asked.

"Know what? Did Rizq tell me what?" Ayda looked at Shams with furrowed eyebrows, trying to recall what it could possibly be that Shams claimed she might know.

"What made you say that just now? About traveling the world?"

Ayda shrugged. "Just the beauty of nature...and how some people really know how to enjoy it, how to take it all in. I wish I could be that way."

"So...no one told you anything?"

"I have no idea what you're talking about, Shams. Go on. What is it that you think I know or that you're worried about me finding out?"

Shams took in a heavy breath. As she exhaled, she said, "I've decided to take a year off after high school, to travel the world."

Ayda's eyebrows went up, then, as her face gradually relaxed, a warm smile came over her face. "That's a great idea, Shams. Do you have it planned out? All the countries you'll go?"

"You're not mad? Or disappointed? That I won't be doing college right away?"

"Oh God, why would I be disappointed? You know how many beautiful things you're going to see? How many wonderful and horrible things you'll experience?"

"But you've only ever talked about college. It was always 'when you graduate high school and are away at college.'"

"Because that's what most people do, not because there is no other path. Plus, art school isn't going anywhere. It'll be here when you get back."

Shams's relief had been short-lived. Swallowing hard, she said, "Oh...um.... I've actually decided I'm not going to go to art school. I'm going to go into law."

Ayda was taken aback. "What? What do you mean? You've wanted to go to art school to be a designer for as long as I've known you. It's been your dream."

Shams nodded. "It was. But then my dream changed. I love fashion design. And art. I always will. And maybe someday I will want to go to school for it. But for now, I want to learn the law. I want to be a judge and put away little shits like Brett."

They were quiet for a few minutes.

"Wow," Ayda said when the words sank in. "I totally didn't expect that. I thought you were headed somewhere completely different. And knowing you've changed directions without discussing it with me first...I feel like you grew up all of a sudden. Like this young girl, making her own decisions, planning her own course, changing her mind and telling me last of all, I feel like it all crept up on me."

She wrapped her arm around Shams and continued. "But I support you no matter where you choose to go, no matter what you choose to be. I'm with you."

"Really?" Shams asked.

"Don't be a clown! Of course!"

"Good, cause I'm going to need you to withdraw some funds for me to be able to travel."

"No, you don't."

Shams crossed her eyebrows.

"Don't you realize that you turn eighteen just before graduation? You'll no longer need my approval to get to your account. It's all yours."

Shams couldn't believe it; her eighteenth birthday was just months away, then she would finally be financially independent, and no one could tell her how to spend her money or how not to. *Not that Didi ever had*, Shams thought. But still, it was a step toward independence, a step toward adulthood.

Shams reflected on her life as she sat staring at the picture hanging on the wall of her mother, father and her two-year-old-self. The girl in the photo was laughing. She was happy and loved. And somehow, even after losing the two people who had been her whole world, even after she'd become an orphan, she had managed to remain happy and loved. She owed so much to Didi, but she knew no amount of thanks would ever be enough. No words could ever communicate how much she appreciated all that Didi had done for her...all the love she had given her.

Searching through the photos on her cell phone, Shams came across a beautiful one of Didi, her, and Rizq. The teenagers were on either side of Didi, kissing her, and Didi was rolling her eyes with that signature half-smile on her face. Shams printed the picture, framed it, and hung it on the wall above the staircase, adding it to the large gallery of pictures that had emerged there over the years.

Chapter Twenty-Eight
SHAMS GOES AWAY

Graduation brought with it new anxieties and new excitements. Finally the day of Shams's departure arrived. As the entire family stood in the airport just before the security check, Shams handed a copy of her itinerary to Ayda.

"If at any moment you want to come home, you do! Even if it means you have to pay a cancellation fee...I'll take care of it."

"Don't worry, Didi. I'm going to be fine, *In sha' Allah*."

"*In sha' Allah*. You have the meds I told you to pack? And you made sure to take that last immunization shot you'd been putting off, right?"

"Yes, Didi. I took all the shots, and I have all the drugs. Don't worry."

Didi nodded, but the stern look on her face didn't fade. "And call me. Call me every day. Call me three times a day."

Shams laughed and hugged her. "I'm going to be fine, *habibti*. You just take care of yourself."

"Don't forget your prayers."

"I've never forgotten my prayers, Didi."

Again, Ayda nodded.

"I need to go because getting through security takes a long time. I'll call you from Venice. Love you, Sitto and Giddo, Auntie Siham. Love you, Rizq. Enjoy college. I want to hear all about it in daily emails." Shams hugged her grandparents, aunt, and cousin goodbye. Then she turned to Ayda.

"I'm going to miss you, but I know Aunt Siham will take care of you. Love you, Didi."

Ayda was too choked up to answer. She wrapped her arms around the girl tightly and didn't want to let go.

"Come on, Didi. She's going to miss her flight," Siham said, gently loosening Ayda's grip.

Shams walked away backwards and waved. Ayda yelled out, "I love you," and a moment later, Shams was out of sight.

"She's going to have a great time, Auntie Didi. She's going to love it."

"*In sha' Allah*," Ayda said. She wrapped her arms around herself, and Siham patted her on the back.

"And you're going to be fine, too," Siham said. Ayda looked at her sister-in-law and gave her that half-grin she was famous for.

Rizq ran off ahead of them calling back, "I'll go bring the car around."

When he was out of earshot, Ayda said, "If it weren't *haram*, I'd go get wasted right now."

"Hell yeah," Siham replied.

The women hadn't noticed Sumayya and Saleh chatting off to the side until the older couple walked over to them, and Saleh said, "Girls, we have something for you."

"Some marijuana?" Didi asked.

When they looked at her with their eyebrows raised, she shook her head and waved off her comment with a swipe of her hand.

"Here you go. Open this."

Siham took the envelope from her mom. Opening it, she found two plane tickets to Hawaii.

"We figured you both deserve a vacation. Your businesses are running well, and your mother and I will look in on them for you while you're gone. Rizq will stay with us, and he's agreed to help out whenever he doesn't have classes. It's only two weeks, but we know it'll do you good."

Siham and Ayda couldn't speak. They stood there dumbfounded for a moment, then they exploded with laughter. "This is too much. Thank you, guys." The women took turns hugging and kissing the older couple, then they hugged each other. If her heart wasn't still throbbing from seeing Shams off, Didi would've screeched in excitement.

"This is such a great idea. I think getting away will be good for both of us," Siham said on their way home.

"Hope it distracts me from worrying about Shams."

But it didn't. Shams called her every day for the first few days. Then she began to call every other day.

"With the time difference," Shams explained, "I can't always adjust my schedule. But I'm good. I promise!"

Then a couple of weeks later, the calls began to come just once every four or five days. And again, Shams assured Ayda that everything was fine, she was enjoying herself, meeting new people.

"That's wonderful, *habibti*. What do you..."

"Didi! Can you hear me?"

"Yes. I was saying, what do..."

"Didi, I can't hear you! If you can hear me, I'm good. I'll call you in a few days! 'Bye."

And on it went. Sometimes it was the time difference, sometimes it was a bad connection. The reason didn't matter to Ayda; she hated it. She just wanted to speak to Shams, to have those few moments together, and so often, even *that* seemed like too much to ask for.

The day before Ayda and Siham's trip, the timing and the connection were both in her favor.

"Don't just sit on the beach," Shams told her. "Do stuff you know you won't get a chance to do otherwise."

"Stuff like what?"

"I don't know. Bungee jumping. Or swimming with dolphins. Or jungle safaris. Or snorkeling. I don't know. Do whatever they offer. Do it all."

"Bungee jumping? Are you praying for my death?"

Shams laughed. "Fine, no bungee jumping. But everything else. Just enjoy it."

"And you don't enjoy yourself too much. I miss you."

"Miss you, too. Once you get back from Hawaii, it'll only be another month before I'm home again."

"But you'll only stay home for a couple of weeks," Ayda answered with a sulk.

"But they'll be a great couple of weeks. Ok, gotta go. Send my salaam to Aunt Siham. Love you!"

Ayda had been lonelier with Shams away than she could admit to anyone. The bookstores kept her busy during the day, but they were well-oiled machines, so she only went to supervise. There was rarely anything that required her attention. She was back to eating dinner alone in the evenings, and the silence which hung all over the house was unnerving. Where were the footsteps, the sounds of books opening and closing? The buzz of the fridge opening and the tea kettle boiling at all hours of the day and night. Ayda tried to remember how she had enjoyed those quiet days before Shams had come into her life. She simply couldn't understand how, only six years before, she had relished that solitude.

"Well, you'd better get used to it again," she said aloud to herself. Staring at the pictures framed on the staircase—the newest additions being one of Shams in Venice and another of her in France—Didi understood that loneliness was part of her future now. Even after Shams returned from her trip, she would be off to college shortly after. This was just one stop on the girl's journey to independence.

The morning of their Hawaii trip finally arrived, and Ayda sat in her car waiting for her sister-in-law to appear. After honking twice and waiting for a few more minutes, Ayda went into the house.

"You always make us late!" she called up the stairs. "Why aren't you ready yet?"

"I'll be down in a second," Siham yelled. "Keep your panties on! God, not everyone has to be early everywhere they go."

"I don't want to be early! I just don't want to miss the damn flight!"

Siham ran down the stairs, suitcase in hand. She stood directly in front of Ayda, exhaled a long and smooth breath, then said, in a voice just barely audible, "I'm ready. Let's go."

As they drove to the airport, Siham double checked their itinerary. Once they'd parked the car, she turned to Ayda and said, "This trip is going to be unbelievable!"

Just as the two women were hugging and laughing in celebration, gathering their things to proceed to check in, Ayda's cell phone rang.

"Is it Mom, calling to check up on us?" Siham asked.

"No, it's an unknown number. I wonder if it's about the shop." She clicked open the line. "Hello?"

"Hello is this Ayda Faisal?" an unfamiliar voice said. Ayda thought she detected a French accent.

"Yes. Who's this?"

"Ms. Faisal, do you know Shams Tawwab?"

"Yes," Ayda said, worry creeping into her heart and causing her voice to shake. "She's my...I'm her...I'm her...stepmom. I'm her stepmom."

"Ms. Faisal, I'm Dr. Paul Maurice. I'm sorry to tell you that your daughter had a bad accident. She's been mostly unconscious since she came to us, about four hours ago. And she has some serious internal bleeding that we're monitoring. I think it would be best for you to come here right away."

"What? What is it?" Siham asked, seeing Ayda's face go white. "What's wrong?"

But Ayda couldn't speak. She began to hyperventilate. Siham pried the phone from her tight grip and listened as the doctor again recounted Shams's condition. She took the name and address of the hospital, hung up, and led Ayda into the airport. She changed their tickets for the next flight to France. Ayda was following Siham through the airport, clutching her handbag and clamping her lips together so tightly they were white.

They waited for a couple of hours before their flight began to board. Ayda was silent the entire time; she only replied to Siham with head shakes and nods. Once they were seated in the plane, Siham began to supplicate in a voice only loud enough for Ayda to hear.

"Please God, heal Shams completely. Only You are the Healer of all ills, so heal her. Have her awaken and enjoy a long, healthy life. Heal her and bless her health and her life."

She continued to supplicate until the plane was soaring smoothly. Ayda had repeated every word Siham had said, and she continued to repeat them even after Siham had dozed off to sleep.

"Please God. She's all I have left, and she has such a bright future. Please don't take her away from me."

Ayda refused to eat anything during the entire eight-hour flight. "I won't be able to keep it down," she said to Siham when the latter tried to convince her to eat her meal. "Just water please," she asked the stewardess. "Or...if you have ginger ale."

Ayda sipped her drink as Siham nibbled at her meal. A few moments later, Ayda said, "It's my fault. She's my responsibility. I was supposed to take care of her. Her mom entrusted her to me so that I would take care of her. I should have never let her go on this trip."

Siham put down her fork and wiped her mouth. "You were planning on sending her away to college, like most parents do. Is that the wrong decision as well?"

"It's not the same."

"It's exactly the same. We do what's best for them and help them choose wisely, but we cannot stop them from experiencing life. How long can we keep them locked away? Even then, bad things happen all the time right in our backyards. There's evil and sickness and all sorts of calamities that are simply unavoidable. Our fate is our fate no matter where we are, whether we're in France or locked up in a room back home. There is no reason to feel guilty. Just pray for her—that's what we can do now."

A few hours later, when they finally landed, Siham navigated them through customs and baggage claim and then converted some money. Outside, she hailed a cab. The drive to the hospital was only half an hour, but to Ayda, it seemed endless. "What's taking so long?"

"Nothing, madam. We will be there shortly," the driver replied.

"Is it very far away?" Ayda asked again.

"No," he replied calmly. "Soon. We will be there soon."

When they finally pulled up to the hospital, Siham paid the fare and followed Ayda up to the reception desk.

"My daughter is here. Shams Tawwab."

The receptionist told Ayda what ward Shams was in but explained that no visitors were allowed in the ICU.

"But you called me and told me she's in critical condition." Ayda was about to lose her patience when Siham stepped in.

"We've come from America. We need to speak with the doctor responsible for her."

The receptionist directed them to the ward but reiterated that they would not be able to see Shams. Ayda was about to tell the receptionist off when Siham hugged her from behind and pulled her away. "She doesn't know why we're here, Didi. We'll straighten it out with the doctor in charge."

The pair made some twists and turns down the hallways, took an elevator, followed by more twists and turns before they finally arrived at the ICU. Siham told the nurse on duty that they were Shams's family and would like to see her and speak with Dr. Maurice.

"Sit in the waiting area. I will call Dr. Maurice for you."

The two women sat in the lounge, their suitcases at their feet.

A white-haired man wearing a long, white coat, his face and hands covered with wrinkles, came marching down the corridor with the nurse at his side. Ayda and Siham rose when he approached. "Ms. Faisal…"

"I want to see my daughter," Ayda interrupted.

He stared into her determined eyes for a moment. "Of course. Come with me."

He led them into the ICU and stood to the side so Ayda and Siham could have a clear view of Shams on the bed. Her head was bandaged, and she was hooked up to several machines. Ayda walked up to her limp body and took her right hand in hers. Siham walked to the other side, wrapped Shams's head in her arm and whispered prayers into her ear.

"You need to know that your daughter's condition is very severe. Until this morning we had some hope she might recover, but as the seconds tick away, so does that hope. I'm very sorry."

Chapter Twenty-Nine
BACK TO THE BEGINNING

The doctor was quiet for another moment before he told them they would only be allowed to stay for a few more minutes, then excused himself to give them some privacy.

Siham, with tears in her eyes, said a few more prayers, then rubbed Ayda's shoulder on her way out the door.

When she was finally alone with her daughter, Ayda's chest heaved as the tears she'd been keeping at bay began to escape.

"I need you to know two things," she said. "First, I have been so very blessed to have you in my life. I know you were a gift, one that I wish I had just kept on the mantle, safe. I have been proud of you every minute. I have loved you since you first came to me and I didn't know what I was supposed to do with you."

She paused to catch her breath and wipe her nose.

"And the second thing you need to know is that...I forgive them. I forgive your father and mother. Remember when I told you that your dad had once promised he would always make it up to me if ever he upset me? He upset me when he had a life—a family—I knew nothing about. But he made it up to me with you. Your parents gave me you, how could I not forgive them? I'm sorry I didn't take better care of you."

Tears flowed from her eyes as she bent down to kiss Shams and hug her as best she could.

"Please forgive me. Forgive me if I've ever wronged you or hurt you. It was never my intention. I love you so much. I may not have given birth to you, but you are my daughter."

She sat in that same position, hugging Shams, until the nurse appeared and told her it was time to leave.

"The doctor said we don't have much time left. I'm not leaving."

The nurse exited the room, and Ayda didn't even realize when she came back to give her a chair.

Ayda continued to speak to Shams, and Shams made no indication that she heard anything. But somehow, Ayda knew she had only minutes left. "I knew you were waiting for me. Thank you. *In sha' Allah*, you're going to a much better place. I love you, Shams. I love you very much. Even more than I loved your father. And he was the most precious thing in my life. Maybe, maybe I'll see you two soon.

"*Ash hadu an la ilaha illa Allah wa ash hadu anna Mohammadan rasul Allah.* Repeat it Shams. Repeat it with me, come on. *Ash hadu an la ilaha illa Allah wa ash hadu anna Mohammadan rasul Allah.*" As Ayda spoke the sacred words for the fifth time, the machines began to beep, and she heard an incomprehensible murmur coming from her daughter. And in a second, she was gone.

Ayda remained beside Shams and repeated her last rites in a steady voice, tears streaking her face. She hadn't noticed when a nurse had snuck in and turned off the beeping machines nor that Siham had been standing beside her ever since the machines had begun making noise. A while later, Siham wrapped her arms around Ayda and led her out of the room.

◆◆◆

The next few days were filled with travel and funeral arrangements. Ayda was too busy for the emptiness to envelop her. Her in-laws, including Siham and Rizq, remained with her during those first few days. It was as comforting as it was suffocating. She wanted to be alone, but she feared the emotions that would attack once the others had left.

Eventually, everyone went back to their homes, and she was left in a home too big with emotions too strong. She had managed to keep her tears to a seeping drizzle over the past few days. Though she feared the dam would burst, she held on to the hope that perhaps—if it could remain intact—so could she.

They reopened the bookstores the following week, and many of the staff and patrons paid their condolences to Ayda. And with each word of condolence, she nodded her head in acknowledgment and walked away, afraid of what might happen to her if she didn't.

It was inappropriate, she knew. And some might have even translated it to disrespect. But in truth, it was the only way Ayda knew how to function: suppressing the pain and plowing forward.

One afternoon, a week or so after the stores had reopened, she looked up from her desk to find her father-in-law standing at the door of her office. "*As salaamu alaikum.*"

"*Wa alaikum as salaam,*" she replied. "Come in, Uncle. Have a seat. What can I get you to drink?"

They talked for some time, then he said, "What have you done with Shams's things? Her clothes and such?"

Ayda looked straight into his eyes, but he looked down. "Nothing."

"When do you plan on going through them?"

"I don't."

"Didi, she will get *sadaqah* if you donate her things to people who need them. There are many..."

"I'm not donating her things."

He looked up at her then, stared at her with the same intensity that she had directed at him just moments before. "Why not?"

"Because I don't want to."

"But that's just wasting..."

"They are *her* things, and they will remain—for as long as I live—*hers!*"

Holding her stare, he rose. "Didi," he said in a softer tone, "she isn't coming back. Keeping her things is wasteful. Other people can benefit from her clothes. She would get the reward of giving out charity. Giving up what she used to own does not mean we are giving her up. We will hold her close, for eternity, in our hearts and prayers. But she is not her things. Think it over. And your mother-in-law and Siham and Rizq, we are all here for you if you need anything." He wiped his tears, kissed her on the forehead, and walked out.

She sighed deeply, exhaling his words, and returned her focus to the paperwork she had before her.

The house was still creepy. Ayda played Qur'an throughout the day to give her a sense that she was not alone. She walked into Shams's room several times a day, just to check. To check on what, she wasn't completely sure, but she did it anyway.

Although Ayda had been praying regularly for several years now, these days she was only going through the motions. She asked God, in her heart, why he'd taken every precious person in her life. Why was she—unlike so many people around her—left completely alone? Why didn't she deserve love? Yes, Siham and Rizq were precious to her, but it was not the same. She asked God the questions without moving her tongue. And although she never received an answer, she felt His acknowledgment of her pain, her loneliness, her sorrow. She felt Him guiding her to reach out to Him, to keep spreading love, to look inside herself for love and shower it around her.

But even as the weeks turned into months, nothing changed. Emptiness engulfed her. She was unable to find pleasure in any of the things she had enjoyed before, unable to laugh or joke.

"Am I going to be like this forever?" she asked Siham.

Her friend stared at her for a long moment. "What is it that hurts?"

Ayda's face crinkled. "What do you mean what hurts? I miss my daughter."

"You will miss her forever. But is that all that hurts? Are you worried about her afterlife?"

"No. She was a good kid, and God is merciful. No."

"Are you worried about what your life will be without her?"

"Of course!"

"But Didi, you had a life before she came into it."

"No, I didn't. I had a job. One I was good at. But I didn't have a life."

"So what about her gave you life?"

Ayda's face dropped. A moment later she said, "Her love. Her love gave me life."

And with those words, the dam that had held strong all those months finally gave way. Remembering all her hugs, all the times she asked Ayda not to smoke, all the times she encouraged her to pray, all the smiles and laughter. Remembering all the different shapes Shams's love had taken, Ayda broke down, crying uncontrollably, falling to the floor. Siham embraced her and allowed her to sob. As Ayda's sniffling began to subside, more than twenty minutes later, Siham said, "Her love is still with you, Didi. But love fades if it isn't shared. Share it, so it can grow stronger."

As the days passed, Ayda slowly picked herself up. She worked regular hours at the shops and visited her in-laws weekly. Rizq worked a fixed schedule, and Ayda liked having him around. His energy reminded her of Shams.

About a month later, Ayda called him on a Saturday and asked him to spend the day helping her with some stuff at home. "Sure, Didi. What do you need?"

"You'll see when you get here."

Rizq stood behind Ayda as she opened the door to Shams's room. A familiar scent wafted up and tickled her nose. And with it, tears began to form in her eyes. But she'd gotten used to seeing through the tears.

Rizq went through and folded all the clothes that were hanging in the closet. He pulled out the shoes and bags and all the other random accessories he could find and placed them in neat piles on or near the bed. Ayda went through the drawers and did the same, then gathered the stuffed animals, CD's, books, yarn, boxes of pictures and yearbooks. When they had organized all of Shams's things as best they could, Rizq asked in a hushed voice, "Now what?"

Ayda stared at all the things piled up around them. "Would you like to keep anything?"

He picked out a sweatshirt, a couple of books, and the knitted hat Shams hadn't had a chance to finish. He put them down beside the door.

"Isn't it strange that in the end, this is all that's left of us? Just random stuff."

"This isn't all that's left, Rizi. This is all we can see, but what's left is something completely different."

She patted his arm, and for the first time, noticed his red nose and tear streaked cheeks. When she put her arms around him, he did not know that it was more to comfort herself than to comfort him. They gathered some things they thought Siham and Shams's grandparents might like to keep. Then they packed the rest of Shams's things in large plastic bags. Ayda decided that the books and CD's would be sold in the shop as used items. The clothes, shoes and stuffed animals would go to charities serving Syrian refugees. Ayda even placed Shams's bed sheets and comforter with the items to be donated. She packed everything up in Rizq's car and gave him specific instructions. "Should I come with you? Make sure you don't screw it all up?"

He chuckled. "I won't screw up, Aunt Ayda."

"Call me Didi. And good. Now come in and eat lunch with me before you go deal with all that."

That evening, after she had showered, prayed and had a cup of tea, Didi opened the door to Shams's room. All that remained was the perfume Shams loved, one purple teddy bear, and boxes of photos and yearbooks. Didi sprayed the bear with the scent and breathed it in as she held the bear tightly. A tear slid down her face as she prayed to God to be merciful on Shams and grant her the highest level of Paradise. Her footsteps filled the silence as she walked back to her room to place the perfume on her dresser and get in bed. The photos she took care of later. Some she kept in boxes, others she framed and hung on the wall of the staircase, including one of Saef, smiling wide. And her wedding photo. But her favorite, she kept by the bed—a purple-framed photo of her and Shams, their arms around each other's shoulders, laughing into the camera. It was the truest picture of Shams's life.

And of Didi's too.

Glossary of Arabic Terms

Abaya:
A full length outer garment worn by some Muslim women.

Alf salaama:
A common phrase said to someone who is suffering any health issue, similar to "get well." It means "a thousand [prayers for] your safety."

Alhamdulillah:
"Praise be to God."

Allah yirhamu (s. m.), Allah yirhamhum (pl.):
May God have mercy on him.

Asr:
The middle of the five daily, obligatory prayers in Islam.

As salaamu alaikum:
This is the proper Islamic greeting, used both for "hello" and "goodbye." Literally, it means "peace be upon you."

AstaghfarAllah:
"God forgive me."

Ayat al Kursi:
A verse in the second chapter of the Quran. It is commonly believed to protect its reciter from harm and is often said in times of difficulty.

Barak Allahu feek:
"May God bless you."

Bismillah:
"In the name of God."

Duaa':
Supplication

Dhuhr:
The second of the five daily, obligatory prayers in Islam.

'Eid:
Holiday. This term is used to refer to either Eid Al-Fitr, which is the first day after Ramadan, or Eid Ul-Adha, which commences on the tenth of the Islamic month of Dhul Hijjah (the month of the Islamic pilgrimage).

El Shafi:
One of the 99 names of Allah. It means "the One Who Cures."

Habibi (m.), Habibti (f.):
A term of endearment meaning "sweetheart" or "my love."

Hadith:
A saying of Prophet Muhammad.

Haram:
Prohibited.

Inna lillahi wa inna ilayhi rajioon:
"To God we belong and to Him we shall return." This prayer is said during times of calamity.

In sha' Allah:
"God willing."

Isha:
The last of the five daily, obligatory prayers in Islam.

La ilaha ila Allah:
"There is no God but God."

Ma sha' Allah:
Literally means "What God has willed." This expression is used to show awe at something while protecting it from the envy.

Mohammadan Rasul Allah:
Mohammad is the Prophet of God.

Sadaqah:
Charity or the reward for giving charity.

Salaam:
Vernacular, short for *as salaamu alaikum*.

Shahadah:
The proclamation that there is only One God, and that Mohamed is His prophet. In Arabic, this proclamation is pronounced *Ash hadu an la ilaha illa Allah wa ash hadu anna Mohammadan rasul Allah*.

Shaitan:
Satan

SubhanAllah:
A term used to hallow God's name; it is a declaration of awe and wonder at God's creation.

Yalla:
Slang Arabic, meaning "come on" or "let's go."

Wa alaikum as salaam:
This is the proper response to "as salaamu alaikum." Literally, it means "and may peace be upon you."

Wudu:
The washing up which precedes prayer; ablution.